Michael Goodell has produced a finely-manicured work that is, while seemingly effortless, boiling over with risks and gambles. The world he's given us is populated with real, living and breathing characters that all have a stake in the game. He asks the big questions, the probing ones. It's a difficult task, handling all these twists and turns and tense reveals, but we are privileged to have a guide as capable and talented as Goodell to lead the way.

—Jared Yates Sexton,
Author of An End to All Things

Before you pick this book up make sure you have the day free. You are not going to want to put it down. Michael Goodell catches you in a web of deceit and won't let you go.

—Evelyn M. Byrne,
Author of the Daughter of Prophecy Series.

Michael Goodell's Rebound is a hardboiled, can't put down, up all night read, that kept me wondering just who the real bad guy was until the end.

—Jean Lauzier,
Author of Dark Decent

REBOUND

To Ken & Ann

To My Discerning Friends —

Michael
Goodell

White Bird Publications
P.O. Box 586
Diana, Texas 75640
http://www.whitebirdpublications.com

This is a work of fiction. Names, characters, places, and incidents are the product of the author's imagination. Any resemblance to actual persons, living or dead, business establishments, event, or locales is entirely coincidental.

Copyright©2013 by Michael Goodell
Cover by E. Kusch

ISBN: 978-1-937690-63-2
LCCN: 2013954636

PRINTED IN THE UNITED STATES OF AMERICA

REBOUND

**White Bird
Publications**

To Emily and Matthew,
for making the adventure worthwhile

CHAPTER 1

Karin's office was in a cluster of medical office buildings in Rochester, one of the handful of upscale suburbs still feeding off the city's corpse. It was about twenty minutes north on I-75, and I made it with fifteen minutes to spare. I found a parking space close to the front door, and settled down to wait.

I pulled Jon's notebook out from under the seat, the one about me. I still hadn't gone through it very thoroughly. I had been more focused on sifting through his dossier, to build as strong a case as possible. This one had seemed like a distraction. It would have no bearing on the matter at hand. At least, that's what I told myself. The fact is, from my cursory glance, Jon had an unhealthy fixation on Sara's death, and my role in it. I didn't relish going down that road again.

On the other hand, I'd come so far, maybe I should see if I could lay that demon to rest along with the other ones. And if I couldn't, I had a good shrink to get me back on track. In fact, my next session was due to begin in—I checked my watch—ten minutes.

So I jumped in. Read the old news articles, though to be honest, I still remembered them almost word for word. The details of her death, my mug shot on the front page of "The Detroit News." The banner headline, "Local Investigator Arrested in Socialite's Murder." Gotta love that word socialite. Wonder what headline writers would do if it didn't exist. Probably make it up.

The basics of the story: The news that her "high-powered financier" of a husband was out of the country on business when it happened. Nice alibi, Olly. A brief rehashing of Sara's career, a lengthy exhumation of mine. The quotes from my one-time or self-proclaimed Grosse Pointe friends, the whole "Seemed like a nice guy, but you wouldn't want to cross him," recapitulation. "Always thought he had a screw loose." "We used to wonder when he'd finally snap."

Rereading those stories, I recalled the special contempt Grosse Pointers felt for those who abandoned them. I remember wondering if the names attached to the quotes were aliases, or whether I had in fact forgotten that much about my life there.

Olly Jensen's appearance at the funeral. Flew in on his private jet, refused all interviews, ignored the cameras and reporters. The bodyguard-encrusted motorcade to the cemetery. I missed the whole extravaganza, because I was cooling my heels in the Wayne County jail at the time, while the Prosecutor kicked himself for letting the police arrest me before making the case.

No hard feelings though. Anybody could have made that mistake.

I caught up on it later in the papers, and a producer I knew at Channel 7 News scored me a copy of Olly's greatest triumph. After tossing a couple clods of dirt on her coffin, he walked away from the grave, right into a media ambush.

He gave an Oscar-worthy performance as the devastated widower, gamely fending off the questions until finally his grief and anger overwhelmed him. You might think me cynical. After all, the guy had just put his wife in the ground. But you have to remember, I'd spent the last three months trying and failing to protect her from him. He was the main suspect, I'd shouted at the TV, and at my trusty bottle of Jack Daniels. Jack became a loyal friend. He never left my side, even when things were at their most bleak.

I guess you could say for a while there, Jack was my only friend. Until Mike came back into my life, having backed off like everybody else at first. But once I was cleared, he was there for me. Of course, we had Jack in common. Then it occurred to me, I hadn't visited old Jack for, what, four days now? Hadn't even missed him. Life can be funny sometimes.

But back to Olly. Once he gave in, he didn't hold back. "The most beautiful girl in the world," he called her. Hey, Olly and I had something in common. Go figure. "Had her whole life ahead of her." Yeah, and she was going to spend it with me. Then, pained look on his face, "We'd talked earlier that night on the phone. She wanted to come back and—" He broke off. His bottom lip even quivered. "Sorry," he said. Oh, Olly was good. "I told her I forgave her, that my life wasn't complete without her."

Here he stopped, looked straight into the cameras. His eyes were curiously dry for someone, even a "high-powered financier," so overcome with emotion. "I guess this, what is it, Cockroft?"

"Corcoran, Corcoran," his eager interlocutors choroused.

"Right. I guess this Corcoran chap just snapped when he thought he was going to lose her." He sighed, deeply, painfully, and concluded with a virtuoso turn, "In a way, I guess I can't blame him." And here, or was it just my imagination, his eyes got real hard. "I don't know but in the same situation, I would have done the same thing."

There it was, a confession. As cold, bold, blatant as

any confession could be. Confession? Hell with that. He wasn't confessing, he was bragging. He was saying, "I killed the bitch. I killed her, and that two-bit private dick is going to fry for it."

The hell with that, Jensen, I swore back then. This isn't over. You killed her, and I'm going to get you if it takes the rest of my life.

I swore it then, and then to my surprise, I found myself swearing it again, to myself, while sitting in my car waiting for Karin. Strange thing, this resurgent lust for vengeance. It came out of nowhere, and threatened to rip my life to pieces again, just like it had ten years before. Because that's when this case began, ten years ago.

I shook my head. Who was I kidding? This case began a long time before that. It began so long ago that sometimes I thought it best to just leave it alone. It would die eventually, once all of us were gone. It would have, too, if Deb hadn't brought it back with that phone call. Was it just two weeks ago, I wondered.

CHAPTER 2

"You heard?" Deborah's voice came down the line like thunder in a desert canyon. I fumbled for the lamp, thinking I should I just hang up. Now, before I got swept away. Instead, I pushed on. I rounded the next bend. Even if a flood was coming, I couldn't turn back. Not yet.

"Of course I heard." How could she think I hadn't? The story had been out there all day. In the papers, on TV, the Internet. Even someone as out of the loop as I was couldn't help but hear about it. But why was she calling me at 3:00 in the morning? We didn't have bedtime chats anymore. Not for the last twenty years.

"I'm sorry," I offered. About the stupidest remark ever to come out of my mouth, but there it hung, somewhere between my lips and her ear. It was too late to call it back, and frankly, I wasn't sure I should. It was a lie, but the right kind of lie. It was the kind of lie people wanted to hear at a time like that.

What was I supposed to say? That I'd been waiting twenty years for the bastard to die? That he had wormed his way into our lives, our love, and had taken the best part of me away? Now he was dead and that felt good. If his death made things tough for his brother, The Mayor, that only made it better.

"He wasn't there," she said.

I greeted that with the respect it deserved.

"He wouldn't have–it's impossible," she replied to my snort. I waited.

"We have to talk."

"It has been awhile."

"About Jonathan."

"When and where?" The best way to defeat a nightmare is to confront it. Then you can get back to sleep.

"Tomorrow, noon, at The Grill."

"Why not just take out an ad in the 'Grosse Pointe News'?"

"I happen to like it."

"No problem. It's your dime."

As a social institution, the Grill ranked just below the Grosse Pointe Yacht Club. The same suspects occupied its tables, along with a smattering of strangers. These were best described as social tourists. Residents of Detroit's less genteel suburbs, they had taken advantage of a sunny autumn Saturday and driven out to browse the galleries and shops, and maybe catch a glimpse of the rich and famous.

It was easy to spot them. They were dressed impeccably in just-right J. Crew sweaters and polo shirts hued properly pastel. Their khakis were pressed, their loafers shined. Their behavior was impeccable, too. Well-mannered, soft-spoken, they made sure their children toed the line. They were determined to pass. In short, they just didn't fit in.

Noon was much too early for Deborah to show, no matter what she had said, so I bought a copy of "The

Detroit News" on my way into the bar. I made a point of showing up on time, determined that a surly precision would dictate my relations with her this time around. There would be no dropping my guard, no revelations. I wouldn't give anything she could use this time. I was here for a job, that was all. I'd let her have her say, and pocket three or four days' worth of inflated fees. I'd get the money up front, too, because she might not want to write that check after I gave her my final report. Normally I wouldn't charge to tell her what a shit her late brother-in-law had been, but what the hell, I could use the money.

I grabbed a stool at the end of the bar and endured Jerry's elaborate double-take.

"Corky? Is it really you?" he cried. I groaned inside. Corky was a nickname I'd never sought and rarely answered to. It was a scar from my youth and Jerry seemed determined to rip it open again. "Corky," he repeated as he bounded down the bar to pump my hand. "Good Lord, it's been awhile."

"Yeah, about ten years. Still going strong?"

"Better than ever." Jerry brushed back his thinning yellow mop. "Well, hell, first one's on me—for old times. Bourbon?"

I stared at him, wondering how much of this was an act. "It's a little early, Jer. Make it a wine—a pinot noir."

"Just got a good one in—Robert Sinskey. They drank the shit out of it last night."

"Definitely the Sinskey then. I hate pinots when they still have the shit in them."

Jerry laughed, a surprisingly rich bass for such a slight frame. "Same old Corky." He set the glass in front of me, and relinquished the bottle for my perusal.

"So what brings you back?" he asked reluctantly, as if afraid of the answer. I was tempted to say I'd bought the old house, was going to get back into the swing of things. Instead, I mumbled, "Work."

"Some celebrity divorce, huh?"

I regretted my charity. "I'll let you figure it out."

He frowned. "I hated the way things worked out."

"Forget it, Jer. That was a long time ago. It's ancient history now."

That little flash of a smile showed how much he believed that. "Hey, I read about you in the paper, that Jensen case. Man, I thought you were going to jail."

"Lost my license for six months while they sorted it out."

"Jesus, Sara Jensen. I mean, that made 'Sixty Minutes.'"

"Forget it, Jer."

"She was killed with your gun."

"Yeah, and she died in my arms." I let some heat spill out with the words. More than I cared to hear, but I didn't like thinking about Sara Jensen.

Jerry brushed back his hair again and gazed out at the sun-spanked lake. "They said you were lovers."

"Occupational hazard."

"So come on, what really happened?"

"I said forget it." That ended the reunion. Jerry shrugged and drifted over to pour drinks for the Peters brothers. John and David were confirmed sailors They spent their summers racing on Lake St. Clair and the rest of the year raising a stake for a run at the America's Cup. They were back home now, arms still tan, faces ruddy. They wore polo shirts and wrinkled jeans, last year's boat shoes worn and faded. They said they were going to start with scotch.

They'd end with Jaegermeisters at closing time, with a dozen hangers-on barely hanging on, lurching through the door to continue the party at their parents' house. Back in college I used to party with them in that ugly old mansion. I used to go on late-night, booze-soaked, swimsuit-shedding, cabin-swapping cruises on the lake, and to pre-ski, apres-ski, finally no-ski parties at their parents' condo out in Aspen. I don't remember if I got older or just uninvited, but here they were, twenty years later, still going strong. Life remained for them one big frat party.

I didn't think they'd remember me, or want to if they did, but I didn't relish the prospects, however slim, of rehashing the good old days, so I hid behind the paper. It was okay. It was my job. Hiding behind newspapers is what private dicks do.

I glanced at the reports of the more sensational crimes. The triple murder on Gratiot, the Comerica Bank vice president who transferred $40 million to an offshore account and followed it out of the country, and the prostitute found in a dumpster behind the Amati Food Center. That last wouldn't have merited mention except whoever killed her had dismembered her, then whimsically reattached her body parts.

Mike Wallis had told me about that yesterday. He was the one who found her, and it took a bottle of Jack Daniels to get him over it. Then again, it took about the same amount to get over a good day. Mike was a good drinking buddy. He never got loud or violent, just mellow, and it never hurt to have a contact on the force. Still, if he didn't slow down, they'd have him taking stolen car reports at the Seventh Precinct, and that wouldn't do me much good.

I scanned the article, curious to see how they could sanitize the tale for what was still called a family newspaper. Disappointed to find the best they could come up with was "shockingly mutilated corpse"—kind of trips off the tongue, don't it?—I decided to flip through to the sports section to check out the latest call for the head (shockingly mutilated) of the Detroit Lions' coach, but my progress was arrested by the photo of a grinning Justin Wade above the fold on the Metro Page.

It was the obligatory human interest follow up. Lots of quotes from anonymous Friends of the Family about just how broken up Justin was, Justin himself having declined to comment. That in itself was newsworthy. The idea that he would pass up any opportunity to speak to his friends in the media, even about his brother's murder, boggled the mind. No doubt his handlers had convinced him that silence would net him more positive publicity than anything he could say.

The article continued with boilerplate effusions about the long-established family (great-grandfather Jared Wade, the lumber baron who transformed the city from a trading post on the Detroit River into a budding industrial center; grandfather Joshua Wade, who turned a sleepy lakeside farm community into the city's most exclusive suburb; the father, Jeremy Wade, who developed most of the land north and west of the city, and Justin himself, the popular and innovative Grosse Pointe mayor and virtual shoo-in for the US Senate next year).

SEE P. 35

The meat of the story wallowed in the tragic tale of two brothers, both scions of the most prominent family in a community of prominent families. One was earmarked for greatness. The other was destined from birth, according to those anonymous Friends of the Family, to end up shot to death outside a Detroit crack house. The reporter rehashed, of course, the drowning of Jessica Wade, their eight-year-old sister. The authorities had ruled it an accident, and the twelve-year-old Justin was even hailed as a hero for his efforts to rescue her, but suspicions lingered that Jon had been responsible, had even drowned her on purpose, and only the family's clout had managed to hush that up.

I put down the paper, contemplating the unlikely prospect of actually pitying Jonathan Wade. They really did a number on him, those Friends of the Family. Never amounted to anything, never had a prayer of doing so. Two brothers estranged, Justin's only contact the past ten years being to bail Jonathan out, to foot the bill for another stay in another clinic, to pay his gambling debts. Jonathan was the only blemish on an otherwise exemplary life.

That was so far from the truth as I knew it, as I had lived it. Don't get me wrong, Jon was as bad as they said he was, and always had been, long before Deborah. The thing was, bad as Jon was, his brother was worse. Though he drew affection to himself like a magnet, I never could understand it. To me, he was a monster, a freak of nature. He had been born without a conscience; sort of a moral birth defect. If I had to choose which brother to spend the rest of my life with on a desert island, I'd opt for suicide.

Jerry showed up to refill my glass. Nodding at the paper he said, "Hard to believe, isn't it?"

"You mean all that bullshit about St. Justin?"

"No, I mean about Jonathan. It just doesn't seem—" He frowned. "Can't let it rest, can you?" I shrugged. "Why'd you come back, Jim?"

"I told you, work. Now, what about Jon?"

He shook his head. "Don't do this. It won't do any good to—" He broke off again, along with all the other locals in the place. I followed his gaze to where Deborah Wade stood silhouetted in the doorway. Details emerged as the door hissed shut behind her.

Her pale skin had aged only slightly in the twenty years since I lost her, and the ten years since I'd seen her last. It had softened, adding character to her high cheekbones and fragile jaw. She still wore her hair long, though there were streaks of gray now in the ebony. She wore a nubbly beige cotton cardigan, the kind with big side pockets, that had gone out of style about the same time I had. I was surprised, and unreasonably gratified, to see that she wasn't a slave to fashion. I thought being a wholly owned subsidiary of Justin Wade Enterprises would have changed her. She hesitated in the doorway, hands plunged into those deep pockets, shoulders hunched slightly forward as though absorbing the waves of silence buffeting her. Then, her eyes adapting to the gloom, she spied me at the bar and made her way over.

She asked Jerry for a glass of Chardonnay. He said

11

okay, then hesitated when she extended a cool, white hand to me. I don't think I had ever received as large a share of Grosse Pointers' esteem as I did at that moment when their silence grew to include me. I stared past her at all those faces which had meant so much to me so long ago.

"How about a table, Jerry?" I muttered. He nodded at the hostess, who transported us to the dim austerity of the Cloisters. The mock-gothic cavern was reserved for the dinner hour, and only the most serious lunches. The handful of people there at that hour graced us with their neglect.

"It's good to be back." I left it up to her to do with that what she would.

"Did I keep you waiting long?"

"About twenty years."

She pulled at her fingers disdainfully. I used to think she should have lived in an era in which women wore gloves. "This isn't about you."

"What was that scene at the bar, then?"

"That wasn't about you, either."

"The way they stared." I said it wistfully. I wasn't trying to hurt her. I wasn't even speaking to her, really, but it did the trick just the same.

"Look, Jim. I'm hurting here." Sure enough, her eyes brimmed with tears.

"So it was about you?"

"No, dammit." I couldn't help but envision her gloves—pearl gray, had to be—slapping the table in emphasis. As it was, the way she spat the words had the same effect. The Cloisters grew ~~as~~ sepulchral ~~as a cathedral~~ as the others lapsed in their neglect, but only for a moment before Deborah's eyes sent them scurrying back to their own concerns.

"It's about Jonathan," she continued in a more level voice.

"As I suspected." It was a mockery, a parody of my role as detective. It was as out of place as I was.

"This isn't going to work."

"Sounds vaguely familiar."

She slid her chair back abruptly.

"Don't go, Deb. You brought me out here, the least you can do is buy me lunch."

She smiled at that. The first I'd seen in years. I'd honestly forgotten how a smile transformed her face from porcelain to rich, soft, humanity. It was genuine, heartfelt, and it went all the way from her lips to her eyes. It enveloped you. A smile like that was so honest, so pure, it was impossible to believe the person behind it was capable of betrayal. I remember once believing I could spend the rest of my life making that face smile that smile.

She picked up the menu. "Okay, you win."

She ordered a Cobb Salad. I went for the salmon en croute for starters, and the breast of chicken rubbed with cumin and cilantro and served with a corn, tomato and black bean salsa, and a stuffed poblano pepper, and a bottle of Patten Valley Pinot.

"You still know how to order," she said as Sondra-our-server-today headed for the kitchen.

"Yeah, I just can't afford it anymore."

"Whatever happened to you?"

"Tell me about your kids."

They were Justin, Jr., 12, and Jessica, 10. A matched pair, straight from the catalog. Money back guarantee. Actually, she told about them well, a line sketch rather than a portrait, enough to inform but not enough to bore. I tried to do the same when she asked me about my life.

"I lived," I said.

"At least one of us did."

The food finally came, and we consumed it with ample helpings of regret on the side. After I poured the last of the bottle and bade Sondra to serve us another, I brought the conversation back to the dearly departed. "So, it looks like Jonathan has smoked his last pipe."

"I just can't believe it," she replied. "It wasn't like

him."

"It was exactly like him," I countered. "Look, you've got to give me one reason not to believe the police report. Otherwise, you're just wasting your money." I raised my glass. "And believe me, it will cost you."

"Money's no object."

I raised my glass again. "My three favorite words."

After Sondra returned with the second bottle, I resumed the discussion. "Now then, Deborah, suppose you explain to me why the guy who turned me on to pot at the age of 13, to cocaine at 16, and to acid at 18, wouldn't have been anywhere near a crack house on Thursday night."

"He just wouldn't have been."

"Give me a break, Deb." Either there was something there, or there wasn't. Blind faith wasn't getting us anywhere. I had to say something to shake out some facts. "Look, I'll take the case. A thousand a day, plus expenses."

"Isn't that a bit steep?"

"Whatever the market will bear, as the man used to say."

"Upton Sinclair's 'The Jungle'?"

"Frank Norris. 'The Octopus'."

"At least I didn't say Sinclair Lewis again."

I laughed. "A few years ago Walden Publishing brought out a book about the beef industry. Their catalog called it the most searing exposé of the beef industry since Sinclair Lewis' 'The Jungle'. If a publisher can't get it right, why should a 23-year-old?"

"Thanks for that, anyway." She smiled again. Things started shaking loose inside me. Things like resolve. "You never would let me forget it." A little more regret for dessert, then, "When did you start reading publishers' catalogs?"

"Oh, that was a little job I did for Steve Goodson. He owns Batchelor Books."

"Isn't that an adult bookstore?"

"There's a 'T' in Batchelor, as in David Batchelor. Steve bought it from David's widow after he got killed in a hold up."

"Nice." She worked the nonexistent gloves again.

"Life in the big city."

"So you were what, security?" I was glad to see she didn't want to believe I'd sunk that far.

I shook my head. "Steve was being shaken down by a cop. So I worked at the store until I got enough evidence to take to the DA."

"You charged him $1,000 a day?"

"More like seven bucks an hour." I grinned. "Retail sucks."

"So you just did the guy a favor?" Her skepticism put paid to any fantasies I might have been entertaining about there ever being a future to our past.

"He's a friend. It's a great bookstore. Besides," I checked the bottle, and emptied it into our glasses. "I needed a job." Hell, I wanted it out in the open. "They'd pulled my license."

"Over Sara?"

"Did she ever talk about—"

"No." Too abruptly.

"I wonder what she said."

Deborah's frown was the polar opposite of her smile. I remembered that, too. She ordered a couple of coffees when Sondra drifted past. I sought a supplemental brandy. It seemed appropriate to the moment. She declined to join me. That seemed about right, too. She refused to meet my eyes, staring instead at the wine swirling in the glass she twirled between her fingers. I let the silence flow. It's a good technique. They offer a whole course on it in detective correspondence school.

"Jonathan didn't even drink anymore," she began falteringly. I almost fell off my chair. I'd gotten my $25 worth. "He hadn't for three years."

"He wasn't just telling you that because that's what you wanted to hear?"

"I knew Jonathan." She still wouldn't look at me. "He'd changed. He—he was motivated. It was like he was trying to make up for lost time, like he didn't want to waste any more of his life." Her smile was a real one, this time, showing me how little she'd put into the others. And this one wasn't for me. I envied the bastard all over again. "He was really starting to open up. I mean, you have to know, don't you, that Jonathan was a brilliant man?"

I nodded. Slowly.

"One day, about two years ago, we were out on his boat." She laughed. She seemed so happy. "He told me, 'I feel like I've been in a body cast for a year. It hurts to walk, but I have to try.'" Then there were tears in her eyes again, and this time they were real. Hell, I don't know. Maybe they were the first time, too. I wasn't prepared for this.

"You were seeing him?"

"Not like that, I wasn't. I—"

Sondra returned with the coffees, and the brandy. "I'll have another," I said.

I thought Deb was going to keep stirring her coffee until it evaporated. She wouldn't look at me so I looked at her. Her cheeks were pink-tinged from emotion. Her eyes were cast down at her coffee, her long black lashes blinking back tears. I gazed at her lips, her fine white teeth, at the white silk blouse she wore. The top two buttons were undone and her skin glowed white down to the hint of the swell of her breasts. I remembered gazing at her like this on other Saturday afternoons, knowing then that soon more buttons would be undone, more of her white body revealed. The first time it happened had been a gift. A gift of life, from life, it had promised to be repeated endlessly. I remembered that first time. I swear, I remembered every time. I remember vowing to forget. The love eventually stopped but the memories never did.

"All right," she confessed abruptly. "Like that. It was, I don't know, special." She touched my hand and I didn't even flinch. "He changed, Jim. You have to understand."

"It doesn't matter. That was a long time ago."

She squeezed my hand. She bought it. She believed me. I don't know why it was so important, but I was happy that she did. She smiled at me, a sad one this time, but a real one. "Thank you for saying that."

Okay, she didn't believe me.

"So you and Jon were what—lovers obviously. Were you planning to jeopardize Justin's political career with a nasty in-house scandal?"

"No, no." She shook her head vigorously. "No, in fact, it didn't last. It was just, I don't know–"

For old times' sake?"

"Oh, please."

"Cause I'm right here."

SEE P. 112

She didn't react, beyond a momentary flaring of her nostrils and the fastidious removal of her hand from mine. "Jonathan was almost all the way back," she recited tonelessly. "It wasn't easy. You don't recover overnight. And Justin–he didn't make it any easier. Jonathan tried to make amends, to bridge the gap, but Justin—he didn't even laugh. He just sneered. He offered him a drink! My God! It was like he didn't want him to recover, like he wanted him dead."

The horror on her face shattered the lifeless facade. Whatever else, this woman cared. Her faith may have been unwarranted, but it was certainly sincere. From where she sat it was easy to believe, but Jon wasn't the first guy to climb out of the pit only to stumble and go all the way back down, and further. Going to that crack house made perfect sense to me. A bullet in the face was an apt coda to Jon's final binge. It's an old story.

She read my skepticism. "It isn't true. He told me he was going to make it all right again. He said he had the answer."

"What did that mean?"

"I don't know. He was so secretive. But he was excited, more so than he had been in years. It was like—"

"What?"

"Nothing." Her lip trembled. She knew.

"Like the old days?" She shook her head.

"Like he was high."

"No. No!" She whispered urgently. "All right, yes. But not, too. He was manic. I mean, he was so happy, so, what, relieved? Yes, that's it. Relieved. Liberated." She grabbed my hand again. No tenderness this time, her nails dug into my flesh. "He wasn't on anything, Jim. Except maybe a crusade."

"A crusade...?"

"Yes. He told me he had a purpose, at last, and was going to see it through. He said he was going to make good on all those I.O.U.'s."

"Well, he had a lot of them. I carried ~~around~~ a $300 chit in my wallet for about five years."

She frowned. "I don't think he meant money."

"Then what?"

"I—I'm not sure. He wouldn't give me any details. Except once, when he—" Her face grew paler than usual.

"What? What did he say?" Was there something there? Was it possible I really did have a case?

"He said he hoped when it all came out, that I wouldn't be hurt."

"Hurt? How? Physically?"

She shrugged. "I have no idea." She grabbed my hand again. "But you can see why I'm suspicious."

I agreed, more to save my hand than out of any conviction. "Okay, I'm intrigued by this new Jon. But I need to know more. Who should I talk to?"

"Karin."

"Girlfriend?"

"He met Karin three years ago, in a program. The program, actually. The one that got him straight."

"And this Karin, is she still clean and sober?"

"She worked there, you ass. She was his counselor."

"Meanwhile, you and he—" I was getting lost again.

"No, that was before, or after."

"It's got to be one or the other."

"It wasn't like that—not with her, not with me. Karin's just—well, you'll know when you meet her. She's something special. She was. For Jonathan, I mean. It was like he was her project, something to work on at home. I don't know if it was very professional, and I don't know anything about their relationship, or—" She sighed. "Oh, forget it. Let her explain."

Deb told me how to get in touch with Karin, and with Bill Jeffries, Jon's partner in some mysterious venture having to do with the stock market, or credit default swaps, or some such thing, she wasn't sure. Finally, she gave me a $4,000 check as a retainer, for which I was sure my landlord would be grateful.

I told her I'd call her in a couple of days with an update, resisted the urge to grace her lips with a social kiss, and went outside to my car.

CHAPTER 3

The drive back wasn't bad. Since The Grill was only three blocks from Alter Road, and it was the middle of the day, it was no great surprise that I didn't see any cops on my way out of town. Which was lucky. Not that I was driving erratically, it's just that a ten-year-old sedan is regarded as a suspicious vehicle in Grosse Pointe. Odds are it's being driven by a burglar, a child molester, or even worse, a Negro. (Though the demographics have altered somewhat over the years, a lot of Grosse Pointers still think that way. Folks might have the latest in smart phones and tablets, but they are less than cutting-edge on social terms. Most Pointers were just getting comfortable with "Black" when "African-American" reared its ugly head. At that point they just threw up their hands and went back to what sounded most comfortable. The more enlightened ones stopped at "Negro").

The cops would stop any car more than six years old on any pretext. Erratic driving, a broken tail light, even a dirty license plate was suitable cause to run a make. One sniff of my breath would justify a breathalyzer, and I had no doubt on which side of the line that needle would stop. I made my escape undetected however, and pulled up in front of my office.

"Office is a charitable term, though I did keep the front third of the loft relatively neat. It was set off from the rest of the mayhem by a weekend's worth of drywalling I did a few years back. I did have James T. Corcoran, Private Detective, stenciled in gold paint on the door, and an extra desk for appearances, but it never really worked for me. Not like the suite I had in the Whitney Building. Now that was classy. Eighth floor, three marble-lined rooms, a real live receptionist, and twelve-foot-high windows overlooking Grand Circus Park.

That was back when I was on a roll. Back when I could command a grand a day from anybody, not just former lovers. That was back before Sara Jensen and the State Board of Review. Back before cops, reporters and lawyers stopped taking my calls. Back before—

But this wasn't getting me anywhere. I had a case, I had four thousand bucks in my pocket, a FedEx signature-required notice stuck to my mailbox, and three flashes on my answering machine. The first was from Sprint, informing me that they'd happily switch me back to AT&T at no charge if I didn't pay my bill, the second from Douglass, Duncan and Steele inquiring whether I had any intention of paying the bill they'd been given by AT&T for collection. The third call was from Mike Wallis announcing that he'd made an arrest in the shockingly mutilated corpse case and did I want to join him at the Walloon Saloon for a celebration?

Not tonight, buddy, I thought. I'm on a case. I figured I could stretch this one into a week or two, pad my expenses and maybe finally turn my life around, again.

Ignoring the fact that I'd already had more fresh starts than Drew Barrymore, I flipped open my notebook, deciphered the number and rang up Karin Champagne.

She wasn't in, so I left a message, deciding after a

moment's hesitation to add that it pertained to Jon Wade. Then I left a message on Bill Jeffries' voice mail, glanced at the clock, and decided four o'clock was too early for another drink. I called Mike at the station but he'd already left. Figuring fifteen minutes wasn't long enough to exhaust all my leads, I grabbed yesterday's papers off the recycling pile and reviewed the accounts of Jonathan Wade's timely demise.

The stories were basically the same, though there were some small discrepancies. The News and the Free Press both said there were six abandoned houses on the dismal block of Manistique where the murder took place, (actually the Freep called it bleak), while the Oakland Press said there were "eight burned-out shells of houses on a block which might have been found in war-torn Baghdad."

The time of death was variously reported as 11:18, 11:23 and 11:32, but there was no disagreement on the other particulars. Neighbors reported hearing voices raised in anger, followed by a shotgun blast and the squeal of tires. The victim's face was blown away. He had a history of drug use, was a member of the prominent Wade family, brother of Justin Wade, Mayor of Grosse Pointe, blah, blah, blah.

Now it was 4:15. Surely half-an-hour was enough? No, I was going to be diligent about this. I owed it to Deb, after all. I figured I'd head over to Manistique, count the number of abandoned houses, and see how many were in fact burned-out shells. Then, maybe I'd drop by the Walloon Saloon and interrogate Mike Wallis, see if there were any details the police had held back. See if there were any clues. After all, Walloon Avenue was just a few blocks north of Manistique.

I grabbed my jacket and was heading for the door when the phone rang. I hesitated. It was probably Sprint, or AT&T, or Visa, or MasterCard, or any of a half-dozen other creditors who would just have to hang on a little longer while I got my life turned around again. On the other hand, it might be important. What the hell, I picked it up.

"Corcoran?" The growl was vaguely familiar and unmistakably menacing.

"Who wants to know?"

"Shuddup and listen. Get off the case and stay off, or else."

"Or else what?" Not the wittiest retort, but this sort of exchange has its own ground rules.

"Or else you'll be sorry," he said, proving my point. It was maddening, the voice was so familiar, the name to go with it hovering on the outside reaches of my memory.

"Tell me what I'm supposed to stay away from, and maybe I will," I snarled. Even if I'd expected it to happen, I wouldn't have expected it to start so soon. Were they watching Deborah? Was she in danger? "Look. What the hell's going on?"

Mike's reedy laughter brought me up short. "God, you scare easy."

"Wallis, you sonofabitch," I laughed. "You goddamn sonofabitch."

"So where the hell are you? I bought you two drinks already."

"I hope they're still waiting."

"Naw, I got tired of talking to an empty chair, so I drank 'em."

I told him I'd be right there, just as soon as I wrapped up some business.

"What kind of business could you have that's more important than—" He broke off. "Hey Jimbo, you got a case?"

I said I did, that I'd fill him in as soon as I got there. I hung up, forwarded any calls to my pager, just in case, and locked the door behind me. I decided to skip checking out Manistique Street. It'd give me something to do tomorrow once the headache wore off. It was shaping up to be that kind of night.

The Walloon Saloon was as dusky as it should be, its smoke-stained fixtures shrouded by dust. The tarnished bowling trophies, the buck with a straw hat and fedora hanging from his antlers, the sputtering Strohs neon sign and the faded "Bless You Boys" banner, all bespoke the neighborhood which once had thrived around this neighborhood bar. The TV at the end of the bar was tuned to the Channel 4 early news, and Darla, the brassy, gravel-voiced bartender, who'd been every local's unattainable ideal thirty years ago, turned wearily at the squeak of the hinges.

"Oh, it's you,' she said, lighting another Winston. "Good. You can babysit him for awhile."

Mike slouched at the end of the bar, as close to the back door as possible. He grinned at me and pointed at the rocks glass sweating on its napkin. "'Nother thirty secs, it would've been gone, too."

I nodded my thanks as I took the stool next to his. "How's it going, Darla?"

She exhaled a violent stream of smoke. "Shitty as ever, Jim. Shitty as ever."

"I'm still waiting for that date."

She grinned. "Well, now that Brad Pitt's makin' babies, you might get it."

Mike swivelled on his stool. "If you're through sweet-talking him, I'd like to tell my buddy how I broke the crime of the century."

I raised my glass. "Shoot."

His eyes clouded over a moment, then he adjusted his silk tie before beginning. Say what you want about Mike, he knew how to dress. Hundred dollar ties, thousand dollar suits, and they looked good on him. He was about 5'10", and slight of build, with a ferret face and thinning sandy hair. He didn't exactly look the part of a detective, but he was a good one, or had been, and still could be when he wanted to. How he could afford the clothes, three ex-wives and five ex-kids on a detective's salary was something I was never going to ask about.

"Justice was well served when they assigned me to this case," Mike began. "Not too many would have had the tenacity and the instincts necessary to close this one."

"Oh, do tell," Darla said through a raspberry cough.

"Well, Doug and I figured we'd go by Ms. Mutilation's flat and see if she left a note or anything—"

"How'd you figure out where she lived? The papers said she was all hacked up."

"That's where the brilliant detective work came in." Mike waved his finger at our glasses. "When they checked her for semen they found her driver's license shoved up there."

"He put it in before or after he killed her?" Darla said, depositing fresh drinks in front of us.

"You know, I forgot to ask. Hell, I bet the Coroner didn't even check. Sometimes Joe gets sloppy when he finds something new." He shrugged. "Luckily, that doesn't happen too often."

"That was damn brilliant detecting so far," I said. "What'd you do next?"

"Like I said, me and Doug went by her flat—first we stopped for coffee at Louis', over on Harper. I think Doug had a Reuben, too."

"It's that mind for details," I said to Darla. "That's what sets Mike apart."

"Yeah, well, I wish he'd remember the little detail of his bar tab."

"Hey, I said I'd take care of it."

"Yeah, for the last month you're gonna take care of it. How do you think the other customers feel, watching you drink for free?"

Mike made an elaborate show of looking around the place. "I don't know. If one shows up, I'll ask him."

Darla's guffaw metastasized into a coughing fit. Mike peeled a hundred off his roll and flipped it on the bar.

"Here, draw me down a bit." Then he went back to his story.

"So when we get there, we knock on the door and it swings open. Doug's got his gun out and he's through the door before I finish pissing myself—asshole watches way too many cop shows. Then he calls, 'You can come in now, Mikey. It's safe.' So I walk in and there's our perp, laid out in black leather, dog collar and all, needle hanging out of his arm."

"OD?"

"Suicide."

THIS SUICIDE PINNED HIS NOTE TO HIS OWN NIPPLE?

"Left a note?"

?

"Pinned to his right nipple so we couldn't miss it. Said he was sorry, that Suzi was one too many cause he really cared about her."

"There were others?"

"Six, to be exact. See, he had a photo album. Kept notes, names and addresses." Mike knocked back his drink and gave a bitter laugh. "Caught a fucking serial killer and we didn't even know we had one."

"How could you not know?"

"He didn't want us to. See, they were all different. Different styles, different M.O.'s. Take Suzi. She was cut up surgically, razor sharp knife, very precise. The others, one was hacked up with a butcher knife, one with an axe. A couple of multiple stabbings, one an ice pick in the ear. He fucked three of em—before or after, I don't know." This last was for Darla's benefit. "He did some at his house, some at their's, some on the street. The only thing that tied them together was they were all women. That and they're all dead."

"So you're going to be famous."

Mike scowled. "Naw, Dougie's taking care of that." He jerked his head at the TV. "He's gonna be on pretty soon. Me, I don't need that shit."

Might raise some questions about his wardrobe, I thought. "Let me buy the detective a drink," I announced.

Darla did a double take. "You're buying?"

"I guess you do have a case," said Mike with a laugh.

"Might as well enjoy it while I can. Be a shame to let it all go to the landlord."

Mike slapped me on the back. "Who's the lucky stiff?"

"Jon Wade." I let it slip casually.

"No, c'mon, really."

"Really, Jon Wade."

"Yeah, but wasn't he the one who—"

"She's my client."

You could just see the life sag out of him. "You want my advice? Leave it alone. Give the money back."

"Drop the case or else?" I said, laughing.

That got a smile out of him. "God, you're a pansy. One little threat and you start bawling like a baby."

"Your problem is, you don't know the difference between anger and fear."

"Yeah, right." Then he looked at me, and there was no humor in his eyes. "Forget about that. Why are you fucking with the Wades?"

"Fucking with the Wades? If Deborah wants to throw her money away, why shouldn't I be there to catch it?"

"It aint that simple, buddy, and I think you know it."

"What? You mean the case? Is there something there?"

Mike's smile was reluctant, and tinged with pity. "Listen to you. 'You mean the case? Is there something there?'" he mimicked. "I just don't want to see you get hurt."

"Again."

"What?"

"Hurt again. That's what you mean, isn't it? Hurt again?"

"Aw for Chrissake, Jim. What are you talkin' about?"

"You know damn well what I'm talking about." I didn't like hearing the rage in my voice. I thought I'd put all that behind me.

"It's got nothing to do with Sara."

"My point exactly," I said. "This is just about money, about getting back to even, about—"

"Revenge," Mike said softly.

My pager went off before I could respond. I checked the number. It was Karin's.

"Jesus, Jim. When you gonna get a cell phone?" Mike said.

"I'm waiting to see if they catch on."

"Catch on?" Darla scoffed.

"Yeah," I said. "I can't just go running after every little fad."

"You got a computer, doncha?" she managed through her guttering laughter.

"Of course I do. Couldn't work without it."

"You work?" Mike put in. "News to me."

"Maybe that's why I don't have a cell phone." I hopped off the stool, and pulled my pockets out to illustrate the point. "Pay phone still work?"

Darla nodded, so I told Mike I'd be back and headed for the phone.

She picked up on the second ring. "You called me?" I said.

"Is this, I'm sorry, uh, James Corcoran?" Her voice sounded red-eyed.

"Yeah."

"You called—about Jonathan?"

I decided not to say anything until she stopped making statements into questions.

"I don't know anything. Really, I don't." Interesting response.

"Weren't you seeing him?"

"No. Well, yes, sort of, I guess." Her voice broke. "I'm sorry, it's just really been hard."

"Listen, Karin," I said quickly before she could hang up. "I'm a private detective. Deborah Wade hired me to look into Jon's death. I think we should meet."

"I don't know. How do I know you're—

"Who else would I be?" Why was I barking at her? This woman was in some pain. So I eased off a bit. "Listen, Karin. I'm on your side."

There was a pause while she worked it out. "Okay, can you come over now?"

I glanced at the bar where yet another drink was waiting for me. "Now? I thought tomorrow might be better."

"I'd feel better if it was now," she insisted. "Please?"

"Well," I hesitated. It felt like a mistake. Then again, I'd made so many, I wasn't sure I could recognize it if I did something right. "Alright, where are you?" I wrote down the address. "No, no, I know where it is. About twenty minutes then."

When I returned to the bar, Mike said, "You ought to leave it alone."

"The hell with you." I grabbed my jacket and left. My key found the lock on the second try, which wasn't too bad. I figured the drive would get me back up to speed.

It also gave me some time to get a read on Karin. I couldn't really blame her for being upset. The way I saw it, things weren't working out between them. She told him it was over, or maybe they just had a fight. Whatever. The important thing was he thought he was losing her, went on a binge and walked off a cliff. So, sure she was upset. She felt like she'd driven him to it. If only she had said this or not done that, or stuck it out a little longer, then he'd still be alive. Basically, she killed him. She didn't pull the trigger, but she killed him just the same. It didn't matter how ridiculous that was. It didn't matter that she was a professional counselor and should know better. She'd probably consoled dozens of guilt-ridden spouses, boyfriends, girlfriends, children, who were feeling the same thing. It didn't matter. This was happening to her. It's always different when it happens to you.

That's the way I saw it, and nothing in that conversation made me think it might be different, except for that subtle undercurrent of fear. But maybe I was over reading the fear angle. Maybe, all cynicism aside, I just really wanted a case. Maybe I really did want to turn my life around again. Maybe I wanted to get back to the big time. I slumped behind the wheel. I glanced at the dashboard clock inching toward 7:00, toward prime drinking time, toward what was starting to feel like a real bad judgment call.

Maybe all I wanted was to feel Debbie Winthrop move beneath me again. To look down into those eyes spread wide in the sudden surprise of feeling me inside her.

I pounded the steering wheel. "Goddamn you, Deborah. Why'd you have to call me? Why couldn't you just leave me alone?"

CHAPTER 4

Eastpointe, located northeast of Detroit, used to be called East Detroit, until the Chamber of Commerce decided association with the struggling city was hurting property values. When they put it to a vote the locals decided, yes, they'd rather be mistaken for Grosse Pointe than Detroit. Of course, when they heard that rationale, Grosse Pointers simply laughed. As if anybody could make that mistake. Eastpointe's official flower is the Petunia.

Karin lived in one of those sprawling complexes littering the suburbs. Two-story, mock chalets housing ten apartments each, set at oblique angles around a pool and recreation area that nobody ever used, they were middle-class slums. I'd always believed no matter how far I fell, I'd never end up there. Still, the people I'd met who lived here weren't so bad. They had brains, some of them. They had goals. They had lives. Some of them were damned good looking.

Like Karin. She opened the door at my knock and ushered me into the living room. "Thanks for coming." Her shoulder-length, straw-blonde hair was a mess. Her eyes were red and her peaches-and-cream complexion didn't fare well under mourning, but none of that affected the quality of the package. She wore a wool sweater and a pair of faded jeans. She was barefoot and I couldn't help admiring the graceful lines of her feet and toes.

The living room was furnished in knock-off deluxe, the kind of chairs and couches you buy from the discount warehouses. Sturdy, built to last, but with a veneer of deprivation kind of like their owner. She cleared a space for me on the couch, sweeping newspapers, a cheap novel, and an afghan aside. Lowering herself into a chair set at a right angle to the couch, she said, "Sorry about the mess."

Waving distractedly around the room, her hand ended up resting in her lap. "I'm a wreck, I guess." She smiled timidly. "I'm sorry."

"No need to apologize," I said, thinking again what a lucky bastard Jon was, or had been.

"Can I get you something to drink?" She was up again, moving to the kitchen.

"Whiskey, if you've got it," I said, watching the way she moved. Her jeans fit snugly, her back was broad. She carried ten or so extra pounds, but she carried them well. Not a slave to her body, I decided, but probably had to be careful the ten pounds didn't become twenty or thirty.

To the sound of opening cupboards and clinking ice cubes, I examined the room. To my right, next to the kitchen doorway, a hunting print hung over a heavy mahogany sideboard, which contrasted with the other furnishings. It held faded photographs, probably of her parents, a brother and sister, maybe. There were a couple of Jon. He looked much older than forty, and his face had filled out. Altogether likable, I grudgingly admitted. His eyes seemed kind, and ready to laugh, with, not at you. In both photos, one taken in winter, the other summer, he wore simple, durable, unfashionable clothing. Maybe he had changed.

In addition to the sideboard, and the sofa and chair

done in a green on black floral print, there was a functional coffee table littered with copies of news magazines and some professional journals, a letter and some junk mail. No coffee table books, no pretension. Across the room, a bookcase dominated the wall next to the hallway. It was simple, just pine boards hammered together. No trim, no finish; definitely homemade. I wondered who made it. Jon? Karin? Somebody else in her life?

The shelves contained a collection of old psych textbooks, a handful of contemporary novels and several more substantial works. There was the usual bric-a-brac, three houseplants, a Walmart stereo and a ten-inch TV.

Before I could reach any firm conclusions about her, Karin returned, carrying two generous glasses. Her breasts, jouncing beneath her baby blue sweater, drew my attention. When she noticed me noticing them she brought her arms close to her sides. This had the dual, yet contradictory effect of stopping their motion while thrusting them forward. I glanced away, then back, at her face this time. Her eyes carried the ambivalence of a shy woman who catches a man appraising her body; embarrassment mingled with pride, with a hint of astonishment that she might be included in his itinerary. I looked for the disdain she should have betrayed at being eyed by a stranger two days after her lover's death. It didn't seem to be there.

I sipped my drink and said, "Tell me about Jon."

She leaned forward to set her drink on the table, and folded her hands in her lap. Took a deep breath to compose herself, and began. "Jonathan came into my life about three years ago, at Shady Grove, a clinic where I work part time? You meet a lot of guys, a lot of people who are there because their family or friends talked them into it, or to keep their jobs, or because the judge said it's that or jail. Most of them just want to get through it so they can get on with their lives."

33

"Which means back to the bar?"

"Or the needle, whatever." Her eyes flickered up at mine, then returned to her hands. She seemed distracted.

"So what about Jon?"

"Jonathan was different. He—you knew he'd been in programs before. He knew the ropes. But he really wanted to change. 'I'm so tired,' he said. 'I want to get back to Go.'" She looked at me again, sadness tinged with concern. "He was haunted, Mr. Corcoran."

"Jim, please."

"Jim." A flicker of warmth. "I'm Karin."

"I know." This with a smile to soften the sarcasm. I glanced at my watch. Going on 7:30. I wondered how Mike was faring. Thinking of him, I took another gulp of my whiskey. "What do you mean, haunted?"

"I don't know. He never would say." She sniffled. "The only time he really got mad was when I pressed him. There was a lot of anger there, a lot of resentment." She glanced at me. "I think that's why he got into drugs, to hide it."

I didn't mean to laugh. It just burst out. Her head shot up. "Sorry," I said. "But how far back is this supposed to go? I mean, even in Junior High, Jon was Mr. Party, and there didn't seem to be any secret anguish."

She shifted uncomfortably. "I didn't realize you and Jonathan were friends."

I said friends would be stretching it. "Let's just say we shared some of the same interests."

She greeted that skeptically, but soon returned to her story. "Lots of people drink, that doesn't mean they have a problem" She hoisted her own glass as illustration. "It's when they can't handle it anymore, when they try to stop but can't, that's when they come to me."

"And you say Jon wanted to stop?"

"He did stop. And you know, that's really strange." Warming to the subject, she tucked her legs underneath her and turned to face me, leaning forward. No longer a grieving lover, she was a professional again, and Jon her favorite case. "Usually, somebody who's abusing to hide something can't begin to recover until they confront whatever it is. Jonathan was different. I had him pegged, almost from the beginning, but whatever it was, he wouldn't touch it. I mean, I don't know if he knew what it was, but it was almost like he was afraid to confront it. He just wouldn't talk about it. When I told him I couldn't help him if he wouldn't open up, he said, 'Well, find me somebody who can.'"

"Do you have any idea what it was? It might be important." I couldn't help it, I was starting to get hooked on the case.

She shook her head no. Folding her arms across her chest, she gazed out the window at the empty grounds.

"Anything at all?"

"No."

"He never gave you a clue? Never said anything? Not in therapy, but after, he never let anything slip in conversation?"

"He hated his brother," she offered.

"Really?"

"Yes, he said he was a monster. He said Justin—I assume you knew him, too?" I nodded. "He said Justin was, and I'm quoting, 'A sick fuck.'" She paused, and blushed, and I liked seeing it. Not too many women know how to do that any more.

"Because?" I offered, thinking I knew the answer.

But she surprised me. "Jon said Justin had a screw loose. Actually, he said he had a whole toolbox loose. He said he had always been scared of him, but lately he was starting to come apart."

I gave her a look. "We're talking about our next U.S. Senator, and you're saying, what, he's nuts?" see p. 10

"I'm not saying anything," she stressed, a professional with her hackles up. "I'm just telling you what Jon said. Me? I've never met the man."

"Well, I have," I replied. "I can see a little bit of what Jon was saying. Justin always was a little blurry around the edges, but the man's a force. I can't see him as a whack job." I shrugged. "You sure Jon wasn't just, what do you shrinks call it, projecting?"

"What do you mean?"

"I mean, Justin may be a bad egg. I won't argue with that. But maybe Jon was making too much of it. Maybe he had another reason, and a damn good one, for trying to undercut his brother."

"You mean Deborah?"

"Is that her name?" It was worth a try.

The way she smiled at me made me wonder how much she knew.

"Deborah didn't matter."

"Get out."

"No, really. He told me all about her, how he went after her just to get her away from some loser. He didn't want her, he just wanted to hurt the guy—hey, are you all right?"

I blinked hard. Detectives don't cry. It's in the book. Anybody saw me, I'd be back before the State Board of Review. "Sorry, an old wound." I rubbed my shoulder. "Kicks up every now and then." I gestured at my empty glass. "Got another one?"

"Are you sure?"

"It's how I do business."

She narrowed her eyes at my tone, but left with my glass. I noticed she took hers, too, but that was okay. She was in mourning. I guess I was too. I drummed my fingers on the coffee table, then called out, "Mind if I smoke?"

She said there was an ashtray on the table somewhere. I took a drag and exhaled a silent, bitter laugh. The only consolation I ever had about losing Deborah was that Jon had lost her too. If he just gave her away, if he just used her to get at me, he must have had a ball laughing at all three of us: me, Deb, and Justin. Then I sat up straight. Unless he was lying to Karin. Maybe that's what the big hurt was, the hidden wound, the haunting, mysterious loss.

God, listen to yourself, I taunted. As if any man could suffer that much and that long over a woman! And where the hell was Karin with that drink?

When she returned, I didn't bother averting my eyes. I noticed she didn't bother with any shows of modesty, either. I wanted to grab her, pull her down, let the drinks fly where they may. I felt in my bones, something about her, she wouldn't have minded. But no, I was a professional. I wouldn't do that. Not this time.

She set the drinks down and asked me for a smoke. She steadied my hand with hers as I lit it.

"Thanks." She exhaled slowly, her lips forming an "o". "Where were we?"

"Deborah." My voice didn't sound too bad, maybe like a three-pack-a-day sixty-year-old.

"Right, Deborah. They kept in touch—she's not happy, you know."

"Of course not."

"What do you mean?"

"Just being polite." She looked at me funny. "So you think his brother had something to do with this Big Hurt?"

"I don't know what to think." She stabbed out the cigarette. "I don't think this 'Big Hurt', as you call it, has anything to do with his death."

"You brought it up."

"You wanted to know about Jonathan," she snapped. "I didn't realize you already knew him, probably better than me." She stood and walked over to the sideboard. Picking up one of his pictures, she wept softly.

"I didn't know him, at least not who he apparently became. I only took the case because I figured Deborah owed me. Now, I'm not so sure."

She turned, her eyes narrowing. "Owed you, how?"

"Doesn't matter. The important thing is figuring out

what happened. Did you and Jon have a fight recently?"

She nodded reluctantly.

"When?"

"Wednesday. Wednesday afternoon." She trailed her hand along the sideboard, a profoundly feminine gesture. "He was into something. I don't know what. He kept talking about turning the tables, evening the score."

"Did Bill Jeffries have anything to do with this?"

She nodded. "I—he was secretive—I was afraid he was going to get hurt."

"Hurt? How?"

She shivered and returned to the chair, hugging herself and rocking slowly back and forth. "I thought he might start drinking again, or worse." She looked at me. "I don't think he did."

"You don't need me to tell you how bad this sounds." She shook her head. "But you don't think it's true?"

"It can't be. He was so—strong."

"Is that your professional opinion or your personal one?"

She stood up again. "Look, Mr. Corcoran—Jim, I don't know what your game is, I don't know what your history is with Jonathan, but I resent your implications."

"Take it easy, Karin." I stood up too. "It's a fair question."

"I don't think so," she snarled, glaring at me. "You act like I'm some schoolgirl who goes all dopey the first time a guy gets her in the sack. Well, it's not true. Look, what Jonathan and I had, it was special. But it wasn't going to last, and we both knew it. So don't you dare suggest that I've lost my perspective here."

"Hey, Karin, hold on—"

"No, you hold on. Maybe you don't like him—you don't exactly have a poker face, you know." She shook her head defiantly. "I don't know what your problem is, and I don't want to know. Maybe you were one of his so-called friends who sponged off him and then threw him away when he was all used up—"

I lunged at her and grabbed her wrists. "Shut up!" I roared.

"You're hurting me," she said in a low, clinical voice. "My wrists, you're hurting me."

I glanced at my hands. I must have been. My knuckles were white. I let go. "I'm sorry," I said, turning to go.

"Wait, we're not done."

Turning back, I saw her rubbing her wrists. "What's the matter?" I growled. "Wanna take another poke at me?"

She blinked in confusion. "I don't know what you're talk—"

"We're finished here, lady."

"What are you going to do?"

"Get drunk."

"You mean drunker."

"Whatever."

"What about the case?"

"There is no case. There never was. You and lover-boy had a fight, he went on a binge and got himself killed. It's yesterday's news."

She grabbed my arm. "It's not true!"

I shook her off. "That's what everybody says, but nobody'll give me anything other than their belief in Jon." I grasped her shoulders and stared deep into her bottomless blue eyes. "Trusting Jon isn't good enough for me. I won't go down that path again. Especially not now."

"Oh my God." She was very good at what she did. Under different circumstances I might have enjoyed watching her face as she figured it out. "You're the one," she whispered.

"Yeah, I'm the loser." I released her shoulders.

"Wait, don't go." She touched my face. "Oh, I am so sorry."

Her expression was so tender, I wanted to take her in my arms right then. Hell, maybe I should have. It would have been the wrong move, but on a day full of wrong moves, maybe it would have worked out all right.

"I had no idea."

"You wouldn't, would you," I managed.

She smiled another apology, and moved back to her chair, trailing a "Please don't go."

I lifted my hands in a helpless gesture. "Look, Karin. I think I'm the wrong guy for this case. I can't go ahead on blind faith. From where I sit, I'm sorry, but it looks like what the papers said."

"But it can't be."

Her insistence dragged me back to the couch. I muttered, "You keep saying that," which got me nothing in return. I hunched forward and tried again. "Okay, you're a professional. What would you think if someone came to you with a story like this?"

"I'd think he probably went on a binge, no question."

"So why's this case different?"

"Because I knew Jonathan." I could tell just looking that she knew how ridiculous that sounded. I just stared at her. She started pacing around the room. "If he were using, I would have known. Jonathan wasn't good at faking—anything."

"This is Jon Wade you're talking about?"

She stopped pacing. "Look, Jim, you're going to have to separate the Jon that you used to know from the Jonathan that got killed, okay?"

"That's a pretty tall order. I mean, Jon Wade unable to fake things? You know what we used to call him?"

"Gumby." She nodded, as if in triumph. "See, I know what he was. I saw him, remember? I know what he was, and the way he changed. When he called me, a year ago August, I was reluctant to see him. When I finally gave in—he can be, could be, very persistent—I couldn't believe it was the same person. He was so genuine, so—so innocent."

I lit another cigarette and walked over to the

sideboard. "This is damn hard," I said, studying his face in one of the photos there. "You're asking me to believe that a guy who spent his life raising deceit to an art form became genuine overnight?"

"Maybe he stopped lying to himself first."

"About what, the Big Hurt?"

"I wish you'd stop calling it that." She walked over to me, and touched Jon's photo. It was as if she were touching me. I felt her proximity almost as a physical force. "Maybe that," she reconsidered. "He never told me what it was, but whatever it was, maybe he stopped denying it. Maybe his whole life, his whole career of plasticity, was a by-product of his denying some basic core of truth." she stopped, and smiled. "I know what you're thinking—psychobabble alert."

I laughed. "I can see your point, and who knows, maybe there's something to it. Hell, maybe he really did change. If so, psychobabble's as good a theory as any."

She smiled again, in gratitude this time. Her smiles weren't quite as good as Deborah's, but they came more frequently, and with less baggage.

"Unless," I continued. "Unless your judgement was clouded somehow. Unless you chose to see him through his eyes because that was the person you wanted to be in love with."

"I wasn't in love with him," she said abruptly.

"Oh, no?"

She shook her head and turned away, her arms crossed. "It's not what you think, or what she—Deborah—thought. We had a special relationship, but it was more like brother and sister. It wasn't sexual."

I raised my eyebrows at this. "I mean, it was," she continued. "For a month or so, but then we kind of figured out that it wasn't what either of us wanted." She worried her ring a moment. "It was like we were both doing each other a favor, and when we found out it wasn't necessary, we stopped."

"Just like that?"

"I don't think he was a very sexual person. I know you're going to laugh again, but he was almost monklike in his behavior."

She was right. I did. "So you two had a celibate relationship, an esthetic coupling, a union of the spirit?"

"I didn't say I don't need or want sex." She blushed again, which I thought a nice touch. "I just didn't need it from him."

I conceded the point, and enjoyed a reprise of crimson. "Suppose you explain Jon's monklike qualities."

She passed a hand over her face, a playful gesture of frustration, I suppose. I could see I was getting to her, and I chided myself for playing that game. This was business, and that's all it was. The other stuff, hell, it was the other stuff that turned you into a used-to-be. "Okay, monk's the wrong word. But he was so single-minded, obsessive I guess."

"What about?"

"Drugs." She shrugged, as if to ask what else it could possibly be. "Maybe he felt guilty about all the people he brought along with him, but he was obsessed with finding the people behind the people selling drugs. 'Follow the money,' he always said. Where it comes from, where it goes. Everything he did was tied together."

"Tied together?"

"This thing he was doing with Bill Jeffries, it was scary."

"How so?"

"He and Bill spent hours on the computer, tracking money, they said." She shrugged. "I don't know if it was legal, what they were doing—probably wasn't. Bill's a hacker."

"You think they were running some sort of scam?"

"Oh, no. Nothing like that," she said with certainty. "He said they were just looking for information. They'd go in, look around, and if what they wanted wasn't there, they'd leave." She hugged herself. "Still, it scared me. I finally told him I didn't want to know."

"You think this had something to do with his death?"

"I don't know, maybe. You'd have to talk to Bill."

"You don't like him." It wasn't a question. It didn't take a brilliant detective to deduce that. Just one look at her face when she said his name would do it.

"The feeling was mutual, believe me."

"So you haven't seen him since Jon died?"

She shook her head. "I tried to. I called him that night when Jon didn't show up, and a half-dozen times since. All I get is that stupid machine."

"Okay." I stood up. "I'll have to check this guy out. At least it's something."

She stood up, too, and took my hands. "Thank you, Jim, for doing this."

I turned away. "I'm getting paid." Then, suspecting that it would be hard getting anything out of Bill, I asked if she had a key to Jon's house.

"His condo. He lived in Butler Woods, on the lake."

That surprised me. Butler Woods was pretty steep for a guy who was supposed to have pissed away his trust fund. "How'd he afford that?"

She shrugged. "Jonathan was funny about money. He just always seemed to have it." She headed down the hall. "Hold on a 'sec."

She returned, having slipped on a pair of loafers to go with an old gray tweed jacket. She was carrying her purse. "I suppose I'd better drive."

"Drive? Where?"

"To Jonathan's"

"Tonight?"

"Of course, tonight."

"Wouldn't tomorrow be better?"

She put her fists on her hips and said, "What kind of detective are you?" Grabbing my arm, she insisted. "Come on."

"I work better alone."

"Yeah, right." She tugged on me and opened the door. "You wouldn't get past the front gate."

I shrugged and followed. I wasn't sure this was such a good idea, but then again I had a history of going with less than good ideas. She had a way about her, a way I could get to like if I wasn't careful. Like I got to like Sara's way. Karin was nothing like Sara, except that I didn't seem to have any will of my own when I was around her. And like Sara, she wanted to get involved. In the case at first, after that, who knows?

I thrust those thoughts aside and concentrated on the road. Karin drove her red Grand Am quickly and well, timing lights and lane changes like an old hand. After twenty minutes I found myself back in Grosse Pointe, for the second time in ten years, and for the second time that day.

About ten years ago Justin Wade pushed through the Butler Woods project, on a fifteen-acre plot alongside Lake St. Clair. The site of the old Butler Estate, the grounds, and the thirty-room mansion, had lain vacant for years. There was a huge controversy, as Grosse Pointers saw themselves as being above something as plebeian as condominiums. It took all Wade's influence and persuasive powers to convince the City Council, and his friends and neighbors, that Butler Woods would become a byword for exclusivity and luxury. In the end, with a sophisticated plan conceived by Narrows Burton, of Thompson Properties, and with a large infusion of cash from out-of-state investors, Butler Woods took shape.

By the time it was finished, everyone agreed that it was the best thing to ever happen to Grosse Pointe. The complex was divided into three main structures, each built to resemble one of the massive manors from the community's Golden Era. Each had eight units, all with separate entries. They were built on a knoll, overlooking a large greenspace which ran gently down to the lakeshore. Justin Wade went from the curse of Grosse Pointe to the town's savior. The following year the grateful residents voted him into the mayor's office.

The security guard at Butler Woods took his time getting out of the booth. About sixty, his uniform wrinkled, his nose a Rudolph red, he ambled over to the car.

"Help ya miss?"

"I need to collect a couple things from Jonathan Wade's condo." She flashed a smile I hadn't seen before. "I'm his girlfriend."

The guard's expression betrayed a wistful memory of the days when he at least had the chance of mistaking himself for the object of one of those smiles. "Yeah, I seen you before. Guess you know where it is." He sighed as he reached for the gate release. "Sorry to hear about your fella."

"Me too."

"Always seemed to be in a hurry, but he treated me okay." Resting his hand on the lever, he added. "Never knew he had so many friends."

"What's that mean?" I asked.

"You're the third car in tonight. Everybody's picking things up. Makes me wonder, did the guy live here, or was he running a storage service?"

"You know who they were?"

"Well, they're s'posed to sign in, aren't they?"

His little show of defiance told me the answer before I asked it. "So did they?"

"Hey, guy's dead, night's cold, and they tipped. Who cares if they sign in?" He turned back to his hut.

"They still here?"

He shrugged. "Could be."

Karin glanced a questioning at me. "Go on," I told her. "Pull in a few doors away from Jon's. We'll just sit and talk for a minute, like you're dropping me off. Then I'll get out, and you drive away."

"Why?"

"In case anybody's still there. Once you're clear, I'll check it out."

"And what do I do?"

"Wait."

I could tell she didn't like the plan, but we were going to play this one my way. She pointed out Jon's condo as we went past. I couldn't see any lights, but that didn't mean anything. She pulled into the curb and we sat in the darkness.

"I don't like this," she said. "Maybe we should come back tomorrow. There might be somebody there."

"Probably just another old friend," I said. "Who knows?"

"Then why this routine?"

"That's the way we detectives work."

I got out, gave a wave and walked up the walk to the recessed doorway. I gave it a minute after the taillights disappeared around the corner, then made my way over to Jon's place. I kept close to the walls, just in case. There were no gunshots, or slamming doors and running feet, just the usual muffled rumblings of suburban American traffic.

I used Jon's key to open the door, and turned on the lights. I had nothing to hide. I was doing a job for the family. The room was neat and sparsely furnished. A couch, a chair, a reading lamp. Books on the shelves, CD's stacked next to the stereo. Nothing out of the ordinary.

It was a different story when I got to Jon's bedroom. The remains of a computer sat on the desk which stood amidst a landfill of paper and torn up books, notebooks and scattered computer printouts. The mattress was cut to shreds. It looked like a giant hamster's cage.

I stood in the doorway while I worked things out. It made sense that they'd start in the bedroom. It obviously doubled as Jon's office. Since the living room was untouched I could assume they'd found whatever it was they were looking for in here. I got down on my knees and started sorting through the debris scattered across the floor. There were bank statements, old phone bills, a copy of his will. I stuck that in my pocket to review later. Who knows, maybe he left me a little something.

I glanced at the computer. Somebody did a number on that, with a sledge hammer by the looks of it. I didn't know enough about computers to know if the hard disk could be salvaged, but maybe it was worth a try. There were a number of prospectuses for old dotcom startups, several of which I remembered following, from afar, from very afar, back when I sat out the Internet Bubble. Not that I was Warren Buffet smart, I was just that broke. There was a whole sheaf of downloads from a website called Dluxe.com, and something called Wade Consulting. That looked interesting. Scanning the sheet, I let out a laugh. Apparently Jon had set himself up as a capital management consultant. That was real funny. The guy blew through an eight figure trust fund the minute he got his hands on the principal, and now he's telling other people how to watch their money? Well, at least he could tell them what not to do. I put that one with the will and turned back to the bank statements.

There was a year's worth, held together by a rubber band. I leafed through them. Jon Wade had been very busy, running as much as $40,000 through his checking account each month. Karin was right, he did seem to always have money. I got up and surveyed the room, looking for canceled checks. It would help to know where all that money went, not to mention where it came from. There had to be records somewhere, unless that's what they took. Whoever they were.

That's when I got that funny feeling. If they wanted the records, surely they would have taken the statements too. I grabbed a stack of them, thinking it might be a good idea to study them someplace else. Glancing at them, I got a shock. They weren't Jon's statements, they were Justin's. What the hell could that mean? Was Jon running a scam on his brother? Was that what he meant by getting back to even?

I was heading back to the living room when I heard the floor creak. It came from the kitchen. I cursed myself for a fool for not checking the place out. God, was I rusty.

I don't know, maybe he was hiding behind the drapes, but the first I knew the other one was there was when he hit me. Hard. I went down. Then the lights went out. Then he kicked me in the ribs. "Forget him, let's get out of here," I heard.

He was grabbing for something in my hand. The statements, I realized. I clawed at his face and felt something warm, moist and yielding. His eyes or mouth, I don't know. He bellowed and kicked at my head, but missed in the darkness. He got my shoulder instead. The force rolled me over, and hurt like hell, but I was well into it now. I scrambled into a crouch and launched myself in the direction I sensed he must be. He was coming at me, too close for an effective tackle. My face smacked into his knee, but I grabbed his legs and went into a roll. He went down and then I was on top. I pounded at his face, getting almost as good as I gave until the other one hit me from behind and I went down again. "C'mon, Sharky. Let's get the fuck out of here," I heard before he kicked me in the face."

I came to with my head resting in Karin's lap. She pressed a warm cloth against my face, stopping the flow of blood. "Did they get the statements?" I managed to ask.

"What statements?"

"There was a bundle—rubber band." I gazed up at her. She was frightened, but under control. There was a welt under her right eye. "What happened?"

"You got jumped."

"No, to you."

"I—I got tired of waiting, so I drove past the house. I saw the lights were on, so I figured it was okay. I was walking up to the door when they went out. That's when I heard the shouting and the noise. I started pounding on the door and calling your name. Then it opened. There were two of them, one white, the other black. The white guy was covered in blood. Then the black guy punched me. I fell and they ran." Her eyes filled with tears.

"When I turned on the lights and saw you lying there and—Oh my God, I thought you were dead. I was so glad to hear you groan. I said, 'Wait, he's not dead, but send an ambulance.'"

I tried to sit up but pain sledge-hammered me back onto my back. I grabbed her arm. "Said to who?"

"911."

"Shit." I tried again to sit. "Karin, I've got to get out of here, now."

"No way, Mister," she said, well into clinical mode. "You've got a broken nose and probably a concussion, and who knows what else. You belong in a hospital."

"Yeah, but I'll end up in jail."

"Why? You weren't doing anything wrong."

"Doesn't matter, doesn't matter, doesn't—listen, when did you—how long?"

"Five minutes? They said they'd be right here."

"Oh shit, oh Jesus. Listen—Oh shit, I hurt, listen, honey—" I gripped her arm again. "Listen, you have to help me."

"No, you're seriously hurt."

"Not me," I tried to yell through gritted teeth. "Find the statements. Are they there?"

She laid my head down gently and stood up. "Yes, I see them. They're scattered all over, some of them are bloody."

"Just grab them, as many as you can, and I don't know, get as much paper as you can from the office, and get out of here."

"I can't leave you."

"You want to know what happened to Jon?" She began retrieving the statements. "Wait, Karin," I coughed. "Take the papers from my inside jacket pocket, too. Then get the evidence."

"What evidence?"

"I don't know, but it must be there. Just grab as much stuff as you can. If you hear a siren, then just get the hell out. You hear me?"

She finished scooping up the statements. "But what about you?" she repeated.

"Don't worry about me. I'll call you as soon as I can." I tried to follow her with my eyes as she headed for the bedroom, but the effort was too great. I closed them for a second, and when I opened them next I was staring into the face of Andy Parsons.

CHAPTER 5

"Well, well, look what we have here," Andy chuckled. "Jim Corcoran. I heard you were back."

"Hello, Andy," I mustered through a cloud of pain. "Still beating up little black kids?"

Andy's grin vanished, replaced by a sneer as he grabbed my arm and wrestled me to my feet. Ten years had shifted his weight around some, but he was still a ~~reached my feet.~~ stood. beast. The pain in my head exploded when I ~~reached my feet.~~ My knees buckled, but Andy caught me. There wasn't any compassion involved, he just had some questions he wanted answered before I blacked out again.

"What're you doing back?" he demanded.

"Working," I gasped.

"Breaking into Wade's condo?" He laughed. "Gone over to the other side?"

"I've got a key."

"Okay, not breaking and entering then. Just entering."

"Give me a break, Andy," I sighed.

He tightened his grip on my arm. "Sure thing, pal. Elbow or shoulder?" I didn't have the strength to try and pull away, which was lucky. Otherwise he probably would have broken one or the other, or both. Then a voice called from the bedroom. "Take a look at this, Lieutenant."

Giving me a little shove that left me sprawled across the sofa, he stalked off, leaving me to muse about the irony of Andy Parsons making Lieutenant of the Grosse Pointe Police Department. I didn't muse for long, though, as unconsciousness offered an inspiration of her own.

When I next awoke I was in a hospital bed. My arms were strapped down, an IV unit inserted in my left. My face was swathed in bandages, my ribs were wrapped, and sunlight streamed through the window. It cast a spotlight on the smartly tailored Grosse Pointe Public Service uniform worn by the officer standing in attendance. "What time is it?" I asked her. She responded by announcing, "Prisoner's awake," into the portable radio unit velcroed to her shoulder.

With that she gave me a dispassionate glance and left. As the door clicked shut, I lay back and took stock of my situation. I was under arrest, that was obvious. I was in the hospital, where I had been patched together. I had to assume I hadn't been formally charged with anything yet, and probably wouldn't be. This was just Andy Parson's way of saying, "Welcome home."

Andy was a bastard and had been as far back as I could remember, and that went back more than thirty years. The Parsons lived in Grosse Pointe, but they certainly weren't of Grosse Pointe. Andy's father had come over in the last wave of Scottish stone masons in the forties, to help build the last of the great mansions lining the lake. He had stayed in the area, mowing lawns and doing odd jobs for various residents, gradually building up what became the largest landscape maintenance company in town. He made enough to ensure that his boys went to The Grosse Pointe

Academy, where Andy was a three letter athlete.

His fame was fleeting, however, and his glory always ended when the clock reached zero. The cheerleaders clung to him when he scored the winning touchdown, but he always went home alone. Knowing he wouldn't be welcome in their fathers' boardrooms, the daughters of Grosse Pointe made sure he never made it into their bedrooms.

Andy's athletic prowess earned him a scholarship to the University of Michigan, but he lost that when he tore up his knee sophomore year. He transferred to Wayne State, switched his major to Police Science, and returned home to the Grosse Pointe Police Force, where he found justice in writing speeding tickets to the future matrons of his hometown.

No, Andy and I went way back, and there weren't any fond memories. Back when Andy was a detective, he found three black kids hanging around the Sanders Ice Cream Shop, licking their cones, and just waiting, he knew, to snatch a purse or steal a car. When he told them to get on home they gave him some civil rights crap about how they could be anywhere they wanted to be. He didn't like their tone, so he took them behind Jergen's Market and beat the bloody hell out of them.

I took the case for their parents, just for expenses, because I was flush then, and I thought pro bono work was good exposure. I didn't know then that it was Andy who had done it, but I had a pretty good idea, and can't say I was disappointed when my hunch turned out to be right. My testimony helped those kids' families win $15 million dollars from the city. Even if the award was knocked down on appeal to a million each, the boys no longer had to caddy at the Country Club of Detroit to earn money for college.

Andy was knocked down too, back to a patrol car. I was surprised he wasn't fired, but I guess cops have unions, too. I suppose his finding Sara's body must have helped restart his career. He did damn diligent police work trying to pin the murder on me, and if there had been anything to it, he would have succeeded. As it was, he got my license pulled for six months, and tore my life apart. You'd think that would be enough vengeance for one lifetime. Apparently not.

Now I had to figure out how I was going to play this. I'd been on the case for less than 24 hours, at least I had to assume it was less, as I still didn't know what day it was, and all I'd managed to do was get beaten up and arrested. The charges wouldn't stick. I probably wouldn't even have to identify my client, but I'd be back in front of the Review Board, and that could get ugly. I'd get through it okay, but I didn't want to have to deal with that right now. Not when I had a case going. And that was the kicker. Suddenly I knew I had a case.

Something about getting kicked in the face, I guess, always gets my attention.

Knowing I had a case was one thing. Knowing what it was, was another. I wondered how much evidence Karin had managed to get away with, or even if she had gotten away. Hell, I didn't know anything, and with my damn hands tied down, I didn't have any way to find out. On top of that, my face itched under the bandages and I couldn't even scratch it.

A while later, the door was unlocked, and Andy Parsons skulked in, accompanied by a tall, slender, honey-brown-skinned man in his late fifties. Andy wore his usual scowl as he undid the straps holding my arms to the bed. "Well, Corcoran, looks like you skate again."

"No charges filed," the other man announced. "In exchange, you promise not to sue for false arrest."

"And you are?"

"Kendall Williams, attorney at law," he replied

smoothly. "Hired by your client."

"How did sh–"

"No names," Williams interjected. "Client confidentiality is part of the deal." He moved quickly to my side as Andy reached for the IV unit. "Are you a trained medical technician?" he demanded. "Then go get one."

Parsons moved reluctantly to the door. I know he had been looking forward to ripping that needle out. When he was gone Williams said quickly, "Things are starting to open up. I've got Ms. Champagne in the car. She'll explain everything."

"Ms. Champagne?" I was momentarily confused. "You mean Karin?"

"She'll explain everything," he repeated. "In the meantime," he announced, flourishing a small leather bag, "I have a change of clothes. As I understand it, yours were a little bloody."

It took another forty-five minutes to get dressed and processed out, and to retrieve my belongings. Parsons insisted on retaining my revolver. "For evidentiary purposes," he explained, wielding jargon like the bureaucratic bully he was.

I glanced at Williams, who shrugged and said, "He's within his rights."

When we reached the car, a sleek gray Lexus sedan, Karin stepped out. She reached for me, then stopped short. "Where does it hurt?"

"It'll save time if I just tell you where it doesn't."

We rode back to her apartment in relative silence, following the example set by Williams, who had taken control of the situation. He and Karin sat in front while I sprawled awkwardly on the back seat. Williams kept flicking his eyes at the rearview mirror as we headed west on Eight Mile.

"Either you're a real cautious driver," I observed, "Or we're being followed."

"Old habits die hard," he chuckled. "And no, we're not being followed."

"But it wouldn't surprise you if we were?"

His appraising eyes settled on me in the mirror for a moment. "It's still too early for that." Something in his tone told me he wouldn't elaborate, so I didn't try.

Back at her apartment, Karin made me as comfortable as she could on the couch, and gave me an iced tea. I would have preferred something stronger, but she told me alcohol was contraindicated for post-concussion syndrome, and her tone brooked no contradiction. She then busied herself fixing sandwiches, pointing out that I hadn't eaten in more than 24 hours.

Williams and I exchanged small talk about the Detroit Tigers having claimed the Major League cellar for the second consecutive year. "When your pitching staff has an ERA of 6.25, it really doesn't matter how many home runs you hit," he observed.

"Makes for some exciting games."

"Especially for the opposition."

"Speaking of the opposition," I segued, "how about you explaining–"

"Ah, Ms. Champagne, let me help you with that tray." He jumped to his feet as Karin entered the room.

Though not broken, my jaw was badly bruised, making it painful to eat my tuna sandwich. Almost as painful as watching the other two chew their roast beef.

When their studied avoidance of my unspoken questions grew intolerable, I voiced one to Karin. "Why were you at the hospital?"

"You mean instead of Deborah?"

"Kendall said his client–"

"Mrs. Wade can't be linked to you in public," Williams interjected.

"It's a little late for that."

"How so?"

"Lunch at The Grill," I said. "Way back, hell,

yesterday?"

"You have a history."

"So?"

The attorney sighed, as if it were so obvious, he should be charging me his regular rate for the imposition of explaining it. "So, you heard about Jonathan's death, and came to extend your sympathies."

I started to laugh, but my ribs argued such action was contraindicated. Instead I groaned and rolled onto my side.

"I concede the story's improbability, but that's the way we choose to play it."

"Who are you?" I demanded, really looking at him for the first time. Up to now he had only been this mysterious agent smoothing my escape from Parsons' clutches. Now I needed some answers.

He flipped a business card at me. Kendall J. Williams, Attorney at Law, and Managing Partner of Fleigher, Kermit and Schneid. I was impressed. Fleigher, Kermit and Schneid was big time. Their headquarters were still in downtown Detroit, but they had offices in New York, Los Angeles and Washington as well.

"Who are you representing in this?"

"Justin Wade is a significant client," he allowed.

"Then he knows about—"

"I know his wife socially."

"How did she find out—"

"I met Ken through Jon," Karin put in.

"Ms. Champagne met with me last night," Williams explained. "Justin Wade knows nothing about you—yet." He frowned. "But you mustn't assume that he won't. The important things is to shield Deborah's involvement from him."

"His wife's paying me, but we have to shield it from him," I repeated blankly.

"I believe that we've erected sufficient firewalls to protect him."

"Protect him." I shook my head—carefully. "I don't

get it."

"Our key objective at this juncture is to preserve plausible deniability on his part."

I slumped back on the sofa, tired, dizzy, and not a little confused. Williams rose from his chair, and tweaked his pant legs, allowing them to hang elegantly, perfectly creased. "You're obviously in no state to discuss this just now. Why don't you rest for the time being? When you're ready, give me a call. If you still wish to pursue this, I'll help you as much as I'm able." He picked up his briefcase, a soft-sided leather one that I knew didn't come cheap. "In the meantime, please do not attempt to contact your client."

"What gives you the right to dictate terms to me?"

Williams smiled coolly. "I don't need to answer that."

"Whose side are you on, here?"

 He smiled again, and chuckled slightly. "Surely, Mr. Corcoran, you of all people ought to know the importance of protecting the client."

Williams extended his hand to Karin, studiously ignoring my efforts to stand. "Ms. Champagne, you will keep in touch, I'm sure."

While she saw him to the door, I managed to reach my feet. This was my case, and I'd be damned if I was going to let some oleaginous corporate shill tell me how to do my job. I didn't care how many strings he was pulling, he wasn't going to pull mine.

Then Karin was beside me, her arm around my back, speaking softly, and easing me toward her bedroom.

"What's going on?" I asked dumbly as she helped me into bed. "I need to–"

"Shhh," she said, touching my lips with her forefinger. "We'll talk about it later."

I woke up when she returned, carrying a mug of coffee

and a plate of scrambled eggs. "Good morning," she chirped. "How do you feel?"

I sat up, groaning only slightly. "Not much worse than a really bad hangover—what time is it?"

"Seven a.m. You've been sleeping for about eighteen hours."

As I reached for the coffee, my ribs fought back. I groaned and slumped back against the pillow.

"The good news is nothing's broken," she announced, handing me the mug.

"Could have fooled me."

"Except your nose." She grinned. "Your ribs are badly bruised, your shoulder's a mess, and your face, well, I'd avoid looking in a mirror for the next few days."

"You seem awfully cheerful."

Her expression turned grave. "I'm just glad it wasn't worse." She hugged herself, and I noticed she was sporting a bruise of her own, on her right cheekbone. "I've never been hit before," she said softly.

"You get used to it."

"I don't think I'd want to," she replied thoughtfully. Then she stood up briskly. "I've got to shower and dress, and I want to check your bandages before I go."

"Go where?"

"To work. Mondays are always busy."

While she was gone I sipped my coffee and negotiated my body into a position in which I could eat without too much pain. I worked out the chronology and decided I hadn't lost any days. I met Deborah at the Wellington Grill on Saturday, and I spent Sunday in the hospital and here. And that was long enough. I had to get to my office. I had to get to work figuring out what kind of case I had. I still wasn't ready to concede that Jon hadn't slipped off the edge that night, but I was starting to suspect that someone might have given him the impetus. I gazed at the bathroom door, behind which I could hear the shower running.

Karin had gotten me this far, and she had kept her head when things got rough, and for that I ought to be grateful. But there was something she wasn't telling me. About Jon, and about herself. How did she know Williams for one thing? Williams was big time. He didn't meet with local cops on a Sunday, and he didn't do pro bono work for two-bit detectives any day of the week. It didn't make sense.

Or maybe it was the feelings she provoked that made me so leery of her. Too close, too soon. Every time she came near me, and she came near me with dismaying frequency, it was all I could do to resist the urge to throw my arms around her and kiss her. Kiss her? Hell, I wanted to rip her clothes off. I hadn't ever felt anything like this. At least, if I were honest with myself, not since Sara. Which was another, or the main, reason I had to get out of there.

I stood up to start looking for my clothes. The sooner I got back to my office, the better I'd feel. After the first wave of pain and nausea swept over me, it wasn't so bad. If I avoided sudden movements, I'd be all right. I found an old work shirt and some faded cords draped over a chair. For a moment I was puzzled, then remembered that Williams had brought them for me yesterday. I buttoned the shirt and began to put on the pants, trying not to think about where he might have gotten them. When I lifted my right leg to step into them a sudden flash of pain heralded a wave of dizziness, and I went down, hard, on my shoulder.

Karin burst out of the bathroom. "What are you doing?" she demanded. She was half-dressed, wearing a navy blue skirt and a bra. "You aren't well, Jim," she chided, kneeling beside me.

"Got to get to my office. Got to get to work," I managed to get out.

"You're in no shape to go anywhere," she insisted. "You need to rest here." As she bent to help me up her full breasts threatened to spill out of her low cut bra. She followed the direction of my eyes and reddened. I gestured at my bare legs. "Put us together, and we're properly dressed."

She smiled ruefully. "And you're going to make me late."

"Then go."

"Not until you promise me you'll stay."

"Give me one good reason why I should."

Karin's expression turned wistful, and her gaze seemed to expand to take in some distant vista. Then, as if reaching a momentous decision, she nodded. She helped me to my feet, and said, "I'll be right back."

She went out into the hall, where I could hear her rummaging in the closet. When she returned she was carrying a file box. "Jon asked me to hold onto this for him," she explained as she set it on the bed.

"What's in it?"

She shook her head. "I don't know."

"You never looked inside?"

"He asked me not to." She shrugged. "Maybe it's nothing, but it'll give you something to do while I'm away."

I sighed. "Okay, I'll stick around–for awhile. Mind if I use your computer?"

She smiled her sense of victory, and nodded. "But Jim, I've really got to go."

"Sure, but aren't you forgetting something?"

She looked confused for a moment, then, remembering her state of undress, she brought her hands to her chest. Then she laughed, at herself, I think, and said, "I guess I don't look very professional."

As she turned to head back to the bathroom I said, "I don't know. I'd come to you for therapy."

She stopped suddenly, and turned, with a frown on her face. She stared at me for a moment. "You got kicked in the head," she said. "You're not yourself."

With that she disappeared behind the bathroom door, giving me fifteen minutes to try to figure out what I meant by that crack, and what I'd hoped to achieve. I kept telling myself that Karin wasn't Sara, and I didn't want her to be, because people like Sara got dead around people like me. When she returned, fully dressed, with her hair dried and brushed, and her makeup in place, she looked like a different woman. Older, much less vulnerable.

I greeted her with a little laugh. "Sorry about that. I meant it as a joke, sort of a compliment."

"Well, it wasn't very funny," she said sharply. Then her features softened. "Well, maybe a little." With a grin, she turned to go.

"Wait," I called.

"What now?"

"Did you get anything from Jon's apartment?"

"Yes, I did what you said. I grabbed the statements, and just anything I could put my hands on."

"Great. Where is it? I can start going through it, maybe figure out–"

She shook her head. "I don't have it."

"What do you mean you don't have it?"

"Ken–Mr. Williams said I should give it to him, for safe keeping."

"Why on earth–" I groaned. "Jesus, Karin, why?"

"He said it was for my own good."

"Who is he, Karin? Who is Williams and what is he doing in this case?"

She backed towards the door, and said woodenly, "I'm sorry, but I really have to go. We can talk about this when I get back."

CHAPTER 6

I spent some time pacing the floor after she was gone. Well, I liked to think of it as pacing, but it had more in common with a runner completing his first marathon than anything reflecting the intensity of my thought process. I wasn't in very good shape, granted, but my mind was alive. Eventually I gave up the pretense of motion, and slumped onto the couch.

The loss of the evidence was critical. I couldn't figure out Williams' role in this. On the face of it, he was my guardian angel, rescuing me from Andy Parsons. But why would he take the statements? And what did he mean, it was for Karin's own good? Sounded like a threat to me. But was he threatening her? Or merely stating the seriousness of the situation? And why was it so serious? According to the police, Jon had been killed at that crack house. If so, case closed. End of story.

On the other hand, I had bandages around my ribs and sandpaper in my throat every time I took a breath. Maybe I was out of practice, but even I knew that wasn't the sort of damage you picked up on a routine case.

So, if the case wasn't routine, what was it? Judging from the beating I got, I had to assume at the very least that Jon was into something that somebody didn't want to see the light of day. Whether that meant the crack house murder was a setup, I couldn't say. But the specific circumstances were immaterial. When somebody kicks the shit out of you, that gives you a reason to keep going. It's in the book. Chapter Three, I think it is. This case was no longer about Jon, and it was no longer about soothing Deborah's conscience. This was about finding those bastards who beat me up, and making sure justice, one way or another, was done. It's like Sam Spade said, when somebody kills your partner, you have to go after them. It doesn't matter if you liked the guy. It's bad business if you don't.

My business had been bad so long that it didn't really matter what kind of decisions I made. Plus, it wasn't my partner who'd died, just my pride. But the principle was the same. If you're going to go after me, you need to understand that you'll pay a price. Otherwise, I shouldn't be in the business.

Taking stock of the situation, I thought maybe I shouldn't be in the business, anyway. I mean, here I was, sitting in Karin's apartment, and I wasn't sure if I was a guest or a prisoner.

I finally decided I needed to get out of there. But how? My car had to be out there where I left it, and my keys had to be somewhere. I don't think Parsons confiscated them along with my gun. But it was a moot point. I was in no shape to walk, let alone drive anywhere. In the movies guys get beaten into unconsciousness by a dozen assailants, and wake up fifteen minutes later with no ill effects, but in real life it doesn't work that way. I was a mess, and I knew it.

I called Mike Wallis' cell phone, but he wasn't picking up. I thought about calling Deborah. After all, she was paying me. But Williams' warning deterred me. I wasn't about to start taking orders from him, but if Williams and Karin were in this together, calling Deborah might jeopardize not just my safety, but hers too.

Wondering if paranoia was also indicative of post-concussion syndrome, I decided to go through the box that Karin had left for me. Maybe it would help me figure out what Jon was into. There were several notebooks filled with newspaper clippings, which reminded me, as if I could have forgotten, that Jon and Justin hadn't been ordinary kids. Just about every move they made, from the time they were five, was documented in the local papers. If they played T-ball, there was a story. Soccer? Same thing. Even going away for summer camp merited a paragraph. What was amazing, though, was Jon kept every article. There were all the headlines of youth, when they were both the best and the brightest, both destined for greatness, both exemplars of Grosse Pointe royalty; Detroit's version of the Kennedys.

I came across an itinerary for the Christ Church Youth Choir European Tour. Christ, I remembered that. I was in that choir. That was big time for me. First trip to Europe. Deborah was there, too. In fact, that was the first time I really noticed her. First time I ever really tried to get a girl to notice me, and to find out everything about her. Hell, it was the first time I fell in love.

What were we? Sophomores? Juniors? That was the first time I kissed a girl. Deborah and me, outside Saint Stephen's Cathedral, in Vienna, street performers working the crowds in the plaza. A light drizzle falling, and it was chilly. Her breath came in little puffs of smoke, and her hair was frizzy under her cap. We were standing there, watching the street magician. I grabbed her hand, and she let me hold it. Then she turned to me, her eyes telling me it was okay. More than okay, it was mandatory that I kiss her right then, right there. And I did. I still remember the feel and taste of her lips, and the heady lightness of being when I held her close...

Jon and Justin and I raised hell throughout that tour, sneaking out almost every night for drinks. It was so cool. What were we? Sixteen? And yet they'd serve us. No sneaking around, paying winos to buy cases of beer at the local party store. We'd just walk into a bierstube, and order whatever we wanted. No problem. One of the chaperones was cool. He let us sneak out, and he signed us in at the end of the night. A couple times he went with us.

There was this weird tension between Jonathan and Justin. It kept building the whole time we were over there. They competed with each other, for everything. Attention, awards, who got to sing the solos. At first I put it down to sibling rivalry, but as time went on, there was a lot more to it than that. The three of us and Deborah palled around, though after awhile the Wade boys' competition got to be too much for her. She started finding ways to split the two of us away from the others. I guess in a way that's what brought us together. I owed my first kiss, the first blush of love, to those two bastards. I'd never thought of it like that before.

Still, late at night, when the lights went out in our hotel, I would accompany Jon and Justin on their forays into the local nightlife. Deborah would never join us. It was against the rules, she would say. She wasn't afraid of being caught, she just didn't think it was right. I would have been happier if she'd been along, but I couldn't complain. I think it was more the thrill of the forbidden that kept me going. I don't know what it was with the Wades, though. The forbidden was old hat for them. They'd been making their own rules since they were ten years old. I guess for them it was more a case of, if they could get away with it, they had a moral obligation to do so,

I don't think they were in it for the fun. In fact, a lot

of times, and increasingly as the tour wore on, they weren't having any fun, and neither was I. The tension came to a head one night in Rome, in an alley near the Piazza Navona. We were staggering back to our hotel, after closing another wine bar, when their constant bickering suddenly flared into violence. Jon shoved Justin and called him a liar. "You bastard," he cried as he lunged at him. Justin met his assault with a right hand to the face. Jon just kept on coming. They grappled, and fell to the ground, rolling around on the sodden pavement, calling each other murderer, coward. It happened so fast, I was helpless to intervene. I stood there gawping at this sudden outburst of animal passion and murderous hatred, until I saw a couple carabinieri take notice of the scuffle and start heading up the alley. I moved forward to break them up.

"Cool it, guys. Cops are coming," I muttered, while getting between them. They finally heard me, and ceased hostilities. When the police reached us, the Wades were both standing, and Justin was laughing his manic laugh, as if they were the best of buddies.

"No, officers," I said. "They were just fooling around. You know how it is."

They chuckled and allowed that they did, but encouraged us to head straight back to our hotel. It was late, and "young boys" like us could come to mischief on a Roman night.

I continued leafing through the scrapbook. Jon's clippings grew progressively darker, while Justin's glowed with the golden aura of the designated heir. Jon was arrested, Justin was elected class President. Jon was shunted off to military boarding school, Justin landed a job as a page for Senator Van de Halen. Justin went to Princeton, Jon disappeared from the papers. There were bail bond receipts, parole reports, hospital bills. I couldn't believe he'd kept them all. From the time he was twenty he kept separate notebooks. Just one for himself, which covered the next two decades–not much there, a life lived in tatters. But Justin's, it was incredible. Six thick notebooks containing every scrap his very public life generated. On the surface it looked like a serious case of hero worship, but I knew that wasn't true. Jon never viewed his brother as a hero, and he certainly didn't worship him.

Then why? Was it envy? Was Justin leading the life Jon felt should have been his? It reminded me of Leicester Hemingway, Ernest's much younger brother. He committed suicide with a pistol. Ernest, of course, used a shotgun.

For Ernest, Leicester was a distant footnote to his life. He barely noticed the kid. When Hemingway was enjoying his greatest acclaim, Leicester was still in the clutches of their overbearing mother. Challenged by his brother's neglect, Leicester followed in his footsteps. He became a big game hunter. He bought a boat and fished in the Gulf Stream off the Florida Keys. He wrote a novel. He wrote a memoir. Everything he did, they said Ernest did it first, and Ernest did it better. I am convinced when Leicester put that pistol in his mouth, his last living thought was, "They'll say Ernest did it first, and Ernest did it better." And then it was easy to pull that trigger.

I set Justin's notebooks aside. I'd go through them later. There wasn't much pleasure in the prospect of reviewing his lustrous career. Pawing deeper into the box I came to a slim notebook, bordered in black, with a crude, juvenile sketch of a skull and crossbones on the cover. Opening it, I was stunned to find a brief compendium of little sister Jessica's life. When had Jon started these things, anyway? I went back to the first notebook I'd looked at. The earliest items dated from the time he was five years old. I shook my head. What kind of kid starts documenting his life from that age? Did he consider himself a child of destiny? Was he saving future biographers a ton of work by assembling it all for them? If so, he'd erred badly. The life he ended up leading wasn't the stuff for biographers; it wasn't even the stuff for bad TV movies. It was shabby, tawdry, and, in terms of the potential he left on the table, utterly offensive.

I turned back to Jessica's notebook. She, too, was a golden child. She, too, lived her life in the public eye. It was amazing how much ink she managed to generate in just eight short years. There was an article clipped from the Grosse Pointe News, reporting that she was the youngest person ever to serve as lector at Christ Church. Granted, a seven-year-old reading scriptures before a congregation packed with the town's best and brightest was unique, but was it worth a front page story in the local rag? Then again, considering the quality of the local rag, maybe it wasn't so surprising.

Jessica played soccer, of course. And she joined a dance program, headlining the annual recital from the time she was five. She was cute, pig tails, freckled face, and dressed in a pink tutu. There wasn't much more than that, except for the bulk of the file, which began with a banner Detroit News headline: Jessica Wade Drowned in Tragic Accident.

It happened up in Northern Michigan at Wolverine Valley. An exclusive compound of seriously overgrown mansions whimsically described as bungalows or cottages, Wolverine Valley covered some fifteen hundred acres. There was a gamekeeper who kept the fields stocked with pheasants and the woods full of deer. There were three lakes on the grounds, plus a river which flowed through to Lake Superior. Its hallmark was rustic privilege. There was a communal dining hall, where each of the residents was obliged to dine at least once. Most of them took all their meals there, except for those who traveled with their own chefs.

I was invited to Wolverine Valley just once, back when I was twenty-three, with the Peters boys. It was a blowout week. Deborah was there, naturally. Come to think of it, that was the week that Jon made his first move on her. Deborah and I weren't getting along just then. Fresh out of college, I was scuffling, trying to figure out what to do with my history degree. She said I should teach, but I couldn't see spending the rest of my life telling the same old stories each year to the same young ears.

I'd applied at a couple of banks, and a brokerage house, resigned to the life of a cubicle slave, but so far no one was nibbling. I was frustrated as hell, and maybe I took it out on her a little bit. Deborah had always had an agenda, a life plan, and part of it included getting married early, raising a couple of kids, and moving into the life, and eventually the house, that her parents had erected for her. I believe she was willing to marry me, back then, but there was a certain economic standard I had to achieve, a certain code I had to adhere to. Slinging burgers at McDonald's wasn't part of the program.

Neither was becoming a private dick. I finally took a job as a gofer for Dick Harting, a Detroit detective. Over the years Dick taught me everything he knew, and shepherded me through the licensing process. After I became his partner, our business began to thrive. Then he died. Of cancer. That's what kills private eyes. Unlike your detective novels, it is rare for a gumshoe to even get roughed up, let alone be involved in a shootout. Most of the work involves poring over records at the county building, or dialing the phone, or these days, sitting in front of a computer.

Of course, that boilerplate description of the mundane world of private detection didn't apply to me. I'd always made my own rules, and played the game the way I thought it should be played. Which was why I'd had my license pulled once, why Sara Jenkins had died, and why I was sitting in Karin Champagne's apartment nursing my various wounds. It was also why I lost Deborah to Jonathan Wade.

Jon hung around us that week at Wolverine Valley, wielding his hangdog expression and his snarky wit, willing Deb to abandon me. This was back when Jon was at the height of his toxicological powers. He could consume more booze than anyone any of us had ever seen, and smoke pot and snort cocaine with abandon. When everybody else was passing out, he was still going strong. It was an incredible display of stamina, and of course, it didn't last. Within six months of that strange Wolverine Valley interlude, he had his first collapse. He landed in the hospital, and very nearly didn't survive it.

By then Deborah and I were history, as were she and Jon, and Justin played the leading role. I was moving on. Mostly it was my decision, I think, though I don't recall any of my erstwhile friends begging me to change my mind. I was twenty-three, a crucial age in the Grosse Pointe ethos. It was time to join the Country Club of Detroit. If you joined, your place in the social stratum was cemented. Later would come the Grosse Pointe Yacht Club, though some, the avid boaters, played it the other way around. Definitely, one or the other was mandatory. Failure to apply meant cession of the rights and privileges of Grosse Pointe society.

I failed to make the grade for two reasons. The first one, the main and overarching factor, was financial. I simply could not afford it. Though I'd grown up a child of privilege in that rarified environment, I didn't have the stuff for the long haul. My father was a self-made man who had muscled his way into Grosse Pointe society on the strength of his boundless enthusiasm, his thick skin, and the bags of money his mortgage company generated. That he had induced Marcia Bascombe, daughter of one of the oldest Grosse Pointe families, to marry him certainly hadn't hurt his prospects.

Gradually, and grudgingly, Grosse Pointe accepted him, if not as one of their own, then at least as the husband of one of their own. As her child I escaped my father's struggles, and moved seamlessly into the life the Wades enjoyed, though in my case the local rag couldn't have cared less whether I played T-ball. It isn't hard to make the grade when you don't realize what a steep slope it is. I was born to it, and the rest came easily. Right up until the recession in the late eighties. My poor old dad made some bad bets on interest rates, and as they continued to climb, his assets were washed away.

I don't think he would have gone out on a ledge that way if my mom hadn't died suddenly of pancreatic cancer. She was only forty-two when she was diagnosed, and three months later she was gone. I was just twelve at the time, and to this day I am ashamed at how little it affected me. But I was young and stupid, and insulated from the horror of death by my friends and my circle, and tea dances and waterskiing on the lake. My father made up for my absence though. He loved that woman, and he nursed her through to the bitter end.

I'll never forget her funeral. Christ Church was packed to the gills. My father wanted to give the eulogy. I remember Reverend Pastor–always loved that name– trying to talk him out of it. He said sometimes things can get away from you; it can be awkward. But my father insisted. He got his way, but Pastor was right. It was supposed to be brief, eloquent, and valedictory. He'd practiced it on me, refining the cadence of his delivery until it hummed. But he couldn't do it. Halfway into it, his voice started to quaver. He gripped the lectern tightly and tried to bull his way through, the way he'd bulled his way through his entire life, up to that point.

It was when he talked about her white dress, of the way the sun shone on her and gave her an ethereal glow–

he was so proud of that imagery–he let out a sob. The church went still. He took a deep breath, and tried to continue. He sobbed again. Great, heart-wrenching explosions of grief wracked his solid frame. He sniffed and sniveled and bawled like a baby in front of us all. The congregation stirred, and murmured, and watched in horror as one, no, not of their own, but damn close, violated just about every rule in the Grosse Pointe manual. He broke down, and had to be led a broken man from the lectern.

He became an outcast, not because his actions were irredeemable, but simply because Grosse Pointers felt so awkward around him after that. While a good, firm hug would have done wonders, people in that town weren't given to giving hugs. Instead, they sought to ignore things they couldn't understand, and the kind of love my father had displayed was one of them. They had no frame of reference, no way of relating, and as a result, they just avoided it. If that meant avoiding him, so be it.

I think it was not so much my mother's death as the community's response that made him take the risks he did. He wanted to bounce back, and the only way he could think of doing it was to become so goddamn undeniably filthy rich that he could buy and sell anybody in town. And that took a whole lot of moolah.

What it did, in the end, was destroy him. Bankrupt, broken, humiliated, he had to quit the Country Club, and the Yacht Club. His last years were spent in court, fending off lawsuits, fighting an indictment by an overly zealous DA who was sure there was some skullduggery going on. In the end he was vindicated. There were no charges brought, because he hadn't broken any laws. Sure, a lot of people were hurt. A lot of people lost money, though none as much as he, who had lost everything.

In a fit of financial planning some years earlier, he had established a small trust for me. Though it wasn't enough to live on, it allowed me to finish college, and to continue, for awhile, under the pretense that life hadn't changed for me. That I was still one of them, One of Us. When I graduated, there was just enough principal left over to throw a party for all my Grosse Pointe chums. There was something noble about the gesture. Somehow, because these things are never kept secret in a town like that, everybody knew I was blowing the last of my paltry inheritance on that blast. For awhile it gave me the cachet I needed to keep going.

But when it was time to step up and join the Country Club, I faltered. Yes, I didn't have the money, but there were bankers in town who would have floated me the loan, with no collateral other than my status. Much to Deborah's dismay, I didn't want to place that bet. It wasn't just the financial risk. It was the slow-dawning realization that I was not in fact of that town, of those people. They had become strangers to me. For how long, I couldn't say, because I had just continued marching along the steps which were so clearly etched on the pavement in front of me. But one day I woke up, looked around, and realized I didn't belong there. I didn't fit in. I didn't even like my closest friends. A frightening discovery for someone as young and naive as I was, but there you have it.

That was when I took the job with Dick Harting. That was when I lost Deborah. It took a couple more weeks before it was over, and another twenty years for me to get over it. Okay, twenty years and counting.

One of the drawbacks to a place as secluded as Wolverine Valley was that it could take hours for an ambulance to arrive, which is what happened the day Jessica Wade died. According to the Detroit News, she was frolicking with her brothers on a rustic wooden diving raft in Watson Lake, the smallest of the three on the property, and the one dedicated to swimming. Usually there was a lifeguard on duty, but apparently he had wandered off to get some lunch. A crestfallen Justin Wade told authorities that she must have hit her head on the edge of the raft when she dived off. Later, he suggested that his brother had thrown her off. It was typical of the horseplay they'd engaged in numerous times before, only this time, a tragedy occurred.

She went under, and didn't come up for a long time. This was not unusual, as she liked to swim under water. She was a very good swimmer. Everyone agreed, from her brothers to her parents, to her swim coach at the Yacht Club. But this time she didn't come up. Justin noticed it first, and started calling her name. Then he dove in, and swam underwater until he saw her motionless body. He struggled to the surface, and called for Jon to help him pull her onto the raft. But Jon was nowhere to be found. Later, it turned out that Jon had swum to shore, in search of help.

By the time some of the adults arrived, Justin had managed to haul his sister onto the raft, and was trying his best to resuscitate her. But to no avail. She'd been under too long. They held her funeral at Christ Church, back in Grosse Pointe. It was a far grander affair than my mother's would be. Every seat was filled, people stood all along the walls, and crowded into the foyer. They clustered outside the front door, and snaked down the wide sidewalk. It was, everyone agreed, the biggest funeral ever, even bigger than that of Mr. and Mrs. Kenneth Herringbone, of Herringbone Motors, who had also drowned, twenty years before, while sailing on Lake Michigan.

The rumors started after the funeral. It was Jonathan who was responsible. He pushed Jessie in the water, and held her down, and then ran away. He wasn't looking for help, he was looking for a place to hide. Justin was a hero, but his younger brother, dare they say it? His younger brother was a murderer. There was nothing to it, as far as I could see, and certainly the authorities didn't waste much time exploring that angle.

Of course not, people said, the Wades bought them

off. They had so much money and power, they just didn't get charged with something as mundane as murder. It was vicious, the way those rumors spread. Funny thing about a town like Grosse Pointe. Packed as it was with the richest people in Detroit, you wouldn't think there would be much class envy, but there was. You might be worth eight million bucks, be able to buy anything you want, and vacation in Europe every year, but let Jerry Winston marry a Rockefeller, and you resented the hell out of him, and her.

That mood fueled the rumors. People wanted to think the worst of the Wades because the rest of the time they had to suck up to them. They had to pretend they liked Jeremy Wade, that they thought his jokes were funny, and his insults hilarious. They had to do it. Otherwise they might not get an invitation to the Wades' annual Christmas Party, which was just the biggest bash in town. Anyone who was anybody got a stiff card for that. And if you didn't, well, maybe it was time to start thinking about relocating to another part of Detroit, or even to another state.

That's the kind of power the Wades had, and that's why people resented them enough to spread lies about their little boy. Justin would have none of it. He insisted all along that Jonathan was innocent. And his word carried weight. After all, Justin was the hero. He was the one who tried to save her life. People absolved him from blame, especially after he stood next to her coffin, looking smart in a tailored suit, his hair combed just so. Standing at attention in front of the mourners, just twelve years old, but suddenly grown to a man. They sat in a mortal hush when he sang Jessie's favorite hymn in his thin, reedy voice. Yes, Justin had greatness about him, even then.

As for his brother, well, the rumors didn't affect him as much as you might have expected. According to the Wade legend, that was mostly thanks to Justin's support. They had always been close, but now they were closer.

Jonathan clung to his older brother like the life preserver they wished Jessie had been wearing. And Justin let him tag along everywhere. You know how competitive boys can be at that age. The twelve-year-old wants to hang out with his twelve-year-old friends. He doesn't want his ten-year-old brother getting in the way. But Justin never told his brother to leave him alone.

You have to remember that I was around for that. I was part of the Wade boys' circle. Justin and I were the same age. If not exactly friends, we shared many of the same buddies. What I saw didn't exactly square with the lionization of Justin Wade. It always seemed to me that far from tolerating Jon's presence, Justin insisted on it. Like he wanted to keep him close at hand. It seemed strange at the time, and looking back on it now, I recalled the sinister smile he flashed at his little brother. Sinister might sound a bit harsh for a preteen's smile, but that's the way I remember it.

Also, it was around this time that Jon started drinking. You might think ten years old is rather young to develop the habit, but it was easy when your big brother did the pouring. We'd all get together at the Wade mansion after school, and hang out by the pool, or play ping pong, or watch tv in their large finished basement. If Justin's mom wasn't home, and usually she wasn't, Justin would open the liquor cabinet and we would have our private preteen cocktail hour.

I gave a cursory glance through the rest of the notebook, where Jon kept copies of the hate mail he'd received. They called him a murderer, or they hoped he'd go to hell. Well, there wasn't much doubt about that. He went there while he was still alive.

But why keep all this? What good could come from reading and rereading those terrible letters?

On the last page of the notebook I found a poem. It was untitled, and unattributed, but it certainly looked like what I remembered of Jon's distinctive scrawl.

Jessie, Jessie,
Life is messy.
Here's to your dying day.

Swimming, boating,
You're just floating,
Waves won't wash you
away.

Pushing, shoving,
Some sick loving,
Boys have nothing to say.

Jessie, Jessie,
Life's still messy
All since your dying day.

Whoa! I read that poem several times. Were the rumors true? Did Jon have something to do with her death after all? Did he drown her intentionally? Had he and Justin concocted the whole story in order to cover up their culpability? That would help explain why Justin wanted to keep an eye on his little brother. Maybe this was the unspeakable mystery Karin had alluded to. I needed to run it past her, maybe come to some conclusion. But that would be later, much later.

I considered calling Deb. Maybe she knew something about it. On the other hand, did I really want to reopen that can of worms? It couldn't be good for Justin, or for Deb for that matter. I was pretty sure retailing stale rumors about Jon killing his little sister wasn't what she was looking for when she hired me.

Sitting there, I was at a disadvantage. I didn't know what if anything was going on between Justin and Deb over this case. And what about Kendall Williams? Again, what role was he playing? What kind of control was he exerting on Deb? I thought again of his warning not to contact her. What of it? I wondered. What can he do to me? To her? I mean, did she even know that he was involved? Had he told her to avoid contact with me, too?

Before I could settle on a course of action, my pager buzzed. It was Mike Wallis. I quickly called him.

"Buddy, whassup?" Mike said cheerily.

"Come get me."

"Come get you where?"

"I'm out in Eastpointe." I gave him the address.

"Eastpointe? You slumming on me?"

"I'm at Karin Champagne's apartment. She's the one who called me at the Walloon."

"You dog," Mike chortled. "Boy, you go to work, you work all the way, don't you."

"Just come get me."

He said he'd have a uniform drop him off, then he could drive my car back. After a painful search I finally found my keys, and wrote a quick note for Karin telling her there may have been a break in the case, and I was looking into it. I'd call her later.

Then I started pulling all the notebooks together, figuring I should just leave the box in Karin's possession. Jessica's notebook I held onto. That was too important to leave lying around. Who knows, Williams might confiscate it. I gave each of Justin's notebooks a quick glance, to see if anything jumped out at me. There was a lot of stuff about the Butler Woods development, including a piece in the Wall Street Journal. That was a big deal, I recalled. Justin Wade was pretty big time for Detroit, but that was the first time he registered on a national level.

"**Developer Tosses Life Raft to Sinking Town**," read the headline, with the typical Journal breeziness.

> *Grosse Pointe, once a national by-word*
> *for exclusivity, has fallen on hard times of*
> *late. Buffeted by neighboring Detroit's*

downward spiral, the community finds itself facing a declining tax base, budget cuts and layoffs. Some of Grosse Pointe's leading citizens are questioning the future of the town they have called home, many for two or three generations.

"I never thought I'd say this," remarks Howard Perryman, long-time resident and former Mayor, "But sometimes I wonder if Grosse Pointe is going to make it."

By not making it, Perryman stresses, he doesn't mean the community will fail, just that it will no longer be the exclusive haven it has been since it was founded back in 1903, by Joshua Wade. "Oh, Grosse Pointe will go on," Perryman predicts. "It just won't be the kind of place where the best people want to live. We'll be more like Sterling Heights, or Eastpointe," he concludes, naming a couple of Detroit's more pedestrian suburbs.

Ironically, the latest proposal to bolster Grosse Pointe's waning prospects comes from Justin Wade, grandson of the community's founder. Wade, president of Wade Investments, a privately held asset management firm, represents a new wave of Grosse Pointe boosters. "We don't have to give up," he insists. "Grosse Pointe is more than a community. It's a culture, a way of life. Do we want to lose it? No, I don't think so."

The way forward, Wade argues, is actually to turn back the clock. "When my grandfather founded Grosse Pointe, it was to take advantage of the lake, which which gives access to the entire Great Lakes system. It was to take advantage of the open land and the opportunity to create some of the most attractive residential architecture in the country."

On the face of it, Wade's proposal, calling for the construction of 24 upscale condominiums, doesn't seem to invite controversy. The plan, which features eight units in each of three buildings, is scheduled to occupy the former site of what the locals call the Old Butler Estate. The fifteen acres of prime real estate overlooking Lake St. Clair has lain vacant since the last of the Butler family moved to Colorado in the early eighties.

Far from being the transformative development Wade promises, many Grosse Pointe residents call it 'an abomination.' "Condos won't save us," Perryman declares. "Condos will destroy the last vestiges of our status."

Not everyone agrees. According to Oliver "Olly" Jensen, one of Wade's backers, "Howard Perryman is living in the—

I stopped right there. Olly Jensen. I'd forgotten about his role in Butler Woods. Probably because I'd forgotten just about everything about that time. Karin would probably say it was suppressed memories. Karin would be right. Whenever I thought about those days, the only memory which came readily to mind was that of Sara's face, or what was left of her face, when she died. After that, there wasn't much else worthy of my attention.

Still, now that I thought of it, the memories started trickling back. I remember thinking at the time, what the hell was Justin Wade doing mixed up with Olly Jensen?

Olly was bad news. My feelings about Justin aside, in public he always kept his nose clean. It didn't make sense for him to have anything to do with that weasel. If Justin represented the horse-riding segment of Grosse Pointe society, Olly Jensen was the stuff they scraped off their boots before heading into the Hunt Club lounge.

Still, despite my best efforts, I couldn't recall what if anything I had done about it. I checked the article's dateline, and yes, it had come out right in the middle of my efforts to track down Olly's assets. Surely I wouldn't have missed that connection? Maybe today I could, when I was so sloppy I got my face kicked in on a routine snoop. But back then, that was when I was firing on all cylinders. In fact, that was–

That was when I was working for Sara Jensen. Trying to get her the best deal possible while she tried to keep Olly, and his thugs, from figuring out where she was living. He didn't like to lose, at anything. And that included marriage. Things got so bad, we decided the only way I could keep Sara safe was to find out something that would put him away for a long time. The guy was as dirty as a dishrag, so it was only a matter of digging. Obviously, I didn't dig deep enough, or maybe I was digging too deeply if I hadn't connected the dots on this story. Maybe I was a bit distracted in those days, but still, I should have been enough of a professional to track that bastard down.

And I was getting close, back then. I'd found a trail, and I was working it. It led from drugs to murder, to the heart of Detroit's blackest holes. This went way beyond Grosse Pointe. Way beyond anything the police there could help me with. I remember talking with Mike about it, asking for advice, help, anything he knew or could find out. What did the Detroit police know about this?

"This what?" he'd said, with a surprising lack of

curiosity.

"Look, Jensen's tied in with some heavy muscle here. Somebody's pulling a lot of strings in Detroit. Don't you want to know who it is?"

"Who who is?" Sometimes Mike could be as inscrutable as Buddha.

"Who's behind all this. Look," I said, flourishing my notes. "It's all right here. Everything except the names and faces."

That set Mike off. "Everything except the names and faces," he howled. He reached for the phone. "Tell you what, I'll call the DA. You can tell Carmine yourself."

"Jesus, Mike. What happened to you?"

"Whaddaya mean?"

"You used to be a good cop." That was the only time I saw Mike lose his temper. I think he would have taken a poke at me, except there was no percentage in that. He couldn't take me in a fight if I spotted him the first three blows. But he was plenty pissed.

"It's easy for you, buddy," he spat. "You just sit back and make things up. You just throw shit and wait for something to stick. No rules for you." He grabbed my notes, my flow chart, my detailed depiction of the chain of command. "What do you think you got here?" He snorted. "Even if you had names here, hell, even if you had this one." He jabbed his finger at the blank space at the top of the chart. "Even if you named Mr. Big, what the fuck good would that do? Probable cause, baby. Ever hear about probable cause? You want me to go to a judge, get a wire on Mr. Big? Why? Cause some buddy of mine has a hunch?"

Flinging the pages in my face, he stalked out of my office, with a "Get me evidence. Get me something I can use."

I tried. Believe me, I tried. But every time I got close, every time I identified a pattern, it dissolved. I was working like crazy in those days. Trying to dot the i's and cross the t's. but I just couldn't get it done. Not in time. Not in time to save Sara. Not in time to save my soul.

But enough of this. I put the notebook with Jessica's. This would bear examination. It probably didn't apply to this case, but stranger things have happened. The thing about having a real case, is, once it gets going, you don't know where it's going to end. It's like white water rafting. Once you enter the first rapids, you have no choice but to hang on and ride it through to the end. If you try to get off, more likely than not you'll end up getting sucked under.

Realizing Mike would be there any second, I flipped through the rest of the notebooks, just in case. When I opened the last one I was stunned to see my own photograph staring back at me. It was from another "Detroit News" article, the one announcing Sara's death. It was chilling, seeing her face again, and reading that story again. It got chillier still when I turned the page and glanced at the follow up articles, with speculation about my own involvement in the case. It got downright Arctic when I continued leafing through, and discovered that Jon had devoted an entire notebook to me, to my career, to my involvement in that terrible night.

CHAPTER 7

When the doorbell rang I moved painfully to let Mike in.

"Took you long enough," he began, then stopped short. "Jesus, what happened to you?"

I told him I'd run into a couple guys trashing Jon's condo.

"Sure, sure. At Butler Woods. Plus, Andy Parsons arrested you. I'm seeing patterns here." He took me gently by the arm. "I told you you shouldn't get involved."

"How do you know so much about the case?"

"I'm a cop. We know these things." He frowned. "But that's not what I'm talking about. You look like you saw a ghost."

I told him I had, the ghost of my career.

"What are you talking about?"

I showed him the notebook. He leafed through it. "Jesus, where'd this come from?"

"Jon Wade. He kept notebooks about everything, and apparently everybody. He's got five or six on Justin, and even kept one for Jessica."

"The one who drowned?"

"Yeah. What do you know about that?"

"For the last time, leave it alone."

"Did Jon kill her?"

"How the hell should I know?" Mike snapped. "I was what, fifteen at the time?"

"What can you find out?"

He shrugged. "I don't know. I could dig around, but why? What does it matter if he did kill her? It's too late to bring charges. It was in another county, and besides, the perp is dead."

"Hell, I don't know, Mike. But something's going on, and I figure every little bit of information's going to help me." I started filling him in on what had gone down the last forty-eight hours, what Karin had told me, the mysterious Bill Jeffries. Mike drew a blank when I said I really needed to track him down. When I got to Kendall Williams, he turned to the door. "Come on, let's get you out of here. You need to rest."

On the way back to Detroit, Mike was his old sardonic self. He grilled me about Karin, wondering if she was "talent." I told him that I was a professional, that I didn't think of witnesses as potential bed mates.

Mike snorted. "Yeah, right." He turned off the expressway at Cadieux Road.

"Uh, Detective," I said. "This isn't the way to my flat."

"Yeah, well, I figured you probably could use a bite to eat, or some other form of sustenance. When was the last time you had a drink?"

I told him that alcohol was contraindicated for post-concussion syndrome.

"Right. And using six syllable words is contraindicated for washed up has-beens like you."

I shrugged, being in no position to debate my status as a has-been. Besides, truth to tell, the thought of a drink sounded pretty good about now. I hadn't had a drink since, hell, just before I got my head kicked in. A wiser man might have given pause at the conjunction of those two incidents, but a wiser man wouldn't have much of a story to tell.

As we ~~pulled up in front of~~ parked at the Walloon Saloon, Mike said, "In my expert medical opinion, a heavy dose of chili fries and bourbon is the best treatment for post-concussion syndrome."

"And how many concussions have you treated, Dr. Wallis?" I inquired while extracting myself from the car.

Mike turned serious a moment, and said, "You'd be surprised."

As the front door hissed shut we were greeted by the sputtering of the Old Vienna neon and the guttering of Darla's laughter.

"Well, well, if it isn't the dynamic duo." She stopped mid-rasp. "What happened to you?"

"I beat up a guy's foot with my face," I quipped, scaling the bar stool.

Mike placed our orders, then said flatly, "So, you won't give up the case."

"There's something there, Mike. I can feel it."

"Yeah, there's something there, alright. A beating, an arrest, who knows what else down the road, and for what? Some drug-riddled corpse you never gave a damn about."

"Oh, I gave a damn about him. I hated the bastard."

"So what gives?" Mike frowned. "It won't get you Deborah back."

"Hell, Mike," I said as Darla slapped our drinks on the bar and turned to toss the fries in the deep-fryer. "I don't want her back. I moved on a long time ago."

If you want to know the truth, it did hurt when Darla joined Mike's laughter. But the important thing is, I tried.

I guess a little bitterness leaked out when I accused Mike of not wanting to see me get back on my feet. "Seems to me, if you gave a damn about your buddy, you'd be trying to help him, not trying to scare him off."

He scowled at me, then shrugged. "Ah, what the hell.

Whaddaya need?"

"First off, I want to know who beat me up, and what they were looking for in Jon's apartment." I tossed back the rest of my drink. "Hell, you get me their names, I'll find out the rest."

"The shape you're in?" Mike snorted. "You couldn't beat the lunch money out of a first grader."

"They grow 'em pretty big these days," Darla put in, much to her own tortured amusement.

"You say it was a white guy and a black guy?" Mike said when Darla's coughing fit subsided.

I said I didn't remember saying anything about them. I suppose I could have, things still being a little hazy, but one thing I prided myself on was my grasp of details.

"Maybe I got that from Parsons, whatever." Mike waved his hand airily. "Okay, let's see, one white guy, one black guy. Well, that pretty much narrows it down. At least we can rule out the Mexicans and the Asians."

"Don't forget the women," Darla added. "That's half the population right there."

Mike rubbed his hands briskly. "Oh yeah, now we're getting somewhere."

I zoned them out while they went off on their reductive tangent, narrowing the suspect field down to a mere forty percent of greater Detroit's population. I tried to recall any details that might help ID them.

"One of them said 'Let's get out of here, Sharky.'" I said. "That was the black guy, because Karin said the white guy's face was bleeding. Sounds like the black guy was in charge."

"Might be worth something," he agreed. "And the other guy, you hurt him pretty bad, you think?"

"Bad enough to keep him from killing me. He was tough, and strong."

"I can check area hospitals," he offered. "Though something tells me they aren't the kind to rely on emergency rooms." He jotted a few lines in his notebook.

"I'll hit a few snitches—" Mike stopped talking abruptly. He gazed blankly at the Old Vienna sign and began tapping his cell phone meditatively on the bar.

"What?" I said.

"Nothing." He tapped some more, then slapped his hand on the scarred and battered wooden bar top. "What the hell," he muttered. "Gotta get something from the car," he announced, hopping off his stool. Turning to Darla, he added, "Don't let him wander off, or get into a fight or anything."

She chuckled. "Don't worry. He moves, I'll clobber him." She kept chuckling until the door hissed shut. Then she leaned across the bar and said, "Watch out for Mike."

"You mean watch his back?" I wondered, gulping my drink, savoring the bite, wondering how I could have gone two days without it.

"No, I mean watch your own back." She met my eyes with a cold gaze.

I stared at her, facing this one-time goddess, this one-time paragon of allure, who had declined apace with her place of employment. "This is Mike Wallis we're talking about–my oldest drinking buddy."

"Yeah, that guy."

"That guy. The guy who's in here three, four nights a week."

"The guy who never pays for a fucking drink," she spat.

"What are you talking about? I saw him fork over a hundred bucks just last Saturday."

"So you're not completely blind," she muttered. "You ever wonder about that wad he carries?"

"Oh, come on, Darla. You can't be serious," I insisted, while the chorus in my head crooned "Yeah, what about that wad?"

"Well, Mike's right about one thing. You're damn easy to fool." Before I could figure if she meant falling for Mike's line of patter, or for her own jest, she set another drink in front of me. "Drink up, you're falling behind." Then she grinned. "Don't worry, it's on Mike's tab."

This was beyond weird. This was hitting too damn close to home. Yeah, the world was a toilet, but the Walloon Saloon was the one place the swirl stopped. But now, if Darla was serious, it was sucking me right down the same vortex. I shook my head. Some things just didn't bear contemplation. Hell, Mike Wallis and Darla were the only constants in my life. If she didn't trust him, where did that leave me?

"You're kidding, right Darla?"

Before she could answer, Mike returned. He had his briefcase in tow, and slapped it on the bar before removing two photos. One white guy, one black guy.

"Look familiar?" he asked.

I gave them both a good look, though they were jumping around a bit, quite a bit actually, considering they were dead. I shrugged. "Not particularly, though this one—" I fingered the photo– "Those scratches on his face ring a bell–where'd you get 'em?"

"You think this Karin could ID them?"

I shrugged again. "Hard to say. She told me the one guy was bleeding." I reached for the photos. "Next time I see her, I'll ask."

Mike pulled them away. "Sorry, buddy. Evidence. Shouldn't even have shown them to you."

"What gives, Mike?"

He made a show of struggling to make up his mind. Then he said, "What the hell, you'll read about it tomorrow anyway."

"Read about what?"

Mike sighed. "Earlier today, while you were still in the clutches of Nurse Ratched, Doug and I went over to do a little follow up on Wade's death. We took along the posse, it being a crack house and all." He drained his drink and gave a little finger whirl to get Darla moving on a refill. I shook my head, having a little trouble focusing as it was. She gave an elaborate double take, which earned her my fiercest scowl. "Anyway," Mike continued. "We rap on the door and these guys–" he flourished the morgue shots–"They come out guns blazing. I'm hiding in the bushes while the team lets loose, and only come out when Doug says it's okay."

"You're one fucking stud, aintcha, Mikey," Darla said. After her warning, I had to view this, what I had always thought as harmless banter, in a whole new light.

"I'm still alive," Mike said, with, was it my imagination, or the booze, a little heat in his voice. "I'm alive, and I'm gonna stay that way. That's the game plan."

"So," I decided, struggling to stay on top of the story. "These guys, assuming they are the same ones, they're tied in with the crack house where Wade got waxed? Maybe Deb has a point. Maybe he didn't go there on his own."

"You think so?" Mike replied. "Wait'll you hear the rest. We went inside, had a look-see. Usual crack house pigsty. Makes you feel diseased just walking around. You think if that dust gets in your lungs, God knows what you'll turn into." He paused for a sip and shudder, then went on. "So we start looking around, and guess whose name is all over the place?"

"Mayor Brown's?" I offered. Hell, I didn't have a clue.

"No, not this particular one," Mike said to Darla's guffaw. "Nope, turns out your buddy Bill Jeffries owns this shooting gallery."

"Jeffries? You mean Jon's business partner owns the house where he got killed?" I frowned into the smoky bar back mirror. "Jesus, maybe that's why he's gone walkabout."

"Could be." Mike slipped the photos back into their folder, and replaced it in his briefcase. "Anyway, it's pretty clear you don't have to waste any time on payback." He tapped his fingers on the bar, then turned to look in my eyes. "Listen, Jim. I still think you should just walk away.

You keep turning over rocks, who knows what you're gonna find."

I said something not quite halfway clever about liking vermin or something, feeling pretty damn light headed. I didn't know if it was the booze or the concussion, but I had definitely hit a down slope. "I'm not quitting, Mike," I announced, with some effort. "The only question is, are you going to help me?"

"Okay, be an idiot, but don't say I didn't warn you." Some more finger tapping on the bar, then he reached his decision. "All right, I'll do what I can. We're definitely looking for Jeffries, as are you. So, let's keep each other in the loop. I'll let you know what we find, you give me any leads you come up with. Deal?"

I said I'd do whatever I could, as long as my client wasn't put at risk.

"Your client may be at risk just by you nosing around."

When I spoke, my voice was hard and cold. "What do you know, Mike? What are you holding back?"

He pushed himself back from the bar, laughing. "No way, buddy. Don't go down that road." He slapped me on the shoulder, which almost knocked me off my stool. I grabbed onto the bar rail. Mike and Darla both chuckled at my distress. "I'm not holding anything back," Mike said patiently. "I'm just saying things could get ugly. But hell, I'll accept your terms." We shook on it, then he asked if there was anything else he could do to help.

"I'd like to find out more about Jessica's death."

"Hell, you can read the clips as well as I can."

"Yeah, I know that. I just thought you might know somebody who knows—"

"Somebody who heard somebody mention something a long time ago—sure, sure. Waste of time, but if you can't waste time for a buddy—"

"Also, this Kendall Williams—something doesn't fit."

Mike grew very solemn. "Stay out of Williams' way. He's bad news."

I scoffed. "What are you saying? He's the managing partner of the biggest law firm in the state. What's he going to do? Work me over in some back alley?"

"Guy like that, he doesn't ever get his hands dirty," muttered Mike. "Guy like that, he doesn't even give the order, it just gets done."

"So what's his story?"

"Hasn't got one."

"What do you mean, he hasn't got a story?" I demanded. "Everybody's got a story. I bet even you've got a story."

Mike jumped up. "What the hell's that supposed to mean? You think I'm mixed up with that S.O.B.?" His composure was gone, his accustomed sang froid out the window. Darla just gazed at him, her expression saying, "Now, this is interesting."

I put up my hands to placate him. "Easy, Mike. I didn't mean anything." I waited for him to settle down, and waved my glass at Darla. Another round. That'd make four for me, and it wasn't even—when I raised my arm to check my watch things started spinning again. I grabbed the edge of the bar to keep from falling off my stool.

"Three drinks and he's falling over," Darla said cheerily. "Even by his standards that's pretty lame."

I told her it was nothing, just lost my balance, but I could tell she didn't believe me. Mike's eyes betrayed a bit of concern, too. Blundering ahead, ignoring the warning signs, that's what I did. That's what's made me the success I am. "So what is it?" I asked Mike. "You guys have a history, or what?"

"What guys are we talking about?" He was being intentionally obtuse now, like he was waiting me out. Like he knew it was just a matter of time before I—

The room sped up, like it used to back in college, when I joined the frat. Took me a hell of a lot more than three drinks in those days. 'Course I hadn't just been beaten unconscious.

"You and Williams," I mustered. "Got a history?"

"Yeah, we got a history alright. Williams, the invisible perp, I call him. I swear his fingerprints were on half a dozen cases of mine. Unsolved cases, mind you."

"But why would Fleigher, Kermit, and Schneid hire a guy like that? I mean, they're about as white shoe as it gets."

"You wanna stay white shoe, you gotta have somebody making sure you don't step in any shit."

"So this Williams, he's what, an enforcer?" I gripped the bar as another wave washed over the deck. "How's he fit in with Justin Wade then?"

"Who says he's got anything to do with Justin?" Mike asked, suddenly all business.

"Williams. He said his number one job is to protect his client."

"Maybe he didn't mean Justin," Mike offered cryptically.

"Then who? Who else is involved with this? Maybe Jeffries?"

"Jeffries?"

"Yeah, Bill Jeffries. The guy you told me owns the crack house where Jon—Whoa." I pulled myself back up by the edge of the bar. "Who's driving this boat, anyway?"

"Buddy, I think it's time we got you home," Mike announced, getting his shoulder under my arm and helping me lurch toward the door.

"Hey, what about your check?" Darla called.

"Put it on my tab, babe," Mike called as he pushed the door open with his other shoulder.

CHAPTER 8

I know I got home somehow, because I woke up in the middle of the night, lying fully clothed on my own bed. I didn't feel so hot, but I didn't feel as bad as I thought I should. Also didn't have that still-drunk-reprieve sensation, the one where you know this is as good as you're going to feel for the next two days. My head hurt, my face hurt, my shoulder hurt, my ribs really hurt, and there was a ringing in my ears which I knew, of course, was the phone which had awakened me. I glanced at the alarm clock. 3:00 a.m.

Maybe it was Deb again. Maybe these wee hour heart-to-hearts were going to become a habit. I picked up.

"Jim? Are you alright?" It was Karin, and she sounded rattled.

"What's going on? Are you okay?"

"Yes, I'm fine." She sounded anything but. "I got your note," she said. "I thought you were coming back here. I thought you'd call. I kept waiting, and then I got worried."

"So you waited until the middle of the night to check

in?"

"No, you ass," she cried, her voice verging on tears. "I've been calling you for hours. Where have you been?"

"I've been here, sleeping."

"Sleeping it off, you mean." Her bitterness was startling.

"Yeah, well, I had a couple of drinks, and—"

"You idiot! Didn't I tell you—"

"—and you were right. Alcohol is definitely contraindicated for post-concussion syndrome. I actually tried to tell Mike that."

"Who's Mike?"

"A cop I know. He's helping me with the case."

She wanted to know what the break was, the one that took me away. I told her I wasn't sure, exactly, but there was stuff in the notebooks that shook me. That was when she told me to wait until she got there.

"What do you mean?"

"I heard from Bill. He called me, and asked for my help. Something in his voice made me nervous. I've just been driving around the city ever since. I'm only about five minutes away."

I hung up and lay back down. Karin was a funny lady. She gets scared, so she jumps in further? Maybe she had a little explaining to do when she got here. Then I decided I might as well get up, maybe put some coffee on. It was shaping up to be one of those nights. I wasn't sure what it meant that Jeffries had finally made contact, but I figured it might shake something loose. Or get us all killed. After what I'd learned about him today, I figured any meeting we might have would have to be in a well-lighted public space.

But why was he asking Karin for help? Surely, if he was involved with Jon's death, she'd be the last person he'd turn to, or maybe the second to last. Deborah Wade wouldn't look too favorably on a request. Not now. Not if she knew what I knew.

While spooning Folgers grounds out of the can I mentally kicked myself for wasting the weekend getting beaten up, arrested, and hospitalized. What I should have done is gone down to Starbucks and picked up a pound of French Roast beans. Now that I was flush again, at least for a little while, I might as well enjoy a good cup of brew. Oh well, at three in the morning, any coffee was better than none.

The machine was grumbling that it was finished when the door bell rang. I pressed the buzzer and made my way down the stairs to meet her. She stood there in the doorway, shivering in a black leather coat, her hair gone wild in the chilly drizzle. Before I could invite her inside, she was in my arms. I held her close. She smelled good and she felt good. Okay, she was crying, but I still counted it as a win.

I led her upstairs, took her coat, and poured her a mug of coffee. She wanted it black, which was lucky because that's the way I drink it, and my budget didn't allow for pitchers of cream, just in case some beautiful woman decided to drop by in the middle of the night.

She wasn't in any hurry to tell me what was happening at first, wasting time checking my bandages and taking stock of my physical condition instead. I finally took her hands and gently pulled them away from the ribs she'd been probing. "What's going on?" I repeated. "We can play doctor later."

She grinned, which I took as a positive sign, for her mental health if nothing else. "I was just so upset when you weren't there," she said. "And angry, too. I don't know what's going on, and I don't think you do either. But obviously something is, or you wouldn't be in the shape you're in."

"So far, so good," I agreed. "You seem to have a knack for this detecting business. But tell me about Jeffries."

"Oh, him." She shuddered. "He gives me the creeps.

Always has."

"But he called you. You said he asked for help."

She nodded.

"What kind of help, specifically? Because I'm not sure we should be doing business with him."

"Why not?"

"I think he might have had something to do with Jon's death."

She shook her head. "He said he didn't."

"You asked him?"

She said no, that he'd brought it up.

"Interesting," I said.

"In fact," she continued. "He was quite insistent about it. That's why he wants my help—to clear his name."

I asked how she could do that. "Can you give him an alibi? Were you with him when it happened?"

She shook her head again, this time with a scowl.

"Okay," I conceded, "But I had to ask. So he doesn't want an alibi. What does he want?"

"He wants me to come clean on what he and Jon were up to."

I told her that would help a lot. "It'd definitely help me," I noted pointedly.

"He wants me to go to the police."

"You haven't, have you?"

She shook her head. "I wanted to talk to you first."

I said that was a good call. "Let's figure out what we're dealing with before involving the cops." I shifted my position slightly on the couch, and she moved closer to me. I tried putting my arm around her, but it hurt my shoulder, so she sort of snuggled against me. It felt nice. Very companionable, but nice. Like we'd been snuggling together for years. "So tell me what they were up to, and what your role was in it."

Frankly, the story she told made me very uncomfortable. In one sitting I had more information than

I'd managed to uncover on my own, but I didn't like the direction it was leading. "You remember how I said Jon and Bill were following the money?" she said. I nodded. "Well, at first Jon was all excited, filling me in each day on what he'd uncovered. Then one day, it just stopped."

Wade suddenly wasn't interested in talking about it. He wouldn't answer her questions other than to say, "It's moving along." When she pressed him, he got angry and told her to just leave it alone.

"And you're sure this was all about tracking down the big suppliers? He wasn't getting involved in the business on a personal basis?"

Karin's expression told me what she thought of that. She scooted away from me, kneeling on the couch and glaring at me. "Why on earth would you ask me something like that?" After I explained Jeffries' connection to the crack house, she shook her head. "I don't believe it, not for a second."

"Why not? You've pretty much said Jeffries can't be trusted."

"Him I could believe, but not Jon."

"But why would Jon be mixed up with him if he were—"

"Oh, I don't know," she cried. I opened my arms and she fairly lunged across the couch.

"Easy," I said, to spare my ribs, and she moderated her approach. I held her awhile, until she relaxed. After a bit she continued in a calmer voice.

"I know it doesn't make sense. All I know is Jon was getting close to the money behind Detroit's drug trade."

"How could you tell, if he wouldn't talk about it?"

"Well, about two weeks ago, that all changed. Jon changed. He got real manic. High as a kite whenever he came over, just bristling with excitement. He started saying, 'We're closing in, baby.' Then, after an hour or so, he'd grow so somber, it was enough to break your heart. When I asked him what was wrong, he just shook his head. All he would say was that sometimes he hoped he was right, and sometimes he hoped he was wrong."

"Wrong about?"

"I had to assume it was the identity of Mr. Big."

"Mr. Big?" I felt a chill pass through the room. Mr. Big. It was a silly name, but that's what Mike had called him, and that's how I thought of him. Had to be a coincidence, didn't it?

"Hey, are you okay?" Karin was good. She didn't miss much. "You look like you saw a ghost."

"That's the second time I heard that phrase today," I replied, absently brushing her hair back from her forehead. She turned her face up toward mine. Her lips were there for the taking. Maybe I should have taken them. Instead, I said, "Tell me about Mr. Big."

"Well, I don't know much," she sighed. "Just what Jon told me, and mostly what he told me was he'd only have one shot at him, so he had to make sure he was right. Otherwise he would go down in flames."

"Go down in flames? Sounds like he was predicting his own death."

Karin shook her head. "It wasn't like that. I mean, there were plenty of times when he sort of warned me that things could get ugly, that there might be danger, and sometimes he thought he should stay away from me, to keep me safe."

When I remarked that Deborah had said pretty much the same thing, Karin scowled. "I never could figure her out. Sometimes Jon spoke of her like she was his big sister. Other times he'd be on the phone with her, and he'd slam it down and yell, 'That's the last time I talk to her.'" She smiled ruefully. "But he went back to her just before the end."

"How'd you feel about that?"

She shrugged. "I don't know. I guess I was kind of conflicted about Jon anyway, and I knew they had a history. I didn't know whether I should be jealous or not, or even if I wanted to be jealous." She sighed, and moved closer to me again. "Jon was a wonderful person, and some of our time together was unbelievably good, but he had an edge about him. I always knew this mission wouldn't be enough. Once he worked it out, he wouldn't relax, he'd be off on another tangent. He was a thrill junkie."

"Sublimating his addictive personality to the thrill of living life on the edge, the rush of working without a net?"

She glanced up at me, grinning. "Ooh, listen to you. And I thought I spoke psychobabble."

"Maybe I know a little bit about that particular personality," I said, beginning the painful process of getting to my feet. "You want some more coffee?"

Karin jumped up. "Allow me. You're still recuperating."

While she was gone I tried to work out what I'd learned, and what I still needed to know. By the clattering of dishes, I suspected she was preparing more than coffee. I wished her luck. My pantry wasn't exactly well-stocked.

We knew Jon was getting close at the end. It sounded like he had a pretty good idea who it might be, but had to be sure. That suggested whoever it was, was powerful, and well known. Other than that, I didn't have a clue. I decided I'd have to pump Karin a little bit more. Maybe she knew and wasn't telling, or maybe she knew but didn't know she knew. The only thing I knew for certain was that I was fading fast. I wasn't sure I'd even be awake when she—

When I woke up next I was back in bed. The sun was shining, or at least there was daylight, and she was gone. The bed was still warm, and I could smell her there. So how 'bout that? I'd slept with another client, and this time I didn't even know it. I wondered how Mike would react to that bit of news. Just as quickly, I realized he would never know. Not unless Karin told him.

So, where was Ms. Champagne? I had to start doing a better job of keeping track of my clients. Then I stopped.

Why was I calling her my client? Deb was my client. Karin was, what? Well, according to Kendall Williams, she was, in fact, my client. My provisional client, I guess you could call her. Fortunately, I was sufficiently aware to resist the urge to shake my head in bewilderment. Head shaking is contraindicated for post-alcoholic binge syndrome. You can look it up. It's in the manual.

Okay, first thing, figure out where Karin went. Then figure out if she is my client. Then, what the hell, figure out a way to get my other client to have a sleep over?

No, this wasn't getting me anywhere. I went into the kitchen to clean out the coffee maker. Seem to recall having used it last night. Or this morning. Something like that.

Turns out Karin's a tidy little house guest. Also good at leaving notes. It was right there next to Mr. Coffee's innards. "I'm at work. Be back around 5:00. Thanks for the bed—don't worry, your honor is still intact."

"Damn," I muttered. A silly grin flashed across my face before my old buddy recrimination reclaimed the scene. Stay away from her, I warned myself. This case is already getting too familiar. Don't you start.

Too familiar? It sure the hell was, I started thinking, as all yesterday's scattered fragments started reassembling. How the hell could this case turn back into Sara's case? Especially when, before Saturday, I'd spent ten years not thinking about her at all. How the hell could I see even a hint of Sara in Karin Champagne?

Sara had been tall, and lithe, with a dancer's build, and long, raven black hair framing an olive face. Her grandfather had come from Lebanon, and built, or expanded an empire in international trade. How a shipping magnate had landed in a city a thousand miles from the nearest ocean was a mystery we had shared a laugh over once or twice, usually when I would murmur something asinine like "How did I ever manage to find someone like you?" Usually about two in the morning, lying sweaty on soggy, twisted sheets.

Sara had been, what, a mystery unveiled? A mystery never to be solved. A mystery whose clues were scattered along with her scent around my office, my apartment, on the street where I lived. I told myself to stay away. It was unprofessional. It was wrong. She was in danger. She was vulnerable, and she had turned to me for help. Instead I was helping myself.

Only problem was, that was my head talking. The rest of me, I had no will of my own. She was my client. I was working for her. I took orders, and her orders, more often than not, were to get undressed. Why, I can't tell you. What she ever saw in me, I'll never figure out. Certainly not now, ten years after we put her in the ground.

That was about the time Olly disappeared. I meant to go looking for him. Track him down, run him to ground and exact my vengeance, Biblical style. Of course, I was distracted, fighting to keep my license. Hell, fighting to stay out of jail. They had nothing on me, other than the fact she was killed with my gun, and she died in my arms. But I had innocence on my side. Granted, that hasn't been enough for a lot of people, but I wasn't exactly helpless. I had a lot of friends, on the force, and in the Hall of Justice. Not that they'd break the law for me, but they were willing to give me the benefit of every doubt.

It was enough to keep me on the outside, but soon enough, I'd used up all my chits, and that's where they ended up keeping me. On the outside. No longer would District Attorney Fred Carmine take my calls. No longer could I call up Police Headquarters and ask for a favor. Oh, I could ask all I wanted, at first, before they stopped even taking my calls, but there was no way anybody was going to stick his neck out for me.

So the whole "Mr. Big" thing died on the vine. The

last time I spoke with the DA was about three months after he decided not to press charges. I'd just gotten my license back, and I was ready to get back into the fray. Item number one, of course, was to find Olly. "He's got to be tied up with Sara's death," I'd insisted. "It's got to be him."

"Sure thing, O.J," Carmine breezed. "You get the evidence. We'll take it from there." Then he hung up, and I started running investigations for a sleazy trial lawyer.

I sat at my desk and sipped my coffee, and watched the bustling city scene unfold on the sodden street two floors below. The guy in the green fatigues climbed slowly out of his sleeping bag in the doorway of the former AAA Office Supplies, in the vacant Mortimer Building across the street. Looks like he survived another night, I thought. He stood up, finally, and stretched, and limped halfway down the block to piss against the wall of the former First Federal Bank building.

The old lady with the purple hair pushed her shopping cart up the sidewalk. She had some words for the fake vet, and delivered them, no doubt in that bizarre tongue known only to herself, then continued on her way. A bus splashed by, mostly empty, mostly covered with graffiti. Time was when graffiti meant something, or so they said. Now it was just an excuse to cover surfaces. It was pathetic, useless, as pathetic and useless as this empty shell of a dying city.

I set down my mug. This was getting me nowhere. I had to act. Right, but how? Where? What to do? Ordinarily I would check in with Mike, but suddenly that didn't seem like such a good idea. Darla's warning stuck in my head. If it was a warning. Just like everything else in this case, it could be interpreted two different ways. But still, caution seemed like the best strategy.

On the other hand, Mike was kind enough to get me home. Then again, he was the one who made sure I needed help getting home. Which made me wonder, with a sickening lurch out of my chair, where were those notebooks? I moved to the bedroom, thinking maybe he'd put them on the dresser. No such luck.

He didn't take them, did he? Why? To find out what I knew? Why would he care? Why was he so interested in this case anyway? Seems like everybody was trying to relieve me of whatever evidence I managed to scrape up. First Williams, now Wallis.

Screw it. What little evidence I had pointed at Jeffries. So a call to him seemed in order. Especially since he was asking for our help. Or Karin's at least. I paused, mid-dial, then returned the phone to its cradle. Something had clicked between Karin and me last night. It felt like we'd skipped right past that whole falling in love stage, and entered the easy comfort of middle age. How was it possible to feel so comfortable with someone you had only just gotten to know? And she felt it, too. That much was obvious.

I couldn't explain it, but I knew it was true. Funny, just yesterday I wasn't sure I could trust her. Right now, she was the one person I knew for certain I could. I'd trust her with my life. Ignoring the painful correlative, that she would then, of necessity, be trusting me with hers, I went back to the phone.

Voice mail, naturally. I left the message. Let him know I was working with Karin, and that we definitely needed to talk.

Then it was time to go see Kendall Williams. But first, a shower. But no, not such a good idea after all. I wanted to take a shower. I needed to take a shower. But with all my bandages, that was a nonstarter. So I took a sponge bath instead, and worked out my strategy. I rejected the idea of calling ahead, deciding to just show up at his office instead. Sometimes all that does is waste an entire day, but I figured, looking the way I did, they wouldn't want me spoiling their lobby. I might not get in to see him, but somebody would do something to make sure I got out of sight. Most likely that something would involve me getting my way. What the hell, it was worth a try.

Headin' downtown, I thought. One of those blocks where the buildings were still occupied, and the sidewalks still got swept; one of Detroit's few Chicago blocks, as I liked to call them. I put on my good suit, and was heading for the door when the phone rang. I picked up to hear Deb's lifeless voice.

"Jim? We need to talk."

"Are you sure—"

"Yes, I'm sure."

"Listen, Deb. Are you okay? Is everything all right?"

"It's fine. It's all fine." Her voice sounded as far away from fine as it was possible to be. I felt a little jolt of electricity scurry around at the back of my neck. "I need to see you."

"You got it. The Grill again?"

"God, no." It sounded like a cry of anguish. "Remember that place we used to go to back when we used to..."

That was rather obscure. "The one with the big—"

"Yes," she sighed. "How soon can you get here?"

"You're there already?"

"Yes, I—" She choked back a sob.

"Fifteen, twenty minutes max."

CHAPTER 9

Twenty minutes didn't leave much time for niceties, such as stop signs and red lights, and speed limits, but it sounded like she was in trouble. It didn't leave much time for feeling around under the seats for a couple of notebooks, either, but I took that time, and there they were, right where I'd left them. A moment's relief, followed by, naturally, another question. Did that mean I could trust Mike, I wondered, making my way through Detroit's indifferent midday traffic, heading for I-96. Or did it mean he'd forgotten I had them with me?

I headed northwest, beyond Detroit's still thriving suburbs, then eight soggy miles through cornfields rusting in the autumn gloom. I exited on State Route 36, and headed north toward Ruggles Creek Park. Back when Deb and I were an item, this was one of our favorite places to get away. Four hundred acres of parkland, with picnic tables and hiking trails, and a big old red barn down in the hollow where the creek burbled through.

A hamper full of cheese and baguettes, and a bottle of Chardonnay, on a drizzly damp day like today, with darkish clouds hovering nearby, promising more rain and heralding the fast approaching snows of winter; we walked hand-in-hand along the trails, scuffling fallen leaves beneath our feet. More than once we sheltered in the barn, caught in a sudden downpour. More than once we made love there. Risking discovery, but so in love with the invincibility of our youth.

Funny she'd want to meet here, I thought, pulling into the parking lot. There was only one other car, snugged up against the thick woods which lined the west side of the lot. A black Yukon. The new Grosse Pointe wagon. Gangbangers and rap videos had tarnished the Escalade, and Suburbans were just too, well, suburban. Yukons fit the bill however. Capable of carrying four kids, a yellow lab, and all the kids' hockey gear, they guzzled too much gas, and had the glamorous lines of a Grosse Pointe matron gone to seed. But they helped justify the expense of doubling the size of the garage, which made it all worthwhile.

I parked across the lot from the Yukon. Don't know why, exactly, but that was the way I decided to play it. I approached from the rear, wishing I had a raincoat in the steady drizzle. Nobody inside. No sign that it was Deb's, though who else would be out here on a day like this? Just crazy young lovers like us, I snorted.

She must've already headed down to the barn, so I cut across the grass, past the daisy chain of picnic tables waiting for spring. The wet grass soaked through the soles of my loafers. Wrong day to dress for the big city, I thought.

The trail was paved as it ducked into the woods, though I knew later on, where it forked down to the creek, it was dirt. Or had been. Maybe someone had thought to pave it in the past twenty years. It was quiet in the woods. Not even birds were out today, just the steady, slithering fall of the trees releasing their dying leaves.

When I reached the fork I detected two sets of

footprints on the muddy path. Waffle-soled hiking boots. They might have been Deb's. They were small enough, plus she had known she was coming out here. She hadn't been dressed for a law office stakeout. But who belonged to the big ones?

Regretting the damage I was doing to my shoes, I hurried down the path. I hadn't gone very far when I heard thrashing in the trees behind me and off to my right. Whoever it was, he was moving quickly, and didn't care how much noise he made doing it.

I wasn't expecting company, so I moved off the trail and hid behind a giant maple. Reflex made me reach for my gun, and recollection made me curse Andy Parsons for confiscating it. My pursuer came to a rapid halt, not more than ten feet the other side of the path. Unarmed, but suddenly beyond caring, I stepped out from behind the tree and confronted—a squirrel, who stopped nibbling his acorn long enough to give me a once-over. When I took a step forward, he chucked the nut and went tearing off. I chuckled at myself, thinking Mike wasn't far off when he said how easily I scared.

But it's amazing how much noise a squirrel can make on a leaf-covered forest floor. That wasn't the first time I'd mistaken one for a much larger creature, though usually it was a deer, or even a bear. But a gun-toting man, bent on mayhem or even murder? Well, there's a first time for everything, I thought as I rounded the bend where the path dipped down toward the creek. Uncertainty was a terrible thing, whether it was where this month's rent was coming from, or where this case was taking me.

To be honest, I couldn't blame my cautious reaction—I decided to use the term cautious, it sounded so much better than cowardly—solely on paranoia. After all, people kept getting dead on this case. What was it? Counting Jon, three already.

I moved cautiously now, as the path got steeper, the surface slick from the rain. A couple more feet, around the next bend, and then there would be the rocks which served as a natural stairway. I wondered how much trouble Deb was in, and how much she was holding back from me. I wondered what she remembered about Justin's dealings with Olly

Granted, that question was straying a bit beyond my brief, but if it helped me get to the truth, then why wouldn't she—

My ruminations were choked off by the sight of the man with a gun who had stepped onto the path in front of me.

"You Corcoran?" he asked.

I slowly raised my hands and took a half-step backwards. "Who wants to know?"

He repeated the question. I shrugged. "She got a bodyguard these days?"

He grinned suddenly. "Yeah, you gotta be Corcoran. She said you were a smart ass." He gestured with the gun. "She's down there."

"You expecting trouble?"

"Way I do things, you always expect trouble, that way it don't surprise you when it shows up." He chuckled. "You know, like a squirrel or something."

I muttered something about squirrels carrying rabies, and moved down the trail. Snarky bastard.

The old barn hadn't aged very well. You wouldn't know it had been red if you hadn't seen it a few years ago. The siding was rotting, and there were gaps in the roof. Not a very good place to sit out a rainstorm anymore.

Deb was waiting inside, under the hayloft where we'd spent those happy hours way back when. Wearing a Carhartt waterproof, blue jeans, and a thick white sweater, she was dressed more appropriately than me. Of course, she always was, even when I was her fashion slave.

She didn't look very happy to see me. She hardly looked at me at all.

I approached her. "What's with the muscle out

there?"

She shrugged. "It wasn't my idea," she said bitterly.

"This one of Justin's grand ideas?" Made sense. His brother gets blown away, why not turn it into a publicity stunt? His family at risk, he acts to protect them, and continues to work for the public good. Or some such saga. Deb's scornful laugh brought me up short.

"You have no idea what you're into, do you?" She turned away and stepped deeper into the gloomy interior.

"What I thought I was into was a nice infusion of cash at a time when I really needed it. I thought I'd milk it for a few weeks, then break the news to you."

"What news?" Just for an instant, there was a hint of life in her voice.

"That lover boy fell off a cliff." I didn't need to be so harsh. It wasn't her fault I'd been strolling down memory lane. "I'm sorry. That was out of line."

"No," she replied, back in zombie land. "That was exactly right. That's exactly what happened. Lover boy fell off a cliff."

"You sure changed your tune in a hurry. What happened to 'He wouldn't have been there. He couldn't?' Four days isn't much time to give up on a guy."

She turned to face me. "There is no story," she announced woodenly. "No case. No nothing."

"You're firing me?"

Another mirthless laugh. "Yeah, Jim. I'm firing you. Thanks for all your effort, but there's nothing left to investigate. Jon went on his final binge, and got the fate he deserved."

I said I wasn't so sure about that.

"Oh really? Why's that?" she wondered. "Still got some unpaid bills?"

That was a low blow, and the fact that it was true didn't exactly ease the sting. "Notice anything different about me?" I offered, passing my hand across my face.

"You think that has something to do with 'the case?' I

heard you got into a bar fight."

Interesting. "Who'd you hear that from?"

"Does it matter?"

"It might. Depending on why whoever said it said it. 'Cause it definitely isn't true."

She strode toward me. "There is no case, Jim. There never was. So just drop it."

Strange she'd have more passion trying to talk me out of the case than she did trying to talk me into it.

"What if I don't?"

"Is it the money, Jim?" Now she was nothing but ice. The contempt just dripped off her tongue. She shoved her hand into her jacket pocket and came out with a check.

I unfolded it. $10,000. "Is that enough? Will that do the trick?"

If I had any integrity left at all I would have returned it. You didn't take payoffs. You didn't take bribes. And from where I stood that's what it looked like. It was too much for saying sorry. It was too much for pity. And it was definitely too much coming from a woman who hated me as much as Deb seemed to right then.

Maybe I would have returned it too, if I hadn't grabbed her, thrown her to the ground and jumped on top of her. Automatic rifle fire'll make a guy do that. "Oh my God," she gasped.

"Keep still," I whispered. "Do you have any idea who that might be?" She shook her head vigorously. "Who knew you were coming here? Justin?"

"No. No one knew, except Howard, and—"

"Howard's the bodyguard?" As she nodded, it became clear that Howard was still with us, as I could hear his gun barking in reply. It sounded like there were two of them. "Wait here," I said, crawling toward the wall. I peeked out through one of the gaps in the siding. I could see them, further up the hill. One had taken cover behind a fallen log, the other behind a tree.

Howard was good, I could see that. He'd taken a

position inside a three-tree cluster, which afforded him adequate protection, and good sight lines. I wanted to move up, lend him a hand, but of course, I didn't have a weapon. I didn't have much time, either. Good as Howard was, he was seriously outgunned. One pistol, even a big sucker like his, wasn't much against two assault rifles, especially in the hands of people who knew how to use them.

They worked well together. One laying down covering fire while the other advanced. No mad rushes, either. They chewed up ground in little chunks. Like they had plenty of ammo, and all the time they needed. It wouldn't take long now. Howard was buying us some time, so we might as well get his money's worth.

I crawled back over to Deb. "Look, I don't know if these guys are after you or me, or why, but we got to get out of here, now."

She nodded, and whispered, "I'm sorry, Jim."

"Forget it. No time for that. That your Yukon up there? Good. Remember that old deer track the other side of the creek? The one where we hid from—"

"Yeah," she said huskily, like a girl gearing up for a fight.

"You go out the back way, the barn will block their view. The path should lead you right up to your car. Go quickly, and try not to make any noise."

"Aren't—aren't you coming?"

"I'm going to give you ten seconds, then I'll make a break for it back up the hill."

She grabbed my arm. "No, Jim. It's too—"

"Listen. It's a diversion. They can't take a shot at me from where they are right now, but that won't be the case for long." I squeezed her hand. "I don't even know if they're after me or you. If they let me go, that answers a few questions."

"What if they chase you?"

"That answers a few, too."

I'm not going to leave you."

"Good. Look, I'm heading out to the northeast, where the woods give out at the cornfield. I'll keep on that line, out to the road. If you get to your car okay, and you have the time, head up 36, I'll flag you down. Don't stop if it's not safe. Now go."

I pointed at the gap in the back of the barn, where several boards had given way. She'd be able to cross the creek and make it deep enough into the woods that they couldn't see her. If there were only two. Maybe they posted another on the trail? For a moment I thought about calling her back, but I forced myself to stick to the plan. If they had a third he'd be busy trying to outflank Howard right now.

I peeked through the gap again on the other side. They were still working their way down to Howard's outpost. It was now or never. If they chased me that meant Howard could catch up to Deb, and get her out of there. That was objective number one. If they let me go, then Howard was doomed. But still, Deb would get away.

It was decision time. I stood up and strode toward the door. No need for secrecy now. I wanted to be seen. I burst into the open, and charged up the hill, clumping through the leaves, crackling the dead fall and snapping twigs and saplings as I ran. I heard a shout, and an answering "Go after him!"

I angled to my right and made for the boundary. I knew if I could get there before he had a clean shot at me my chances were at least fifty-fifty. It's tough to track somebody through a cornfield. Lucky the meet hadn't taken place three weeks later. After harvest I'd be a dead man.

I could hear him thrashing some distance behind me, and cursing when he slipped and fell. I glanced back to see him slide down the slope on his back. He didn't go far, but it gave me an even bigger lead. The other guy was still trying to maneuver on Howard, whose gun had gone silent. At first, I thought maybe he was down, but then I saw him. He'd left his shelter and was working his way back toward the spot my pursuer had abandoned. "Clever, Howard, clever," I thought, resuming my escape.

When I got to the boundary, I found they hadn't done any better preserving the fence than they had the barn. I cleared the dangling barbed wire without breaking stride, and then was thick into the cornstalks. The rain had resumed, and my shoes were shot. My suit was soaked and splattered with mud, and it was my one good suit. Leaves whipped my face, each slap sending waves of pain up from my nose. My chest was on fire, and my ribs felt like they were breaking out of their cage. Corn silk slashed my eyes, and some guy I'd never seen before was trying to kill me. At least there weren't any crop dusters.

I've always had a good sense of direction, which was lucky now, because the last thing I wanted to do was start running in circles. Though that would be hard to do unless the farmer had been drunk when he planted. The rows ran in a straight line to the east, parallel to the highway. I needed to angle northeast, and I needed to hurry if I was going to get to the road in time to flag down Deb.

I paused, trying to hear the other guy over the sound of my rasping breath. Let's face it, I'm in no kind of shape for cross country running. It's amazing the adrenaline boost the sound of live rounds will give you, but eventually physics takes over, and objects in motion are bound to collapse in a sodden, sweaty, gasping heap. I heard some thrashing, off to the south, which was good news. I couldn't hear any more shooting, which may have been good, may have been bad.

On the move again, I cut across the rows this time, trying to be as quiet as I could. I was putting my money on Howard, mainly because I always root for the good guys. Whether Howard was in fact a good guy, I didn't know, but he was shooting at the guys who were shooting at me, so that made him, at the very least, one of the less bad guys.

When I finally reached the road, the Yukon was just sitting there idling, back door open and waiting. Deb returned my wave as I trotted to the vehicle. I was pleased to see Howard behind the wheel. He started moving before I could yank the door shut.

"You got away," I gasped.

"Now I see why you're a detective," he deadpanned. Glancing in the rear view he added, "Thanks for the diversion."

I asked if he'd been in the service. "Yeah, Special Forces. Got out after Somalia."

"And now you work for Justin Wade."

He just laughed. Two short barks, and that was it, though they told me a lot. One, he didn't work for Wade, and two, he wasn't going to tell me who he did work for. The message was as plain as the nose on my face, which was pretty plainly throbbing just at the moment. But me, being me, I plowed straight ahead. I didn't get to where I am today by ignoring the obvious.

"So you don't work for Wade," I offered to his back as he negotiated the highway.

"What are you, just a roving body—"

"Jim, just let it drop." Deb's first contribution to the conversation. No "Thanks for getting me out of there." No "Thanks for putting your life on the line, for saving my life, and Howard's." No "Thanks for ruining your one good suit even though that means you won't even get through the front door of Fleigher, Kermit, and Schneid." Wait a minute. That had to be it.

"Kendall Williams."

Howard's face in the mirror had lost what little charm it had possessed. Turning in the front seat, he pointed a finger at me. I noticed his hands were particularly large, and there were blood stains around his fingernails. "I'm not playing twenty questions with you, Corcoran."

"That's okay. I only have three or four," I replied.

"For you, that is. I might have twenty for my client."

"Listen, pal. I don't have to take your—"

Deb put her hand on his arm. "It's okay, Howard. I think he has the right to know."

"It's not your place to think," he said harshly. She recoiled as if she'd been slapped.

"Look, somebody's going to have to tell me what's going on," I insisted.

"The hell we do," he sneered. "You know who you are? You're nobody. You're yesterday's news. You're yesterday's snoop."

"Bullshit," I snapped. "I'm right in the middle of this."

"You don't know what you're in the middle of," Howard came back. "And if you're smart, you'll just walk away."

"If I were smart I wouldn't be here in the first place." I admit, it was lame. But it got a little laugh from Deb. It was a sad laugh, but a laugh just the same.

Howard slammed on the brakes and slithered to the side of the road. He put the Yukon into park. "Okay buddy, this ride is over." He opened the door and came around the front.

"No, Howard," Deb begged as he opened the door and started to haul me out. "They're still out there."

"No, he's still out there." He had me around the chest, and it felt like at least one of my ribs was stabbing me in the lung.

"You got him, then," I gasped.

His response involved flinging me to the ground. Towering over me, he said. "Yeah, I got him. Didn't even break a sweat."

With that he turned back to the Yukon. "Get back in the car," he ordered Deb. She frowned. I remembered just how much she liked getting ordered around. To my surprise, she pulled her legs back inside. With a sorrowful glance at me, she shut the door.

I climbed shakily to my feet. "Tell Williams he'll have to talk to me, sooner or later."

Howard stopped at the sound of Kendall's name. When he looked at me his face was a road map of confusion. Then he grinned. "You're fishing," he laughed. "You don't know nothing."

A flash of brake lights and then he was gone in a cloud of spitting gravel.

And mud. Gravel and mud splattered the front of my suit, but at least the rain would wash it off. It came down harder, and it wasn't warm. I figured I must be a couple of miles from my car. Twenty minutes if I ran, though staggering was more likely. When I inhaled someone stuck a knife in my ribs, or my heart, or my lungs. Hell, my liver for all I knew. I was all messed up inside. Howard was not a gentle man.

That gave me pause. Deborah mixed up with him? She wasn't a free agent. Then again, I realized, neither was I. Howard may have gotten one of them, but the other was still out there looking for me.

I hadn't been in the Yukon for long, but we'd been moving away from the park. That put more distance between me and my pursuer, but it also put him between me and my car. The only advantage I had was he didn't know where I was. On the other hand, he knew where my car was, and if he had any brains, he'd already started doubling back. Stake out my car, and sooner or later he'd get me.

Unless he saw his partner first and bagged it. Of course, not being a—how'd Mike put it?—a washed up has-been, he probably had a cell phone, and was calling for reinforcements right now. I had a choice to make, and it wasn't pretty. I could walk back up Highway 36 to the Expressway, diving into the ditch every time I heard a car, or I could try to get back to my car before he did.

Whatever I did, I'd better hurry. I was soaked to the bone and hypothermia was not out of the question. What I wouldn't give for a glass of warm whiskey right now. I wondered if alcohol was contraindicated for being chased through a muddy cornfield by a man who wanted to kill me. I wondered if Karin would consider giving me a warm bath and a soft cotton robe to snuggle up in.

While I was doing all this wondering, I noticed that I was moving in a half-jog back down the road toward the park. Guess I made up my mind. Then, waking up slightly, I veered back into the cornfield, this time on the other side of the road. No sense in being too inviting a target.

It turned out to be a shrewd move because not more than a minute later I heard a car careening out of the parking lot. He was coming my way, and he was in a hurry. I crouched down, waiting for him to slam on the brakes. Instead, he kept going, still accelerating as he passed me. I got just a glimpse of him. Not enough to make him out, but enough to see he was dripping wet. And none too happy. He had a phone plastered to his ear.

I waited in the steady rain while the roar of his engine receded in the distance. If it was a trick, it was too subtle for me. Maybe I was safe. For the time being. Still, discretion being the better part and all that, I stuck to the cornfield until I reached the lot. Moving as quickly as I could manage, I crossed the road and ducked behind my car. No gun shots. I considered that a good sign. No shouts, no running feet. It didn't look like he'd shot out my tires or anything, so maybe my luck was still holding.

The car started easily. Not too surprising. If he was in too much of a hurry to shoot my tires, he wouldn't take the time to screw with the engine. I headed south on 36, figuring I'd circle around, come back in on I-94. Might take an extra forty-five minutes, but it was better than getting ambushed. Plus it would give me a chance to think.

The good news was I could pay off my bills and have enough left over to buy a pitcher of cream. And a nice steak dinner at the London Chop House. Or maybe I'd tear up the check and mail it back to Deb. Show her what kind of integrity I had. Show her that I couldn't be bought. Show her that it was going to take more than a lousy ten grand to get me off this case.

I wasn't quitting, I knew that. Of course, that was about all I knew. That and the fact that Mr. Williams and I needed to have a little heart-to-heart. The bastard had played me like a fool from the beginning, and it was time for him to pay. He could pay with information if he wanted, or he could pay with blood. I really didn't give a rat's ass one way or another.

If he wanted to take pot shots at me, fine. It went with the territory. But what the hell was he doing with Deb? I didn't know what kind of game she was playing, but I was a good enough detective to know she wasn't penciling in the starting lineups. The way she complied so meekly with Howard's orders. That wasn't the Deborah I remembered. She didn't follow anybody's orders, meekly or otherwise. Or maybe she had changed, being married to Justin Wade. Maybe that lunatic had sucked all the life, all the light out of her. Maybe that's the way she lived now, meekly, timidly, like Donna Reed in George Bailey's alternate universe.

Maybe, but she did a hell of a job of faking it back there in the barn. There was a whole lot of the old Deb down there. There was a whole lot of hatred, too. Contempt, scorn, disgust...

Okay, okay, I get it. But maybe that was all an act. Maybe she was doing it to drive me away. Get me so pissed off I didn't care what happened to her. Laying her life on the line to spare me whatever was coming if I didn't get off the case. I snorted. Yeah, right.

Still didn't answer the big questions. What was waiting for me down the road? Who was waiting? And what did any of this have to do with Jon's murder?

I approached I-94, the rain still drumming down. All three eastbound lanes were clogged. As I shoe-horned my way into the creeping traffic, for just a panic-tinged

(see p. 124)

moment I wondered if this was a set up. Then I chuckled. You'd have to have a ton of muscle to block an entire Interstate Highway. Plus they didn't even know which way I was heading. They'd have to shut down every highway. I wasn't sure even the Feds could pull that off.

Unless it was the Feds. Maybe the guy put a tracking device on my car? He and his buddy did have quite the armory with them back in the woods. I decided to get off that line before I started peeking out the window for black helicopters. Anyway, it was still daylight. Those black ops choppers only worked at night.

We crept along, the right lane squeezing into the middle into the left to give room for the EMT's to do their thing. A black Mercedes had t-boned into the buttress of the Rouge River Bridge. Must've been going at a pretty good clip. It was almost cut in half. Chiding myself for my paranoia, I was just starting to accelerate when I heard a shout. One of the cops was pointing my direction as he jumped into his car. He hit the lights and the gas, and nearly hit my bumper as he came up behind.

I hit the blinker and pulled over. What could this be about, I wondered, not giving a shred of credence to my recent speculation. I was parked on the bridge, overlooking the river flowing heavy and brown in the steady rain. Leaning over to pull my registration and proof of insurance from the glove compartment, I heard him shout, "Freeze!"

I glanced back to see the barrel of his revolver staring me in the face. I froze. Put my hands up, and waited. Not for long. He sprang for the door, ripped it open, and ordered my ass outside. Compliant, as one must be in these situations, I stepped out slowly, and asked, "What's this ab—"

My words choked off when my mouth hit the hood, his hand jammed up behind my neck. I recoiled reflexively from the pain in my nose. This earned me a sideswiped foot across my ankles, and then I was on my knees. I felt the cuffs clamp down, before I was yanked to my feet and frog-marched back to the waiting cruiser. Unceremoniously shoved inside, I sprawled on the seat, feeling the blood from my rebroken nose dripping down onto my only white shirt. At least I've got other ties, I thought, so the day isn't a total loss.

The cop called it in. "Apprehended the suspect on the Rouge River Bridge—doing traffic control for that Merc– heard the APB on the way out."

"Half hour—that's a damn righteous collar," the dispatcher said. "Read him his rights?"

"Naw, we can do that at the station." A glance over the seat back. "He's not talking."

If I was going to the station, that meant this wasn't related to the case. This was something else entirely. Maybe AT&T was pressing charges for back payments, I didn't know.

"Am I under arrest?" I bubbled through the blood. He nodded in the mirror. "You gonna tell me what for? Or do I have to guess?"

"Why don't you guess?" I guess he thought he was clever. I guess he was expecting high fives, nomination for cop of the month, and instant promotion, I don't know. But this was the smuggest cop I'd seen since waking up in Andy Parson's arms way back, hell, Saturday? Getting arrested two times in three days, not too many private eyes could make that claim.

"Did I forget to return a library book?" I offered.

He snorted in reply. "Pretty cocky for a murderer."

"Murder?" He had to be joking. Although, given my situation, it wasn't very funny. "Who am I supposed to have killed?" I wondered.

He told me to sit tight, we'd be at the station soon enough. And we were. Barring accidents, there weren't enough people left in Detroit, even downtown, to create traffic jams. Plus it doesn't hurt to have a pair of flashing lights on top of your car. The cop whipped up to the curb out front, and hauled me out. He had an audience, and their hands were resting on their guns. Guess they figured I was a dangerous man.

Inside, they formally charged me with the murder of Gus Reynolds. They read me my rights, then hauled me over to Detroit Receiving to get my nose treated. It was after five before I landed in my cell. First I made a call. Not to my non-existent attorney, but to Mike Wallis. Luckily, he was still at the station, because you can't make collect calls to a cell phone. I figured the only other good piece of luck I had was it was a Detroit cop who'd picked me up. If it had been a county sheriff, I might still be behind bars.

As it was, it was eight p.m. before Mike could get there. He chuckled at my face, and the nice orange jumpsuit they'd given me. "Jesus, turn my back on you for a second and look what happens."

"Yeah, what did happen?" I asked, not really in the mood for chit chat. "Who the fuck is Gus Reynolds?"

"Some hired gun, got himself shot out at Ruggles Creek Park." His look grew stern. "Know where that is?"

"Of course I do," I answered, with a bravado I didn't exactly feel. It was falling into place. The other gunman, seeing his dead partner, must have called it in. Gave the license plate on my car, the only one in the lot. Made sense. Also made sense that whoever he was working for had enough clout to get the report processed so fast. Williams again?

Still, it was just dumb luck that I got nabbed so quickly, but that seemed to be what I was running on lately. Dumb luck. Dumb rotten luck.

But this complicated things. I wasn't sure how I could get out of this without bringing Deborah into it. Unless I figured out a way to implicate Williams. Well, that was a thought worth hanging onto.

"How's this gonna play, Mike? You know I didn't kill the guy."

"But you were there." It wasn't a question. "Maybe if you come clean with me, I can pull some strings." He shrugged. "Ain't going to be easy. Murder rap's a bit more serious than a parking ticket."

"I figured that. Would it help if I said I didn't do it?"

Mike grinned. "Well, it's a start." He shot his cuff, checked his watch, and said, "What were you doing there?"

"Meeting a client."

"That client?"

I nodded. "Getting fired by that client, actually."

"Why there?"

"Old times sake, maybe." I ignored his elaborate double take. "I don't know why. She picked the spot. She sounded pretty upset on the phone. Hell, Mike, the more I think about it the more it sounds like a setup. But it's a pretty elaborate setup. I mean, if they were looking to take me out, why would she be there at all? And then there's Howard."

"Howard?"

"Her bodyguard. He was holding them off."

"Them?"

"Yeah, there were two of them. I made a break, to see who they were after. One went after me. I guess Howard got the other one."

"How sure are you?"

"'Yeah, I got him. Didn't even break a sweat.' That's how sure."

"Howard said that?"

"Yeah, just before he threw me out of the car."

"Maybe you should start at the beginning," Mike suggested.

So I ran through it, even mentioning Deb's name. Technically she wasn't a client anymore, so I wasn't actually breaking any rules.

Mike stood up. "Well, there's nothing I can do about this tonight."

"I figured that."

"Look, Jim, I'll do what I can, but I can't promise anything."

"Maybe you can track down this Howard guy."

"Yeah, how'm I gonna do that? Big guy, ex-special forces, blood under his fingernails. Lotsa guys answer that description, except for the blood, and we gotta figure he knows how to use a bar of soap." He turned to go.

"You could pay a visit to Kendall Williams, I suppose."

Mike froze. "Now, why would I want to do that?" he asked with a touch of menace.

"Find out who Howard is."

"You think he works for Williams?"

"Hell, Mike, I don't know. But Williams' fingerprints are all over this case. All I know is Howard got pretty rattled when I told him to tell Williams I'd be talking to him."

Mike walked back over to the table. "Listen, Jim, you don't know what you're into. You got paid off, so leave it alone. I'm begging you, drop the case."

"What's going on, Mike?" I spoke softly, trying to get the import of the thing across to him. "You've been pushing me away from this from the beginning."

"Of course I have," he shouted. "Jesus, look at yourself. You're a fucking mess! Whaddid I tell you right from the start? Nothing good can come from this."

"Yeah, but what does that mean?"

"What does that mean? You're sitting there, face busted up, cracked ribs, black eye. You're in a goddamn jail for Chrissakes. That's what that means."

"But why, Mike? Why?" I raised my hands, palms up, like I was praying. "Why's this happening to me? What do you know that you're not telling me?"

He shook his head at me, sadly. "Why's this happening to you? 'Cuz you're washed up. You're out of practice. Your reflexes are too slow. Your instincts a

shot. Hell, buddy. I don't know why this is happening."
He came over, clapped a hand on my shoulder, a flash of a
grin when I winced reflexively at the contact. "But you've
got to let this go. You aren't thinking straight, and it's
gonna get you killed." He said it gently, so unlike his
usual sardonic self, it almost brought tears to my eyes.

"Maybe you're right, Mike." I slumped back down in
the chair. "Maybe I just got a little crazy. Seeing Deb
again, revisiting old memories."

"Like Sara."

I nodded sadly. "Yeah, like Sara. Earlier today I
actually thought she had some bearing on this case."

Mike shook his head in disbelief. "Why would you
think that?"

"Something Karin said, about Jon trying to track
down Mr. Big. That's the term you used back when I was
on Olly Jensen's trail."

A cloud crossed Mike's face. Just a hint of, what?
Panic? Fear? Doubt? So faint I almost missed it. Then he
shook his head, sadly this time. "Get some rest, Jim.
You've been through a lot." He headed for the door again.
"I'll call in some chits, try to get you out of here."

CHAPTER 10

Sometimes it's good to have a friend on the force. Next morning Mike showed up with the Watch Captain in tow. "I laid it out to Captain Greene," he announced. "No way you're a murderer."

"Let's just say the case is still open," Greene conceded. He shoved the envelope with my belongings at me.

"So I'm free to go?"

"For the time being." He splayed the release documents on the table. "Must be nice to have friends in high places."

I shot Mike a look but he deflected it with a quick head shake. So I signed the forms, waived counsel, and for good measure, promised not to press charges for police brutality. That seemed to satisfy Greene. Then we were out the door. Mike said we could get my car out of impound later, "But first you should get changed, before they bust you for a fugitive."

I was still wearing the orange jumpsuit. They had given me back my suit, but it lay in a rotten, rumpled, still-soggy heap at the bottom of a plastic bag.

"Friends in high places," I remarked. "You got more clout than I thought."

"That wasn't me, you idiot. I gave it a shot, but they were clamped down tight on your ass."

"Then who was it?"

Mike said, "Carmine."

"Carmine?"

"Yeah, your old buddy Fred Carmine. Seems your footprints keep showing up in some investigation he's running. You need to talk to him."

I said talking to him never did me much good, maybe I'd take a pass.

"I'm not the one telling you," Mike corrected. "If it were me, I'd say, stay away from the DA. You're off the case now, so let it drop."

"Maybe I should."

"Maybe it's too late for that," Mike countered. "His words were, 'I want Corcoran in my office before noon today.'"

I said I'd have to cancel my spa appointment.

Mike didn't laugh. He pulled over to the side of the road and turned to me. "Listen, you can't just go in cold. We gotta figure out how to play this."

"What do you mean, 'play this?' You think I need an attorney? Maybe I should hire Williams to represent me."

"Not funny, pal," Mike spat. "But Jim, you gotta think this through. I don't know what Carmine's working on, but odds are it's this case."

"Makes sense."

"So maybe you ought to play it close to the vest. Give him something—you know, a recap of your investigation—but no details. Just stick to the basics. You went to Jon's house, you got beat up. You snooped around, you got fired. You're off the case."

"Maybe I shouldn't be off the case," I suggested.

He pounded the steering wheel. "Jesus Christ, Jim! I

thought we settled this last night."

"Yeah, but if Carmine's looking into—"

"Shit. I should've left you in jail." Then, with a lighter tone, "Hell, I should arrest you right now for criminal stupidity."

I told him I got it. "Still, I can't help but think Deborah's in trouble. If you could've seen the way Howard bossed her around."

"Don't worry about Deborah. She's Mrs. Justin Wade, after all. She's part of the one percent. People in real trouble don't have bodyguards. People in real trouble run from bodyguards."

"Yeah, but she was scared," I insisted.

"Damn right she was scared. She'd just escaped from a gun fight. You think she'd ever been in one of those before?"

"So you think—"

"I think Howard had to get tough to keep control of the situation. I think he was smart enough to figure they weren't out of the woods yet, and he didn't want her doing something stupid. Then she would've been in trouble. Not to mention him."

"Could be." I tried to think it through. Sounded plausible enough. "I just hate leaving loose ends. What about the two guys who—"

Mike said they were dead, so just leave them alone. They were dead. Jon was dead. The case was dead, so just leave it alone. Cash that check and move on. "Tell you what, meet me at the Walloon around six. Buy me a couple drinks, and I'll give you all your loose ends wrapped neatly in a bundle."

I shrugged. If Carmine was on the case, he had resources way beyond anything I could muster. If there was justice to be done, let him do the heavy lifting for awhile. I was tired of getting my ass kicked.

When I told him maybe he was right, Mike put the car in gear and pulled back into traffic. Then he said I had a new enemy on the force.

"Who's that?" I wondered.

"That rookie cop who arrested you? Name's Henry Nelson. He's got a real hard on for you."

"How come?"

"You were his first collar. He was damn proud of it, too. Half hour from call to bust, it's the kind of thing legends are made of. Then your buddy Carmine comes along and screws it up. I just wouldn't break the speed limit if I were you. I mean, he's looking at you, hard. He's a real hot head, thinks he's Robocop or something."

"Yeah, he was a smug little bastard," I agreed.

"Sure, smug little bastard who put you back in the hospital."

"Well how 'bout I was blindsided? Maybe I shouldn't have signed that release."

"Forget it," Mike chuckled. "With your luck in court, you'd probably be convicted of being the 20th hijacker."

I washed up and changed at the flat. I was tempted to check the flashing messages on my answering machine, but Mike was waiting to drive me back to the impound lot. "You got enough for the fines?" he asked.

"Guess I'll use plastic," I replied. "I think I've got one that hasn't melted."

"You should use that kiss off and get out of debt," he suggested.

I thought it over. Maybe I should. Maybe it wouldn't be the most ethical thing I ever did, but what the hell. Maybe what I needed was to get back to even, start over again. Again.

By the time we reached the impound lot, I told Mike he had a deal. "Thanks again, buddy," I said. "See you tonight." I headed toward the office, with just a moment's pause at Mike's "No, *thank you*," flung at my back. Why the emphasis? Was he just expressing his relief that I was out of danger? Or was he out of danger?

As I approached the office, Henry Nelson, the one

who'd arrested me yesterday, was coming out the door. He faked a punch, and laughed when I flinched. "Tough guy, eh?" he sneered. I thought about giving him a little shoulder as he went past, but after Mike's warning, decided against it.

Got my car, muttering about the fees when I wasn't supposed to be there anyway. The clerk said, "Yeah, yeah, tell it to the judge." Thought it was funny, too. Easy to be a comedian, I guess, when you supply your own laugh track.

Before driving away, I thought to check under the seat again, see if the notebooks were still there. Figured I should do it before I left the impound lot, though if they'd taken them without leaving a note, they sure as hell weren't likely to give them back. For just a moment I thought maybe I'd be tipping them off by checking, but then figured, what the hell, I was off the case anyway. If somebody wanted them, I'd just hand them right over.

As I pulled out of the lot, I checked in the rear view mirror, just in case. Nobody there. I thought it over and decided, yeah, the case was definitely over. I deposited Deb's check. I wasn't proud, but I needed the money. I took a grand in cash. Ten crisp hundreds. Nothing like it, having money in your pocket. Then, on a whim, I rented a safe deposit box, and stuffed the notebooks inside. Maybe someday I'd pull them out. Like when I was ready to write my memoirs. Or pen them. I think that's how those literary guys talk.

Then I headed downtown to the Justice Building. Got there around 11:00, but they let me cool my heels awhile. Fred Carmine had been District Attorney for the past fifteen years. He was good at what he did, but he lacked that special something that would have let him rise in the criminal justice hierarchy. That special something called tact. Working in the cesspool that was Detroit, he broke some of the biggest cases in the history of the state, and if he took it to trial, he was going to win it.

The problem was, he didn't know when to shut up. He stepped on more toes than a drunken ballerina. A pity, too. He should have gotten some credit. He should be sitting in an office in Washington by now, way the hell up the DOJ ladder. They could use him there. He could be a prosecutorial role model. All the work he did, all the crimes he investigated, all the cases he tried, and there was never a whiff of scandal. His kind of justice was always clean.

Which had made it doubly odd that he hadn't given me the time of day ten years ago. Ordinarily he would have sunk his teeth into a case like that. Instead, he just let it drift away. I couldn't figure it out then, and I couldn't figure it out now. Maybe I'd ask him about it, if I ever got in there.

They finally summoned me at 11:58. I know, I'd been checking my watch every three minutes. At least I beat the deadline.

Carmine had a corner office, with one wall of windows overlooking what was left of downtown Detroit, and a nice view of the river out the other. He had a huge desk, and unlike other highly placed prosecutors, it wasn't spotless. Instead it was heaped with files and evidence boxes. He obviously still worked his cases. He didn't fob them off on his minions. Maybe that's why his work was so clean.

He bounded out of his chair as I entered, and came around the desk to pump my hand. Carmine was short, and barrel round, with a bald head and a wide, flat nose. His grip was fierce. He stayed in shape. I figured I could learn something from his example, and maybe I would as soon as I learned how to stay out of the hospital.

And jail, I reminded myself, as he came right to the point.

"Jesus, Corcoran, ten years on and you're still getting arrested?"

I shrugged. "Comes with the territory, I guess." I

paused, then gave him one. "Thanks for helping out."

He waved his hand dismissively. "Don't know exactly what went down out there, but no way you killed him. Maybe you can shed some light, though?" He let that dangle a second. When I didn't respond, he told me to sit, and retreated to his desk.

"So, what did happen?"

"I went to meet a client. She fired me. Somebody started shooting."

"Just like that, huh?"

"Yeah, just like that. I'd never seen them before, and I figure, being off the case, I'll never see them again."

He said I could see one of them if I wanted, "Downstairs, in the morgue."

I told him I would if he wanted me too, but it wouldn't do any good. "Like I said, I didn't know the guy. I don't even know if he was shooting at me, or at the client."

He hunched forward. "Why would anyone go after Deborah Wade?"

"Whoa, Fred. Who said anything about Deborah Wade?"

"I think it was me," he breezed. "Let me think. Yeah, it was definitely me."

"You're skating pretty close to the edge," I cautioned. "That's not like you."

"Oh, for Chrissakes, Jim. You said yourself she fired you."

"I said my client fired me. I didn't say who she was."

Carmine picked up a pen and tapped out an energetic beat on one of the files. Then he flipped it across the desk. "Okay, play it that way. I don't care." Then he grabbed one of the files off the desk. "But I do need to know what you've come up with. I mean, every time we get a lead, you've already been there, or you're walking into the middle of it. So how about it? Let's play on the same team. Whaddaya say?"

"What do I say?" I temporized. What do I say? Should I come clean? Sure, Mike said I should play dumb. It made sense at the time. Get out from under this case and move on. Otherwise, I was back in the middle of it, and maybe next time they wouldn't miss. One thing was clear, I didn't owe anybody. Except maybe Karin, but stillI didn't know what was going on with that.

"I don't even know what you're talking about," I said, settling on a strategy. "What are you running? Who's involved?"

Carmine frowned. "I don't know how much I can tell you," he began.

"Ditto."

That earned me a scowl. "Don't be coy with me, Corky, or I'll get that murder rap reinstated."

I tossed the scowl right back at him. "Tell you what," I said. "You don't call me Corky, maybe we can deal. You give me some names, maybe I can give you some back. Maybe we have the same names, maybe we don't. But I'm not sticking my neck out here. Been down that road one time too many."

He mulled it over. He sat there, deep in thought, staring down at the file folder. He sat there so long I thought maybe he'd forgotten me. Or he'd developed a case of narcolepsy. Finally, he glanced up, and choosing his words carefully, he said, "Maybe I should have listened to you back then, after Sara Jensen died..."

"Olly? He's still in play?"

"Back in play might be a better way to put it," he said softly.

I should have come clean right then. I should have dumped everything in Carmine's lap. Would've saved me a world of hurt if I had. Maybe things would have worked out differently.

But I didn't. If I had chosen to, I could have read his words as an apology. It was about as close as a DA's ever going to come to one. But I didn't do that, either. Instead, I got up. I leaned across his desk, and said, "Yeah, thanks for that, buddy. Thanks for listening, now. You want me to give you something? You figure out how to give me back the last ten years, then maybe I'll think about giving you something."

Then I was out the door. He could have stopped me. He could have had one of the uniforms drag me back in. Hell, he could have locked me up as a material witness. He didn't do any of that, though. He just let me go.

I ran some errands, bought a new suit to replace the Ruggles Creek Martyr, so it was almost three by the time I got back to the office. First thing I did was replay my messages.

First one was from Karin. She'd come by after work but I wasn't there. Call her? Ah yes, I'd kind of forgotten about her. I wondered what kind of loose end she was going to turn out to be. There was something there, I thought, and now that Sara'd been put to bed again, who knew where it might lead.

Second call, Karin. Not quite frantic. Maybe a little miffed. I thought I detected a subtle undercurrent of suspicion that I was out boozing it up again. "Not this time, sister," I said.

Next four, two hang ups, and two more from Karin.

Number seven, also Karin. About twelve hours ago. This time she finished, "I'm frightened. Please call–no matter how late, no matter how drunk you are."

That hurt. But there were still a few flashes from this morning. First one, Karin. "Jim, where are you?" Big emphasis on "are," the sign of a seriously pissed off woman. Oh well, have to deal with that later. The next three were business. Always a welcome sign. Two skip traces and a nasty little divorce.

Maybe things were looking up. I called and got the details. The skip traces were no brainers. I'd get them done before meeting Mike. I talked to Ben Wethers, the lawyer handling the divorce, found out what he needed.

Told me to talk to the wife, get a feel for the situation. I figured I could do most of it from my computer. Maybe a little stake out, if I couldn't figure out how he'd covered his assets. Looked like another 750 bucks, plus $250 each for the skip traces.

Last message was Karin, wooden voice, left ten minutes before I got home. Said she had to meet somebody, then she'd be home around 5:00. Call her. If I wanted to.

I would. I did. I had to let her know how things had played out. How played out I was. Working out the details in my head, I realized there were way too many still-unanswered questions, too many loose ends for Mike to tie together, pretty ribbon or not. Jeffries, for example. He could be a threat to Karin, or to Deb. Well, maybe not Deb. She had a bodyguard.

Shoving those thoughts aside, I turned to the computer, got a line on my two deadbeats, wrote up quick reports and e-filed them to the requesting agencies, with the promise of hard copies posted tomorrow. I worked up a game plan for Herman Gallup, the philandering soon-to-be ex. Money in my pocket, money in the pipeline. Things were definitely looking up. By then it was 5:30. Quick call to Karin, then off to the Walloon, if she'd let me.

I wasn't sure how this was going to play out. Might have to put Mike off for a night. Maybe I could buy some time, tell her I'd be out there around 8:00 or so, had some loose ends to tie up, then I'd tell her all about it.

No answer. What a waste of speculation. I told her to call my pager, and explained a bit of what had happened yesterday, without going into too much detail. That was better for a face to face, or face to train wreck, given the shape mine was in. Of course, that got me thinking about the details I was skimping over. Somebody out there wanted me dead. Why? Because I was on the case? But Deb was buying me off. Wouldn't that mean I was no longer a threat?

No, something wasn't adding up. Those guys, Gus the stiff and the other one, they represented some new angle, a different party. It was crazy. I no longer knew who Deb was, what her game was. According to Mike I didn't need to know. I was well out of it. I didn't owe her anything, certainly not any more of my blood. She'd dragged me in, somehow opened a can of worms, and now she wanted out. So be it. I was current on my rent.

Grabbing my coat, I headed out into the drizzle, headed for a reunion with good old Jack, and a tumbler of ice, and whatever package Mike was going to drop into my lap. A black Yukon was idling at the curb about halfway down the block. For a moment I thought it might be Deb. Maybe she'd changed her mind. Maybe she wanted me back on the case. I wondered if that meant I'd have to give her back the check.

I eyed the Yukon as I approached. You didn't see too many late model SUV's on my block. There was someone behind the wheel. A pretty big someone at that. Suddenly I started to think maybe I should go the other way around the block. Or maybe I forgot something back at the office. I could try calling Karin again. She sounded pretty upset earlier. Kid's probably worried sick. Yeah, that's what I'll do. Who needs Jack Daniels, anyway?

As I turned back, the Yukon clunked into gear. Figuring the worst that could happen probably already had, I continued at a steady pace toward my door. As I was reaching for my key the vehicle stopped right beside me. I told myself not to look. Then I told myself if I didn't look I was a coward.

I didn't look. I reached for the door. Not used to being a coward yet, though I'd gotten plenty of practice recently. Just give me a few days for all the hurts to stop hurting, I told myself, and whatever gods were listening. Then I'll go back to being a tough guy. Right now I just want to breathe without somebody sticking a knife in my lungs.

"Corcoran," the voice came.

I turned. It was Howard. He was climbing out from the driver's seat. "What're you doing driving Deb's car?" I wondered.

He chuckled. "S'not hers."

"So what do you want? I'm a busy man."

"Yeah, I can see that. Walking up and down in front of your building." He snorted. "What're you, on strike?"

"Forgot something. Had to make a phone call."

He reached for his cell phone. "So, use mine. You can call while we drive."

I didn't move. "Where're we headed?"

Howard shrugged. "Don't know. I could give you a lift, maybe."

Turning back toward my door, I said, "Thanks anyway, Howard. But it's a personal call."

"You don't think I can keep a secret, Corcoran? Now, that hurts my feelings." Howard's voice sounded awfully cheerful for someone with hurt feelings. I glanced over my shoulder. Sure enough, he was moving around the front of the Yukon, heading my way.

I turned to face him. "So what's it going to be? Kidnapping?"

He laughed. "Of course not, just doing a favor."

"Like I said, I don't need a lift anywhere."

"Oh, but I think you do." Howard unbuttoned his jacket, and flared out the left flap, just enough for me to catch a glimpse of his holster.

"It's like that, is it?"

"Yeah, 'fraid so." He shrugged. "Didn't have to be, if you'd play nice for once."

I weighed my options. I could call his bluff, force him to shoot me. Gunshot wound, that'd be a refreshing change from all the beatings. Then again, he wouldn't have to shoot me. I'd already seen enough of his strength. Or should I say felt? I glanced around, thinking maybe today I'd get lucky and there'd be a cop nearby.

Fat chance of that. I returned his shrug, and then I headed to the car. He opened the front door, which I thought was a nice gesture. "You wouldn't happen to be going past the Walloon Saloon, would you?"

Howard snorted. "That place still open? We used to call it the Ptomaine Palace back in the day."

"They've got a special going now. You get food poisoning, your next meal's free."

He glanced over at me, a grin on his face. "Probably could've gotten to like you, Corcoran."

Something about his valedictory tone made me feel squirrelly. "There's still time, Howard. I could buy you a beer and a plate of chili cheese fries, you could tell me old war stories."

"Enough new ones still being written, you ask me," he said by way of reply. He turned right and accelerated down the I-94 ramp.

"Where we headed?" I asked uneasily. Detroit may be crime-ridden and falling apart, but it seems bad things only happen to me when I leave the city limits.

"Little visit with an old friend of yours."

"We going to the cemetery?"

Another snort. "You don't quit, do you."

"I wouldn't know where to begin."

"Seriously, you don't know when to stop," he replied, the edge back in his voice.

"Actually, I did figure that one out."

"What's that mean?" He turned to face me, even while swerving around a slow moving car poking along just ten miles over the speed limit. Nobody pays any attention to speed limits in Detroit. Doing so would suggest you were law abiding, and that'd just make you a target.

"Means I'm off the case."

"Since when?"

"Since last night. Part of the deal that got me out of jail. Again."

He chuckled. "Yeah, heard about that. Those Detroit cops work fast, don't they?"

"So what's the deal?" I asked, suddenly tired of this charade. "Where are we going?"

"Mr. W says we should talk."

"Mr. W? As in Kendall Williams?"

"Got it in one. Like I said, you're one hell of a detective."

The rest of the drive passed in silence. I looked out the window at the littered embankment, and the roofs of houses poking over the edge of the ditch. We passed an overgrown golf course, a couple of abandoned motels, and a vacant strip mall. Depressing as ever, depressing as hell. I wasn't surprised when we took the Moross Road exit. Where else would Williams live but Grosse Pointe?

When I was growing up he wouldn't have lived there, not with his skin color. Back then it didn't matter how much money he made, or how much power he wielded. He wouldn't have been welcome, and he wouldn't have wanted to be there, even if he had been. Guess things had changed over the years, after all.

When you think of it, it was probably Butler Woods that set the change in motion. Funny, based on that article I read in one of Jon's notebooks, all those Grosse Pointe traditionalists had been right. Justin's condos had definitely changed the community. Only it didn't detract from the town's aura of exclusivity, it just changed its monochromatic hue. Butler Woods made Grosse Pointe modern. That old, staid community was once again where people wanted to live, and this time, if they could cover the mortgage, they could. Williams wasn't the first Black to move to Grosse Pointe, and he wouldn't be the last. But that didn't mean they were about to start erecting public housing, or busing kids in from the ghetto. And it was people like Williams who would make sure of that.

We took Moross to Kercheval, turned left, and drove past the flanks of the Country Club. Heading for

Provencal. Naturally. Where else would Williams live? Howard slowed at the guard house and flashed his ID. Provencal was where the really huge mansions were, which only the oldest names and the biggest balances called home. This was where the Perrymans, the Thurstons, the Herringbones and, damn it, the Wades lived. I guess Williams had really hit the big time.

As we passed the Wades' I wondered how Deb was faring. Was she home tonight? Maybe balancing her checkbook, trying to figure out how to cover up the check. I wondered if Justin was there. I wondered how much he knew. I wondered what in the hell was going on when Howard turned into the next driveway. Had Williams bought the Jensen mansion?

I hadn't been in the Jensen's house since the night Sara died. She'd called me, around ten p.m., on a windswept night with a steady rain ~~steadily~~ turning to snow. I'd been trying to reach her for hours, but she wasn't picking up. Even drove past her condo a couple times. No lights. No sign of life. Boy, I'd gotten that one right. I could've just let myself in. Had my own keys by then. I shook my head at the bitter irony. Seems you can't let sleeping dogs lie after all.

I'd gone home. Nothing else to do. I was at a crossroads in the case. I felt like I was this close to breaking through Olly's Chinese Wall. I was about to lay him wide open, naked to the world, like one of the strippers out on Eight Mile. But there were a couple more doors to get through. I thought maybe Sara might unwittingly hold a key. I needed to talk to her, but all I could do was wait.

When the call came she sounded rattled. No, she sounded scared to death. In fact, she sounded a lot like Deb had sounded yesterday. Now that was a coincidence I ought to file away. She said she was at the house. That was it. At the house. No need to give me an address. No need for an explanation, just she was at the house and she needed me. Now.

I got there as quickly as I could. In those days I wasn't driving a fifteen-year-old Oldsmobile, either. I tore through the suburban night in my Porsche 924, breaking all sorts of laws and speed records, and screeched to a halt in the driveway. I bounded up the steps to the door, ringing the bell and pounding on the heavy oak slab. When no one came, I tried the handle. It was unlocked and the door swung slowly open onto a darkened hallway. I entered, calling her name. She answered, her voice a strangled sob. "Jim. I'm up here."

I wasn't sure where up here was, but I took the steps on the circular staircase, two at a time, and landed in the wide, polished oak-floored second story hallway. "Sara?" I called.

"Down here!" Her voice was panic taut, you could play an "A" on it if you had a bow. I raced down the hall and burst into the room just in time to run into somebody's fist. I went down in a heap and woke to the roar of a gun. A kick to the gut, and whoever it was, was gone. I staggered to my feet, ready to go after him, when I heard her moan. I ran to the bed, where she lay with half her face gone. The bullet had entered just beneath her left cheekbone, her perfect cheekbone, shattering that china doll face. Her blood was flowing, staining the bedspread and pooling around the gun lying next to her head. I picked it up and tossed it across the room.

She was trying to say something, but I said, "No, baby, don't talk. Just lie still." It was hard to believe she was still alive. I picked up the phone and was calling 911 when I heard heavy footsteps pounding up the stairs. I was about to jump up and try to retrieve that bloody gun when she clutched at my sleeve. It was a terrifyingly fierce grasp she held on me, a shuddering, trembling, suddenly weakening grip. I cradled her head in my arms, and this time listened when she tried to speak. Her lips moved drily, distantly, and her one good eye was brimming with tears. My eyes moistened as I bent to kiss her lips as she gave me her last breath.

And then the cops were in the room, and I was thrown on the floor and tossed into the ashpit of hell.

The driveway was a narrow cobblestone lane, closely lined with fir trees and shrubs, whose needles and leaves brushed the windows of the burly SUV. After fifty yards or so, it opened up into a large, circular forecourt, with the obligatory fountain in the middle. There were three other vehicles there, two more black Yukons, and a gray Lexus which I figured was Williams'.

When Howard pulled up in front of the house the door opened and a guy who looked like his twin came down to open my door. "He's waiting," he said, more to Howard than to me.

"He's waiting?" I said. "I hope you didn't ruin the surprise."

Howard sniggered. I could tell he was warming to me. "Don't worry about that, shitheel." Okay, maybe warming was a bit optimistic.

I walked inside, Howard on one side, the other guy on the other. "You got a name?" I said to the one on my right. "Or should I call you Howard Two?"

His tight little smile said as long as he had to take my shit, he would. But the minute he was free, watch out.

We walked down the long, dark corridor, past the staircase, and turned left into the living room. It was deep and wide, about twenty by thirty, with a sixteen foot ceiling. Lined with polished oak, with heavy, brooding oils on the walls. Ancestors, by the look of them. Not Williams', but somebody's. There was a fire crackling in the oversized hearth, with four armchairs gathered around it. Little cherrywood side tables stood between them, one of which held a drink.

Williams sat in one of the chairs, next to the fire, impeccably dressed in grey wool slacks and a v-necked sweater over a light blue Oxford shirt. His tasseled loafers reflected the fire glow. He nodded at my book ends, and they released my arms.

"Mr. Corcoran, what a pleasure to see you again," he said easily while motioning to the chair across from him. "Won't you sit down?"

I glared at him. "No, I don't think I will," I snarled. "Sort of a personal thing with me. I don't like to get too friendly with my kidnappers. Helps ward off that Stockholm Syndrome."

"Stockholm Syndrome?" Williams' laugh was gentle and easy, and as far as I could tell, genuine. Maybe it showed he was a genial soul. Or maybe it was just an indication of how much in control of the situation he was. "Well, Mr. Corcoran. I can see you're feeling better." He gestured at the chair again, and asked, "What makes you think you've been kidnapped?"

I could've come up with a half dozen reasons, or I could have accepted his hospitality. But frankly, I wasn't in the mood. I didn't feel like saying anything, or doing anything, except covering the space between us in two steps, leaping upon him, my two hands locked around his scrawny neck, and squeezing the life out of him. And I would have, if Howard and Howard Two hadn't reattached themselves to me before I got half a step into my charge.

"Easy, killer," Howard said genially. "Why don't you have a seat like Mr. Williams says? Behave yourself, maybe you can even have a drink."

"Yes, of course," Williams interjected. "Where are my manners? What will you have? Jack Rocks?"

Good old Jack. Nothing like it to ease into a conversation with Mr. Big. That much I'd figured out.

What I ought to do is refuse. Show that bastard I can't be bought. Show him he can't kill me with kindness. On the other hand, what I was getting from these guys was they were going to kill me anyway. With kindness or guns or their bare hands, I didn't know, and I'm sure they didn't care. So I might as well have a taste, something to remember life by on my long slide into hell.

So I sat. I sat and I waited for Howard Two to bring me my drink. I wasn't exactly proud of myself, but then again, it had been about a decade since I had been.

When it came, I took a big gulp, and let me tell you, it tasted good. I took another swallow, this one more modest, more becoming of a man who knows how to hold his liquor. In your left hand, I always say. That way your right's free to shake hands.

"Well, Mr. Corcoran," Williams began easily after my fidgeting subsided. "You're a hard man to dissuade, I'll grant you that much."

"Yeah, I've heard that." I jerked a thumb at Howard. "That's what your muscle here keeps telling me."

"Sometimes, maybe, listening wouldn't be such a bad thing."

"Okay, so I'm listening now," I shot back. "But I'm not hearing anything."

The attorney gazed coolly at me. "That's because I'm trying to figure out how much to tell you."

"Well, it's a bit of a cliche, but why don't you start at the beginning," I offered. "Don't worry, I'll let you know if I'm getting bored."

"Oh, you won't be bored, I can assure you." He laughed easily again, as if he were having the time of his life. As opposed to the time of my life. "The question is, how much do you need to know? How much—"

"How much do I—"

"Do you need to know," he repeated, talking over my indignation. "And how much can I tell you without putting you in jeopardy?"

"Since when are you concerned with my safety?" I demanded. "Maybe you should have given that some thought before you sent your thugs after me yesterday."

"See, that's exactly the kind of blowback I've been trying to avoid," he replied in such a reasonable tone that I wanted to believe him.

"You mean it wasn't you?"

Howard snorted in the background. "Jesus, Corcoran."

"That's enough, Howard," Williams said sharply. "Why don't you and Rafe go check the perimeters?"

"But what about—"

"Don't worry, I can handle him." As soon as Howard was gone, Williams' tone changed. He became more abrupt, more urgent. "Listen, Corcoran. Things are starting to happen, and happen quick. Yeah, I tried to keep you out of it. I've got too much time invested in this to have some amateur start mucking around—"

"What do you mean amateur?" I demanded. You can kick me, hit me, point a gun at me. Put me in the hospital or put me in jail. But don't go questioning my professionalism. I've spent too much time in front of the State Review Board to take that lying down.

Williams raised his hands placatingly. "Okay, wrong choice of words. What I meant was, you were mucking around in something you didn't understand."

"Yeah, well, that's an understatement."

"Exactly."

"So what was I mucking around in?"

He scrunched forward in his chair, the firelight capturing the glittering energy in his eyes. "I've been working with Jon Wade for the last two years, trying to crack open the whole Detroit drug trade. Look, you know the City's a shithole, right?"

"How could I not?" I live in it after all. "But what's that got to do with—"

"Poverty breeds crime and crime breeds poverty.

Detroit would be bad enough without the drugs, but the drugs make it that much worse. So the question is, where do they come from?"

"Mexico, Venezuela, Afghanistan," I ventured. It wasn't a tough one. Anyone who'd ever watched "60 Minutes" knew the answer to that one.

"Of course, everyone knows where they come from," Williams conceded. "But how do they get here? I mean, why is Detroit ground zero for America's drug scourge?"

I shrugged. "I figured it was just because of the poverty. Like you were saying."

"Sure, that's part of it. There are always going to be drugs in a city like Detroit. But the numbers, Mr. Corcoran. They don't add up. There are too many drugs here. Too many lives being torn upside down, and it's been like that for years."

"And the cops can't keep a lid on it."

"Can't? Or won't?"

"You mean you think—"

"I mean I know," he shot back, thumping his chest. "I know it in here." A tap to the head. "And here. I just can't prove it."

Taking a sip of my drink, I slumped back in my chair. So Williams is a good guy? How does that square with what Mike called him, the invisible perp? According to Mike, Williams is as dirty as they come. If anything, I would have bet he was the one behind Detroit's drug problem. Now he says he's trying to fight it?

"So why try to run me off? Why not fill me in, let me help?"

"Who are you? Can I trust you?"

"What the hell's that supposed to mean? You think I'm involved?"

Williams shook his head. "No, I mean, when you first showed up, ransacking Wade's condo. What was I supposed to think?"

"I thought you and Karin were tight though, through

Jon."

"Ms. Champagne's another story altogether," Williams said ~~with some asperity~~. "Let's keep to the subject at hand." *sharply*

"Which is what? Drugs? Or Wade? Or what am I doing in the middle of it?"

Chuckling lightly, he said, "Yeah, something along those lines." He got up and headed for the wet bar in the corner. "Going to freshen this up. Yours okay?"

I don't know who was more surprised, him or me, when I said I was fine.

Drink in hand, Williams returned to his seat. "Two years ago Jon Wade came to me with a proposal. After a lifetime of substance abuse, he was on the mend. 'It's time to work out my salvation,' he said."

"The more I learn, the less I ever knew about the guy," I observed.

"No, you knew him exactly right," Williams countered. "Wade was everything you ever thought he was. I should know. I spent half my billable hours keeping him from destroying Justin's career. Which is why I was so completely blind-sided by Wade's proposal. He wanted to figure out where the drugs were coming from, and put a stop to it. 'This stuff doesn't happen in a vacuum,' he said. 'Somebody's bankrolling it, and somebody's making a fortune.'"

"Yeah, I would've put good money on it being you."

Williams snorted his reply, and got up to put another log on the fire. "Why me?" he wondered, positioning the log with the poker.

"Oh, hell, lots of things. The way you mysteriously showed up at the hospital."

"I should have thought you would be grateful."

"Yeah, I was. But it didn't add up. I mean, why you? Guy like you doesn't go around doing pro bono work on weekends."

"Obviously, I was there at Ms. Champagne's request,

and out of consideration for Jon—our history."

"And to keep the brother's name out of it," I added.

"Of course. The man's a good client."

"Okay, it makes sense, in light of what you're telling me," I conceded. "But why confiscate the evidence?"

"You mean the materials the woman gathered?"

"Yeah, the woman," I said sarcastically. "Ms. Champagne. Karin. Somehow, I get the idea you don't like her."

"Don't trust her, would better describe my attitude."

"What's not to trust?"

Williams suggested, ever so gently, that perhaps my judgement was slightly skewed by emotion. I didn't care for that, and I let him know it. Especially in that house. It was just tacky as hell. On the other hand, what did I know about Karin, other than the little mouse scurrying around in my brain whenever she was near? "So you took the stuff to keep it out of her hands," I concluded.

"Yes, that, and frankly, within the context of my previous remarks, your hands too." He smiled placatingly, and I shrugged, as if to say, "Yeah, I get it."

"Plus, I needed to know what was in it," he continued. "Jon called me the night he died. He said he had cracked the puzzle. He was cackling, bizarre as that might sound. Said he'd cracked the puzzle, and was I going to be pissed off at what he found."

"He didn't tell you?"

Williams shook his head. "Not then, and of course, he never had a chance to do it later. I told him to be careful. I—"

"There was nothing you could've done," I said, to allay what looked an awful lot like survivor's guilt. "I guess no matter how much he changed, he was still impulsive."

A sad smile. "Yeah, that sums him up. Impulsive." He sighed, then continued. "Jon said not to worry. Even if something happened to him, he had all the evidence we needed to put the guy away for a long time." A shrug, then, "After he was—gone, I waited, thinking maybe he'd put something in the mail. When nothing came, I headed out to his place. Got there just as the ambulance was pulling away. Ms. Champagne was there, rather upset if you want to know. Tears, sobbing, the whole nine yards."

"I told her to get out of there," I complained.

"As I suggested, perhaps there is an issue of trust," Williams observed coolly. "Anyway, I walked her to her car after the police finished with her."

"She talked to the cops?"

"She had no choice, really, at least not once she returned to the condo."

"Returned?"

Williams nodded. "She'd put the evidence in her car, she told me. Then, unable to resist, she returned to the condo, she said, to make sure you were okay."

"And ran into Andy Parsons."

"Yes, your old friend was still securing the premises. I've seen a lot of pompous buffoons in my time, but let me tell you, Parsons is in a class of his own." Williams tossed a grin my way, and added, "Even if I weren't already involved in the case, I might have shown up to pry you away from him, just on general principle."

I conceded that Parsons didn't seem to be mellowing with age.

"That is an understatement. He was adamant about keeping me out. He kept going on about keeping the crime scene secure, for the CSI team, he said. I think he watches too much TV."

"Well, they don't get a lot of chances for real police work out here, do they?"

"Certainly not when you're not around," Williams murmured. "I'm sorry, that was a cheap shot," he replied to the look on my face.

"What possessed you to buy Olly Jensen's place, anyway?" I asked, hoping to get a shot of my own in.

"I got a good price," Williams said mildly. "But that's another story. Let's finish this one first."

I agreed, adding that I assumed Parsons hadn't let him into Jon's condo.

Williams shook his head, sadly. "Nope. Locked up tighter than a drum. For all I know, everything left inside is buried in some evidence lockup."

"Except for what Karin got."

"Except for that, and I must say, she did a pretty thorough job, especially considering how upset she was."

"I still don't see why you don't trust her. I mean, she handed over everything to you, didn't she?"

"Did she?" he countered. "All I know is she handed over everything she said she had."

"Judging from her reaction when I found out what she'd done, I figure you got it all."

"But we're still missing the crucial evidence." Williams hunched forward in his chair, reaching out to me, pleadingly. "Don't you see, Corcoran, if we don't find it, Jon will have died in vain."

"But what can I do?"

"You've got to find it."

"I don't even know what I'm looking for."

"I think you do. I think you've been looking for it for at least the last ten years."

"The last ten— What do you—" I slumped back in my chair. No. It couldn't be, could it? "This have to do with Olly?"

Williams shrugged again. "Who knows? But I think he's a good place to start."

"That mean you're hiring me?"

He chuckled. "Sure, why not?" Rising, he added, "Need a retainer?" He headed for the door before I could tell him no. "Will $5,000 be enough?"

Okay, so maybe I wouldn't tell him. Funny how, after years of scraping by, suddenly everybody was throwing money at me.

He came back with the check, and we got down to business, trying work out a game plan. Trying to figure out who might have the evidence, what form that evidence might take, and the best way to go about retrieving it.

"I still think this Champagne woman holds the key," he insisted. "Maybe she doesn't even know she knows what she knows, but that's where you need to begin."

Right on schedule, my pager went off, the beeping blotting out the discordant memory of my once thinking the same thing about Sara.

"You really need a cell phone, Mr. Corcoran. No one carries pagers anymore."

"No one but doctors, and private eyes who can't afford phones," I replied as I checked the number. "But right now, I need to borrow yours. Or a land line. This is a call I need to take."

CHAPTER 11

Williams offered his office, in case I needed privacy. Given his feelings about Karin, I thought that would be a good idea. She picked up on the first ring.

"Oh, God, Jim. Where have you been?" Her voice was shrill, more frightened than angry, but angry enough as it was. I told her I'd explain it soon enough, but what was the matter?

"It's my apartment. They were here–oh, it's horrible."

"Who was? What's wrong?"

"Somebody was here," she replied, in a suddenly calm, clinical voice, as if the professional had taken over. "They searched the place. They weren't tidy, either. Everything's jumbled, oh, and they broke all the picture frames. Even the ones of Jon–they tore them up." Her composure didn't last long.

"Listen, Karin. I'm not far away. I'll be there as quickly as I can."

Williams, upon hearing the news, didn't hesitate. "I'll have Howard run you over," he decided. Then, leveling a cool gaze at me, he said, "Looks like I'm not the only one who suspects her."

I returned the gaze, adding, "I don't want anything to happen to her."

"Not this time, eh?"

"Maybe you should tell me exactly what you know about Sara Jensen," I said, stepping toward him. Naturally, Howard chose this moment to make his appearance. Taking my arm he said, "What is it with you, Corcoran? Always picking fights—and you know you're not very good at it."

I shook his hand off my arm. "I was just asking a question," I jutted my chin at Williams. "It's still out there."

"In due time," Williams replied with an easy grin. God, I'd like the chance to wipe that smugness off his mug. "But right now, I think there's a white horse you're supposed to be mounting."

"You mean I don't get to ride in the Yukon this time?"

Williams laughed, and I joined him. What the hell, he was a client now.

Then we were gone. Howard didn't have much to say, especially after I let him know we were playing on the same team now. No dust up tonight. It took about fifteen minutes for us to get there. Traffic was light. Not surprising for 8:30 on a drizzly Tuesday night. I thanked him for the ride, and then I was out the door.

The Eastpointe cops were just finishing up. Unlike Detroit, where you had to make a reservation a month or two ahead of time to get a house call on a B & E, Eastpointe police lived for this kind of excitement. When I got to the door a detective was handing Karin his card, and assuring her they'd do everything they could to get to the bottom of this one. After a brief exchange with me, during which he acknowledged recognizing my name, or notoriety, I wasn't sure, he made his exit.

A moment later she was in my arms. Again. And

crying. Again. This time there were a hell of a lot of conflicting thoughts and emotions. Williams' words stuck in my head, and then there were those doubts that I'd already been wrestling with.

On the other hand, there was the feeling I got holding her like that. It was a feeling a lot like, whaddaya call it? Love? Maybe love. Maybe I just wanted her to check my bandages again.

But no, there was business at hand. This time I wasn't the taker. This time I had to be the one in charge. I gave a low whistle as she led me inside. They did a number all right. It looked a lot like Jon's condo, but we knew there were different perps this time. "You checked the place out? Is anything missing?"

"I don't know. I—oh, who can tell?" She had done some cleaning. Much of the debris was assembled into piles. I wasn't sure she should have done that. She said the detective had said the same thing, but she just couldn't stand the mess. There was still plenty of work to do, though.

We moved slowly through the place, one room at a time. There weren't that many rooms, just the kitchen, living room, and her bedroom. And the bathroom, which was totally trashed. They had ripped up the shower curtain, and emptied all her soap bottles, and the cornucopia of liquids and gels women put on their hair. The toothpaste tube was emptied on the floor.

In the kitchen, they'd cleared everything out of the cabinets; dishes, cups and saucers, all shattered on the floor. Karin knelt next to the pile she'd swept, to pick up a shard from a teacup. "This was my grandmother's," she sniffed, before letting out a gasp. "Oh my God, no!" she cried, springing to her feet and racing into the living room. I followed, and found her on her knees, in front of the sideboard. She flung the door open, and sighed in relief at the set of fine china still intact. "These were my mother's," she said quietly. "It's pretty much all she left me after she died."

There was no reason I should have known that her mother had died early, too, but it somehow seemed expected. I asked how it had happened. She shrugged. "Car accident. She and my Dad had a fight, and she stormed off. This was at our cottage, on Lake Michigan. It was raining, and she lost control of the car." She shook her head, sadly. "It was my junior year at Michigan when it happened. I guess my Dad blamed himself. I suppose he never really got over it."

"To this day?"

She shrugged again. "I don't know. I haven't seen him in years. He just drifted away. Didn't even come for my graduation."

I knelt beside her, and offered my arms. She moved into them, and I held her, more gingerly than I wanted, ever conscious of my still tender ribs. She started crying again, and I let her. She needed to let it out, but still, we needed to finish the post mortem. After she settled down, I asked the question I should have asked first.

"What did you tell the cops?"

"Nothing, really," she replied. "I thought I'd let you decide what to do." And then, for the first time, she looked at me. "Good Lord, Jim. What happened to you this time?"

I filled her in, gave her the short version, skipping over the whole shootout in the woods chapter. Maybe we'd get there someday. But first, we had to figure out why she'd been searched, and what she might have had that somebody wanted. I helped her to her feet, and led her to the couch. Together we swept the trash, the ripped up magazines and books from the cushions. Then I sat with her.

"Why would someone do this?" she wondered.

"What do you think?"

"It must be about Jon," she decided. "I don't know why, but what else could it be?"

"Did he leave anything with you?"

"Other than the box?" Her face instantly assumed the same kicked-in expression I was sure mine held, and we jumped up and ran for the closet. Naturally, it was gone.

"Was that it? Was that what they wanted?" she wondered.

"You honestly never looked inside?"

She shook her head. "No, Jon said not to, so I didn't." She gazed up at me. "We couldn't function without mutual trust. That was so important to him."

"Okay," I gave her. "But that doesn't really answer the question. Did he give you anything else to hold onto?"

No, there was nothing. Only what was in the box. That didn't help, but I had one more card left to play. "Do you know if he added anything to it just before he died?"

She thought it over. "I don't think so," she said hesitantly, then suddenly, "But he did ask me about it, where I kept it. That would have been last—Tuesday? Tuesday or Wednesday."

"Damn," I muttered.

"What is it?"

"It might be the key. Williams said he was working with Jon, trying to—" Karin's derisive snort cut me short. She'd never struck me as the type of woman to snort, but she gave a convincing performance. "Something the matter?" I asked.

"Jon working with Williams? That doesn't make sense."

"Why not?"

"Well, I wouldn't say he hated him, but there was no love lost between them." She said she thought it was because of his brother.

"Yeah, Williams said he spent a lot of time cleaning up after Jon," I offered.

"Stabbing Jon in the back is more like it," was her bitter retort.

"How so?" She took a step closer to me, crossing that

boundary where the electricity started again. I wanted to reach out to her, to hold her again, and feel her body against me. It was insane. We were dealing with murder, betrayal, and a series of intertwined mysteries. There was danger both implicit in the case, and explicit in the disarray in her apartment, yet here I was acting like a thirteen-year-old. I led her back to the couch. This time I took the chair.

"Jon kept a notebook on him," she announced. "He showed it to me once. There were injunctions, restraining orders, threatening letters. It was like Justin was trying to pretend Jon didn't exist, and was using Williams as his eraser."

Yet another notebook. That was interesting. I wondered if he had one on Karin, and what it would say. But as for the one in question, "Actually, that kind of squares with what Williams said, that half his billable hours were spent trying to keep Jon from destroying Justin's career. It makes sense when you think of it."

She couldn't argue, but I could see she didn't want to let go of her hostility.

"It's funny," I remarked. "That first day, when I met Williams at the hospital, I thought you two were allies, and you were keeping me on the outside. Now it seems you don't trust him any more than he trusts you."

Karin said at first "Ken told me to hold you at arm's length. He said we didn't know anything about you, what your motives were, who you were working for."

"Except that you both knew about Deb."

"Yeah," she said, shaking her head, a curious disconnect between words and action which has always intrigued me. "But Ken said he didn't really know whose side she was on."

I did a double take. Whose side she was on? "I wonder what he meant by that."

"From a couple of his comments, and things Jon said, I gathered that their marriage wasn't doing that well."

"Well, good for her," I said, and laughed at her bemused expression.

"You're still not over her, are you."

"Hell, Karin, I don't know," I confessed. "But I don't feel like talking about Deborah Wade right now."

She laughed lightly, a good sign considering the wreckage surrounding us. "But what about you?" I pursued. "Made up your mind about me?"

"Made up my mind?" she asked, startled, like a Senator caught telling the truth. "About what?"

"Whether you can trust me. I mean, you're not holding back now, right?"

"Oh, that—the case, you mean." A hint of blush began tinging her cheeks. She toyed with the edge of a tattered Afghan draped over the back of the sofa. Then she looked up, straight into my eyes. "No, I'm not holding anything back now."

The ambiguity was oppressive, and from my perspective, it was totally out of place to be playing these games. We had work to do. Maybe we couldn't make progress on the case—I had the feeling what I needed was hidden in that box—but at the least we had to find out if anything else was missing. Who knows, maybe something else would trigger another revelation.

We continued to inventory her possessions. There weren't very many. The spartan aspect of her living room, which I'd noticed that first visit, wasn't just for show. That was the way she was. "I never cared that much for things," she explained. "They just don't mean anything to me."

Before long we were finished, and we concluded that the box was all they'd taken. Which confused her. "What could possibly be in there that would make somebody trash my apartment? And why would they anyway? I mean, wouldn't you check closets first? And if that was what they were looking for, why keep going?"

"This is way beyond search and destroy," I agreed. "Cops'll do that sometimes, if they have a search warrant, and they don't like the suspect. They're none too careful about what they break and what kind of mess they make. But they'd never do something like this. This is personal. This is insane. The big question is, why?"

"I don't know, I don't know, I don't know."

"Could it be a patient? Somebody you couldn't help, or wouldn't help, or thought you had helped? Somebody who slipped a gear and blamed you for it?"

She thought it unlikely. "I don't deal with the mentally ill," she explained. "More just substance abusers and the like. Usually the only ones they hate are themselves."

"And they're the only ones they're likely to hurt?"

"Exactly."

"Which leaves us nowhere," I decided. "But somebody's got it in for you." After a moment I had an idea. "What about Jeffries? If he dislikes you as much as you—"

She cut me off with a shake of her head. "It couldn't have been him. I'm positive."

"How can you be so sure?" I asked, wondering if they were somehow involved. Maybe the whole hostility act was a red herring to throw me off their scent. Keep me suspicious of him, and keep him well-hidden, and I would never suspect anything between them. Then she gutted that theory with a confession.

"I was meeting with him when it happened."

"I thought I told you to stay away from him."

"Well, he wanted to meet, and you had, if you recall, disappeared for two days. What was I supposed to do?"

I had to give her that one. It wasn't really my fault, but it's hard to rely too heavily on somebody who keeps finding himself in a hospital or in jail. Still, Jeffries. She was playing with fire. "What did you talk about?"

She said he was scared. He was looking to clear out. Things were getting too hot. "You should have seen the look on his face when I asked him about the crack house.

He said he had nothing to do with it."

"I wonder how that happened?" I said. "Mike was pretty sure about it. I mean, it's not the kind of thing you do by accident."

"Well, he doesn't want to pursue it. He said, 'That's just one more reason to get out.' Plus, he's pretty sure his phone's bugged, and I figure as tech-savvy as he is, he ought to know."

"Any idea who that might be?"

"He didn't say, just that he wasn't going to sit around waiting for the second shoe to drop."

"Did he mention any names? Anybody at all?"

She shook her head. "Just Ken Williams, but that's ancient history."

"Not to me."

She shrugged. "What's there to tell?"

That got me started. I didn't want to believe it, but maybe Williams had reasons not to trust her. "What's there to tell? He waltzes in, takes all the evidence we picked up at Jon's place, then stonewalls me. Seems to me there's a lot to talk about."

She looked at me as if she'd been betrayed. Maybe she had been, but her sudden coyness had gotten my hackles up. "I don't know anything," she said flatly.

I tossed a shrug at her. "Maybe not, but you at least know what Jeffries said about him."

She got up from the couch and started gathering the scattered papers. I resisted the urge to help. This was no time to change the subject. She tidied for awhile. I waited. Finally she sighed and said, "He said he's frightened."

"Of what?"

"Of what he might do," she answered petulantly.

"And what might that be?"

Back to cleaning. This time I decided to help. "Where do you keep your garbage bags?" I asked, heading for the kitchen.

"In the cabinet below the sink," she answered, a little

life back in her voice.

I brought out the box, and together we started on the living room. She kept a running commentary on the books and other items she was discarding, telling me why she'd kept that particular textbook or novel, with the constant refrain of her disbelief at the disarray. There wasn't much I could say to comfort her. In fact, the more time we spent cleaning, the more concerned I grew. This was disturbingly personal.

I asked her if there had been some other man in her life she hadn't mentioned.

"Not since I was 22," she said.

"Three years seems like a long time to hold a grudge."

Grudging was a good description of her smile. "Do you ever not flirt?" she asked.

"How was I flirting?" She shrugged aimlessly. "You mean you're not 25?"

This time her smile came more naturally, and she stepped over and gave me a little hug. I resisted the urge to hang on. "Thanks for trying," she said, before heading toward the bedroom.

I helped her unfurl the crumpled sheet left on top of the bed, then froze at her gasp. The mattress had been slashed open, not once but several times. Long gaping wounds in the fabric, the stuffing puffed out like frozen white blood. "Why? Why?" she repeated.

Still stunned by the violence, we turned it over. It looked good enough at least for tonight, though I thought it more likely we'd go to my place for the night. Or maybe a hotel. I could afford it now. I was flush with cash.

"It might be a little lumpy, but it should do for one night." I stopped abruptly, realizing in my tone was the assumption that I would be there, too. She mouthed her agreement, either oblivious to or acquiescent in my assumption, I wasn't sure. But I helped her spread the sheet over the corners, and tucked the ends under the

162

mattress. The top sheet next, and then the comforter, miraculously spared the vandal's knife. Then she pulled a couple teddy bears out from under the bed, and tossed them on top.

"Twenty-five," she said, abashedly acknowledging her toys as she passed, heading no doubt to the kitchen. I grabbed her arm instead, and pulled her to me. She came as if hurled there, her lips open to my own as I began to kiss her with an uncalculated frenzy. Her tongue was in my mouth, her fingers snarled in my hair, and my passion mounting like a thing possessed.

And then we were apart, my hands to my face. We had gotten too close, too fast, and my nose had pressed against her cheek. The pain was excruciating. It buckled my knees and I sat heavily on the just made bed.

"Oh, poor baby," she said. "I forgot."

"So did I," I answered huskily.

She pushed me gently onto my back, and undressed me. Then standing before me, she removed her own. Her body had the ripeness and plumpness of voluptuous womanhood. She stood before me, not quite embarrassed, but not entirely comfortable, either, her left arm drawn up, her fingers curling strands of hair behind her neck while her right rested on her belly.

I opened my arms to her and she came. She lay beside me, cautiously, and stroked my hair while gazing into my eyes. "I don't know where to touch you," she whispered. "I don't want to hurt you."

I told her there was one place where I knew it would be safe. She chuckled, deep in her throat, and ran her hand down my body. She guessed right, and grasped me. I grew hard and suddenly wanted her with a passion that astonished me. She responded to my sudden urgency, and mounted me. We rocked and moaned and gasped and groaned, and all too quickly, it was finished.

She collapsed next to me, and pulled the comforter on top, and we snuggled awhile as first time lovers ought

163

always to. It was enough to share gentle kisses and promises of what the next time would be, and the next, and who would do what to whom and when. Still, despite the intimacy, and the fruition of the plan that had been born unbidden from the moment I first saw her, I knew we had unfinished business, and I knew, despite my deepest desire to postpone it, that it wouldn't wait.

I rolled onto my side, and we lay there, face to face, our bodies learning each other's contours and finding our comfort zones. I told her in a few days the ribs would be better, and she could see what my nose looked like in its natural state.

She said, "I remember, from the time we met. Can you believe it was only Saturday?"

"You liked what you saw?"

She snorted. "You staggered through the door. God, you were so drunk. I remember thinking, 'This guy's supposed to help me?'"

When I asked why she didn't throw me out, she replied with a sluttish grin, "Because you were so damn good looking."

"You did a good job of concealing it."

"It's what I do," she replied solemnly. "Conceal things. It goes with the job."

I wanted to tell her she did a good job of revealing with me, but she'd given me my opening, and it was time to go back to work. I agreed with her instead. I told her she had done nothing but conceal things from me, almost from the moment we'd met.

I felt her stiffen against me, and tried caressing her back to complacency. It didn't work. "Was this just part of your investigative technique?" she asked icily?

I protested that it wasn't. I didn't work that way— most of the time, I hedged, silently. I said I hadn't planned on it, but I'd wanted it, "From the moment I saw you, your face blotched from emotion, your eyes red from tears, tangled hair and naked feet, I wanted you. I wanted you like I never wanted anybody, ever before."

"Even Deb?" she asked softly.

"Even Deb. She was the first, and really the only for the longest time. I thought she always would be, until—"

"Until Sara?"

I pulled away from her. I sat up, and stared. "How'd you know about Sara?"

She stared back, startled by my reaction. "Ken told me—when we were waiting at the hospital—he said it was one of the reasons not to trust you."

I shook my head. "Sara was—I don't know—I keep fighting her memory, ever since I met you. I—"

"Since you met me?" She scrambled onto her knees. I couldn't help but drink in her body. "What do I have to do with—"

"I know," I almost whined it. "That's what I keep insisting. You're nothing alike. Nothing. You don't look like her. You don't act like she did, except, except the way you jumped into the case."

"Are you saying I shouldn't have?"

I gestured around the room. "Look what happens when you get involved." I reached for her hands and she came willingly to me. I held her, and buried my face in her hair, and breathed deeply of her scents. "I can't help thinking, if only I'd kept Sara at arm's length, she'd still be alive. And when you wanted to go with me out to Jon's condo, I told myself that. I told myself not to let you come." I kissed her gently on her eyelids, and said, "I don't want you to get hurt."

She said, "Nor you, either." Then, lying back on the bed, she drew me down beside her, and just like that we were back to companionable intimacy. "But what if I hadn't gone with you that night?" she murmured. "Who would have saved you?"

"I wouldn't have gone then if it weren't for you. And there wouldn't have been anybody there the next day."

"But all the evidence would have been gone," she

insisted.

"All the evidence is gone," I replied. She sighed her frustration, and then we simply snuggled awhile. And then we touched each other with more purpose. Then the playground was open again, and the children frolicked on the swings and the slides, and played tag, and capture the flag, and ring around the rosie, until we both fell down. And then I watched her shower, and then she gave me a bath, and then we got dressed and addressed the traffic wreck of her apartment.

CHAPTER 12

Next morning Karin dropped me at my office on her way to the Detroit Medical Center, where she worked at the Psych Clinic two days a week. We were both a little groggy, having stayed up until nearly three putting her apartment back together. Still, I was amused at the whole suburban-commuting-couple effect of it all, she dressed smartly in her calm, collected, professional costume, and me in my usual heading-to-the-Walloon mismatched casuals.

Speaking of the Walloon, Mike called last night, around 11:30, in his cups and wondering where I'd been. I gave him the abridged version, though not abridged enough because he went ballistic when I mentioned Williams' name. "What the hell you doing, Jim?" he stormed. "Didn't I tell you to stay away from him?"

"Not a lot of choice, Mike. Howard dropped by and asked me politely to come out for a visit."

"And you went along? Just like that?"

When I told him the polite request came along with a glimpse of his pistol, Mike changed his tune. "What'd they want?" he asked in a more sympathetic tone.

"Did you know Williams lives in Olly Jensen's old place?"

"Right next to the Wades' isn't it?"

"Yeah, that's the one. Seems curious to me."

"I'm telling you, stay away from him," Mike repeated for the sixtieth or so time.

I told him that might be a little difficult, what with him being a client and all. That's when he hung up. At first I thought maybe his cell phone had died. They do that sometimes—actually, Karin offered to take me phone shopping after work, set me up with a G3 or a Raspberry, something along those lines.

When he didn't call back after a half hour or so, I tried ringing him, but it went straight to voice mail. In the end, I decided not to worry about it. There was plenty to do in the apartment, and tomorrow's schedule was wide open.

Actually, by my standards, today's schedule was jam-packed, with those two skip trace reports to type, and the research on Herman Gallup's assets. The fact that my projects were likely to take up four hours at most gives you an idea of just how moribund my career had been before Deb decided to toss me a bone.

I still couldn't figure out her change of heart. Heart? Change of personality. One day she's tearing up every time she mentions Jon's name, and the next, she acts like she wishes he was dead. Well, actually, he was dead, so maybe she—

Oh hell, I wasn't going to figure that one out. I went to work on the reports, which were pretty cut and dried. Fifteen minutes each, and another five to seal and stamp and walk downstairs to the mailbox in the lobby. When I got there, I noticed a second notice from FedEx. Oh, right. First one came, when? Must've been last Friday. I first saw it on Saturday, after my fateful lunch with Deb.

I shrugged. What the hell, maybe I'd head over there

now, and work on the gray divorcee this afternoon. Guy like me, he likes to stay busy. I ran back upstairs to lock up, and took a moment to phone Mike. Got his voice mail again. Did that mean we were having a spat? I chuckled. Spats and Mike were two terms that didn't get along.

The line at the FedEx office was about fifteen minutes long, which gave me a chance to study the surroundings. Clearly the folks at FedEx didn't waste a lot of money on decorators. The walls were probably beige once, before mutating into that color best described as industrial smoke. The kind of shade that comes from decades of exposure to heavy smokers working in a foundry. But there were scuff marks, scratches, and holes in the drywall to break up the monotony. The holes probably came from too-little people wrestling with too-big boxes, though given the slowly moving line, the rage quotient was probably higher than the average dingy, cramped, neglected will call center.

When I finally reached the window, the fat woman with magenta hair and a chartreuse sweat suit pursed her swollen ruby lips while reading the number on my call slip. I had the feeling their ripeness had more to do with ingesting carbohydrates than injecting collagen, but who knows? Maybe after work she slipped into something sexy, like a muumuu, and was the life of the party down at the bowling alley.

But she did nothing for me. Other than fetch my package, that is. It was a 10-by-13 envelope, about two inches thick. I checked, but the return address was one of those pack-and-ship centers. Hoping it wasn't a letter bomb, I tossed it on the passenger seat and headed back to my place. On the way I stopped at O'Reilly's, home of the best corned beef sandwiches in town. What the hell, I was hungry, I craved corned beef, and I was rolling in dough at the moment.

I grabbed the envelope on my way out of the car, and took a booth along the right wall, beneath the grimy picture window. The tinny speakers were playing some kind of not-close-to-ever-being-famous country western singer who was twanging out a tale of love and loss and getting beat up in the honky tonk parking lot by his ex-wife's ex-boyfriend. A Korean War vet, by the looks of him, was tapping his thumbs mostly in time on the Formica counter, with a mug of thick black coffee steaming beside him. I could smell the brew from where I sat, and decided coke would better complement my sandwich.

"Unless you want to make a fresh pot of coffee," I told the perky young thing who waited on tables here between classes at Wayne State University. She scowled at me like I was her history prof the day she flunked the final, and said she just made that one a couple hours ago. I was going to explain to her the pot life of institutional coffee grounds, but decided to just stick with the coke.

By the time she slapped the plate down in front of me, I'd pretty much lost my appetite. When I opened the envelope the first thing I saw was Sara's picture. Not just any picture, but her crime scene portrait. She was still lying on the bed, and half her face was still missing. It hit me like one of Howard's fists. I never saw it coming. I got angry before I got scared, and then I got mad and started riffing through the stack, searching for other photos. Finding none, I looked at the second sheet. On it, in Jon's nearly indecipherable scrawl, was "Corky, that was just to make sure I have your attention."

Well, he certainly did, and what came after served to hold it. "If you're reading this, I'm probably dead," he wrote.

They say the key to good writing is to write a first sentence that makes the reader want to read the second one. If the second one is even better than the first, you've probably got a hit on your hands. Based on Jon's work so far, I figured this had the makings of a best seller.

Having spent the better part of my life despising him,

I felt a twinge of pity when I read, "You're probably wondering why I'm sending this to you. Sometimes I wonder myself. The main reason is this: there's no one else I can trust. Well, there is one, but I don't want to see her get hurt."

I figured I knew who that was, and she'd already been hurt once, when she got punched in the face. Or maybe twice if you count when Jon got himself dead. I had to make sure the tally didn't reach three.

It was almost as if he was reading my mind, because the next thing Jon wrote was "She's a good woman—did me a lot of good and probably could you too, but I don't want her involved in any way. She might be in danger anyway, so maybe you should look in on her. You have to anyway, because I left a box with her. It has some notebooks which will back up the story I'm about to tell you."

He gave Karin's name and number, along with repeating his admonition that I not let her get involved. "I know how she operates, Corky, and you too, for that matter."

Nothing like cheap shots from beyond the grave to put me off my feed, not to mention the damned nickname. I skimmed most of the letter, then left half the sandwich on the plate, and a few bills on the table. I scooped up the mess of papers and headed back to the office. On the way I chewed over the rest of his sprawling introduction, where he had written, "So why choose you?"

A good question, one which had popped up almost immediately upon opening the envelope. Why me, indeed? He threw in some gratuitous speculation. Maybe it was the ultimate payback, he mused, since the very act of opening the envelope put me in play, which is to say put me in danger. There was that, but then again, maybe it had to do with Sara Jensen, and how she died, and how it messed up my life.

"Yeah, we never got along, but you didn't deserve

that—hell, you didn't deserve any of it."

Thanks, pal, I thought. Really means a lot, coming from you. He went on to say if things went right, that is to say if they didn't get me first, I could reel in some big fish, and make a name for myself, again.

Then he repeated, "But the fact is, you're the only one I can trust. I can't go to the cops 'cause I don't know which ones are dirty." I didn't either, he stressed, urging me not to "talk to any friends you might have left on the force."

Nice. The guy must have had a ball writing this crap.

So what about Williams? I thought they were supposed to be working together. Jon didn't mention him by name, but he made an oblique reference to "people you think are allies who turn out to be playing you all along."

And then there was Deb. According to Jon, Deb was tied up in the whole mess. "She doesn't know how tied up she is—hell, she probably doesn't even know she's tied up, but when this comes down, she's going to hate me worse than you do. Hell, she'll hate me worse than I do."

Back at the office, I slipped the envelope into a drawer. Jon's letter, especially his remarks about Deb, had opened up a can of speculative worms, which I dearly wished to wriggle around with, but before I could do that, I had to finish off the Herman Gallup research. If this was going to go the way I thought it was, I wasn't going to have time for anything else, except maybe trying to stay alive.

Gallup's grieving-widow-wannabe picked up on the second ring, and after I introduced myself, she launched into a tirade about her "asshole, deadbeat" hubby. She was just glad the bastard was sterile, so there weren't any kids wandering around wearing his genes.

I let her rant for awhile. It's part of what we do. Sometimes private detectives function as confessors, or therapists. Maybe that's why Karin and I hit it off so well. I spent some time thinking about her, and recalling last night, while the wife rambled on. I could tell she was feeling better. Her invective was getting more and more cheerful. She was putting strings of words together in a remarkably original fashion. Me, I was starting to get depressed. Oh, to be loved like that...

Finally, I put a stop to it, and got us down to business. I explained my function, which was basically to figure out what Harold's assets were, and to make sure he wasn't hiding any, "So you can get what you deserve after the hell he put you through."

Hey, c'mon, a client's a client.

Turns out hubby was making things awfully easy for me, and wifey was making them even easier. He did everything online, and she had all his passwords.

"I'm surprised he gave them to you, things being the way they are."

Actually, he hadn't. She'd installed some keylogging software, which had enabled her to learn all his secrets. Which made me wonder why she needed my services, not that I was going to mention that. Like I said, a client's a client.

"Hell hath no fury like a tech-savvy woman scorned, eh?" I said instead.

She got a kick out of that, laughing in a kind of cacophonous, high-pitched shriek, which made me feel a little sympathy for poor Harold.

Anyway, she gave me what I needed and I told her I'd send a report to her attorney. The actual work took closer to two hours than the thirty minutes I'd promised myself. I may be the last person on earth still using dial up, but eventually the right screens popped up.

Harold wasn't rich, but he was well on his way. No doubt this divorce would be a bit more than a speed bump on his road to wealth. He had about $600,000 spread around four brokerage firms, including one online account that he traded in pretty heavily. I checked the history and was reassured that he had done so for the past four years.

No unusual activity, and no big withdrawals. It looked like the divorce was going to catch him off guard.

I entered the details of Harold's net worth on a spread sheet, and emailed it to the attorney. Ben Wethers was beyond doubt the best, or, depending on your gender, the worst divorce attorney in town. He only handled wives. In fact, there were consistent rumors floating around that he handled wives in more ways than one, that he took the divorce attorney's ancillary task of hand-holding to a higher level than was customary. Maybe it was true, I couldn't say. I figured it was probably embittered, recently impoverished, ex-husbands who started them.

I'd never seen any corroborating evidence, and I'd worked pretty closely with Wethers over the years. In fact, it was the occasional case he'd tossed my way that had kept me going the past few years, that and investigative work for ambulance chasers.

Still, it was true that Wethers only handled attractive young divorcees. You never saw him handing out his cards in trailer parks. In fact, he'd been Sara's attorney. Which got me thinking. We'd never talked about her after she died. Of course, that might have had more to do with me fighting for my professional life than anything else. There were a couple years, even after I got my license back, that even guys like Wethers wouldn't come near me. Hard to believe divorce lawyers need to worry about their reputation, but there you go.

Thinking about Sara naturally led me back to Jon's bombshell. He made some hints that there might be some answers to that mystery in the package. God, would I like to put that one to bed.

With Gallup dispensed with, it was time to jump back in. It was only 3:00, and Karin wasn't due back until six or so. I poured myself a ~~mug of~~ coffee and opened the envelope. Rereading Jon's letter, more carefully this time, it struck me again how critical that missing box was. Which gave me pause. If in fact it contained indictable evidence, Karin might be in more danger than I'd first assumed.

I didn't know exactly what Jon thought he was giving me, but if it was enough to put someone away, that same someone might begin to wonder whether she had read it. Somehow I didn't think her assurances that she hadn't looked because Jon had asked her not to would carry much weight with these people. Actually, given what had transpired thus far, they were more likely to eliminate a problem without going through the formality of interrogation.

I finished the letter and turned to the first sheaf of stapled documents. That's when the phone rang.

"Corcoran, got something for you," Mike growled.

"What's that?"

"No, you'll want to see this. Know where the fishing pier is?"

"On Belle Isle?"

"Nope. Riverside Park. How soon can you get here?"

I tried again to get some sense of what was going on, but Mike remained coy. So I said, "Give me fifteen minutes."

After stuffing the pages into my office safe, I gulped the rest of my coffee, and headed out again. I wondered what Mike had, and how it might pertain to the case. He sounded downright smug, almost triumphant about it. For just a moment I considered the possibility that he was setting me up. But I dismissed it, for a number of reasons, among which trust and friendship didn't rank that highly.

The most convincing argument was timing. If he were planning to kill me, or more likely, have me killed, it would be more plausible to do it at night, not in the middle of the afternoon. I revised that assessment as I approached the rubble-strewn parking lot. Riverside Park was a wasteland.

Never one of Detroit's jewels, it was developed in the late 1970's after the local gas company donated the land to the city. In a style typical of the City, the park was built on polluted soil. Periodic clean up efforts were largely unsuccessful, until finally the City closed the park. Of course, in a city like Detroit, posting "Closed" signs and stretching chains across the parking lot entrance pretty much guaranteed an uptick in patronage. However, since the park closed, the Recreation Department no longer serviced it, not even bothering to empty the garbage cans. As a result, the park was not only polluted, it was filthy.

Feeling cynical, I negotiated the potholes and broken glass in the parking lot beneath the gray, soaring steel superstructure of the Ambassador Bridge. The struts grumbled and groaned as trucks rumbled overhead, pulsing with international trade.

The handful of squad cars, an ambulance, and three unmarked sedans in the lot reassured me that, unless Mike had a hell of a lot more clout than I gave him credit for, I wasn't about to be ambushed. I parked and headed over to the suits and uniforms clustered around the pier. Mike was there, conferring with the forensics team, but before I could approach him, Officer Nelson placed his hand on my chest.

"S'a restricted area," he announced, a nasty grin stealing across his face when he recognized me. "Corcoran, huh? What're you doing here?"

"I got a call. Supposed to meet somebody." I suppose I could have just mentioned Mike's name and saved myself a lot of trouble. But this punk had pissed me off, and I didn't feel like making nice. Hey, what can I say? I got laid last night, I woke up this morning feeling almost normal for the first time in a long while, and what the hell, I hadn't seen the inside of a hospital or jail in a couple of days.

"Like who?" Nelson demanded. "The stiff?"

The stiff? I didn't think people actually used words like "the stiff." Nelson must read too many detective novels. "Stiff, huh? Don't suppose it's got a name?"

"Probably does. Don't they all? But what's it to you?"

"I'll let you know when I figure it out," I said, starting to ease past him. Not too bad, I thought. We were almost civil.

That's when his hand made contact with my chest again. Maybe he was just a little overeager. Maybe his adrenaline was up. Who knows, maybe it was Nelson's first corpse. All I know is his move came down closer to a shove than it did restraint.

"Listen sonny, why don't you do your job and let me do mine?" I kind of brushed his hand away with a "and if you ever touch me again, I'll rip your arm off."

Naturally the little prick went for his gun as soon as my back was turned. "Freeze, asshole," he shrieked, the terror he meant to impart with his order quavering in his own voice.

I grinned and turned, and said, "You guys never learn, do you." I also ducked the left he threw at my nose, and danced back, keeping him at bay. Yeah, I really was feeling good today.

Right on schedule Mike shouted, "Henry, what the fuck are you doing?"

I glanced over and gave him a wave, "Took your own sweet time, Mike."

He wasn't buying any of my sunshine, being busy ordering Officer Nelson to holster his weapon.

"But this dirtbag was resisting arrest," he insisted.

I choked off my derisive snort when Mike barked, "Can it, Corcoran." Oh, that's right, we're having a spat. Mike then asked the cop what the charges were.

"How 'bout assaulting a police officer?" he essayed, his face growing beet red, whether from rage or embarrassment, I couldn't tell. Either would have been justified. Henry Nelson was not having a good day.

Mike surprised me by actually taking the time to listen to Nelson's story. For a second I thought he was going to okay the collar. Maybe I could hang myself in my cell. Happens all the time.

In the end, though, he just suggested the rookie cop put a little less zeal into securing the perimeter, then led me back to the pier. "Jesus, Corcoran. Can't you just show up like other people? You know, quietly?"

"Sorry, Mike. That punk just rubs me the wrong way."

"Yeah, a broken nose'll do that, I hear." He shrugged. "Punk's the right word, though. I don't know how he got through the Academy. Hell, he wouldn't even be here if he hadn't already been here."

"How's that?"

"Said he likes to swing by the park every once in awhile, keep the homeys on their toes. Me? I think maybe it wasn't so innocent."

"You think he had something to do with it?"

"Naw, maybe just some kind of shakedown. Said he pulled into the lot, this old black guy starts jumping up and down, waving his hands. So he goes over. Turns out the old codger is out trying to catch a river cat, gets his line snagged. Thinks it's a log or something. He tries to jiggle the hook loose, but nothing doing. So he reels in, figuring he'll just break the line, when the body bobs up to the surface."

"Must've given him a start."

"'I like to jumped outa my skin,' is how he put it. The old guy's a hoot. You should talk to him."

"That why you brought me out here, to trade one-liners with a river rat?"

Mike shook his head, said there was somebody he wanted me to meet.

There was still a group standing around the coroner, who was bent over the body. It looked pretty fresh, couldn't have been in the water for more than a few hours. I wandered over to one of the uniforms. "What's with this guy?"

"Robbery it looks like. No watch, no ring, no wallet." Then he stopped talking. Squinting at me, he asked, "What's it to you?"

"Mike Wallis called me."

"Oh, sure, you're Corcoran."

I wasn't sure why everyone else was still hanging around, but maybe they were just enjoying the view.

The three days of drizzle and overcast had given way to blue skies and sunshine. It was warm, too, for that time of year, in the low sixties. Still, there was that unmistakable tinge in the air, the one that said winter was coming whether you liked it or not. The trees on the Canadian side were turning, and if you looked upstream, the period piece towers of downtown Detroit looked nice glowing in the sunlight.

Downtown Detroit always looked nice, from a distance. It was only when you got up close and personal that you realized how hopeless everything was. From this vantage point, you couldn't tell that half the towers were empty.

But this wasn't accomplishing anything. If Mike wanted to introduce me to somebody, what was he waiting for?

"Well?" I said.

He gave it right back, "Well?"

"You wanted me to meet somebody?"

Mike nodded his chin at the ground.

"What're you talking about? I know Joe." Joe Condon and I went back quite a few years. Every so often in my career somebody would get dead in one of my cases, so I'd developed a good working relationship with the Wayne County Coroner. That might have been tarnished a bit during Sara's inquest, but Joe was then and now remained a professional. He glanced up at the sound of his name and grunted, "Corcoran."

"Not Joe," Mike corrected. "The corpse."

I gave it another glance. "So?"

"You don't recognize him?" Mike sounded skeptical.

"No. Who is he?"

"Your old pal Bill Jeffries."

My jaw must have dropped, or maybe it was the way the blood drained from my face, but it was enough to convince Mike. "You really didn't know?"

"Never met him. Never even talked to him. Just left him a bunch of voice mail messages," I replied absently, my mind racing. "How long's he been dead?" I asked Joe.

"Well, I won't know for certain 'til I open him up," he said, grunting as he rose from his crouch. He peeled the latex gloves off and handed them to an assistant. "But if I had to hazard a guess, I'd say 12 to 16 hours, 24 max."

I did the math. It was almost 4:00 now, and Karin had called me at 8:00 last night. That was well within Joe's time frame.

"How soon can you narrow that down?"

Mike glanced sharply at me. "What difference does it make?"

"None, I guess," I temporized. I had to think quickly. The chances that Karin had something to do with this were slim, but I wanted to be the one to find that out. Not the DPD, and especially not Detective Mike Wallis. Still, my stupid, panicked reaction had put him on my scent.

"Then why ask?"

"Hell, Mike, I don't know. It just hit me, realizing it was him." I gave him a hard look. "You know, one of those loose ends?"

The little up beat at the end had the desired effect, as in, "one of those loose ends you were going to tie up for me?" Mike got it. Say what you want about him but he did subtle about as well as anybody. He was also a pretty deft hand at discretion, and asking questions he didn't know the answer to in front of a half-dozen cops and detectives didn't fit that bill.

He turned to his partner and said, "You wanna finish up here, Doug? I need a drink." That was met with knowing glances. Everybody knew Mike's MO. He clapped a hand on my shoulder and said, "Come on, first one's on me."

CHAPTER 13

Darla presided as usual over the silent chamber of the Walloon. Well, silent in terms of customer chit chat. Dr. Phil was doing a good job of filling that void. Actually, the bar was surprisingly full for 4:30 on a Wednesday. A retired sailor dozed at the far end of the bar, his head resting next to a half-full rocks glass. A World War II vet, by the looks of his cap. The USS Hudson, it read, and there were a half-dozen battles stitched along the brim.

Over in a corner, a grizzled, battered down bar fly sat staring wordlessly at his own half-empty rocks glass, while his redheaded, dishwater-weary, way past her sell-by-date companion sat staring wordlessly at him. Whether they were worn out from a fight, gearing up for another one, or just catching a breather between rounds, only time would tell.

Even Darla was out of sorts. She stubbed out a smoke as we came in, and greeted us with a glance of such baleful loathing that I actually took a half-step backwards. Mike, though, was having none of it. He might do subtle well, but he was as blind as a bank regulator when it came to blatant.

"Jesus, Darla. Looks like happy hour in here."

"Up yours, Wallis," she rasped. "Oh, and what's this? You finally tracked down lover boy?"

She filled a couple tumblers with ice and drowned them in bourbon, clunked them down in front of us, and said to me, "You should've seen him last night. Kept checking his watch and saying, 'Where the hell is he? He said he'd be here.' Shit, I thought he was gonna cry."

"You try spending four hours with Little Miss Sunshine," Mike said, eyes asparkle. "You'd be crying, too."

Darla guttered up another laugh, in spite of herself. "So where were you?"

"Got a better offer," I replied, figuring I might as well join in the spirit. I had to hand it to Mike, he knew how to cheer her up. Which made me wonder again about her warning me. Was it a joke or not? Maybe I should just ask her point blank in front of Mike.

"You're healing up good," she observed. "Couple more days, you won't look like a raccoon no more."

I scowled at her guffaw, and dove into the drink. When she finally stopped coughing, I said, "Going on two days without getting beat up."

"Two days? I thought that was Saturday."

Mike said it was, but then I had to go pick a fight on Tuesday, too.

She lit another cigarette and scoffed, "Oh really? Who was it this time? A meter maid?"

"Close," Mike said, grinning slyly. "It was a cop."

"A cop?" This set her off on another jag of wheezing laughter. "Not you?"

"If it'd been him, he'd look worse than me," I offered, my first contribution to this charade. "No, it was Officer Henry Nelson, and if he's one of Detroit's finest, well, that tells you all you need to know about this city. Anyway, it wasn't a fight, he slammed my face down on lood of my car."

"Yeah, he was arresting Jim for murder." Mike tried to contain it, but in the end he succumbed to laughter.

"Who'd you kill this time?" Darla's attempt to join his mirth was abbreviated by another coughing fit. It was either the bits of her lungs splattering against the wall, or the ticking of his internal alcoholic clock, but something roused the old guy at the end of the bar. He jerked awake and stared wildly until his eyes settled on his drink. He grabbed the glass, drained it in one go, and tapped it on the bar for another.

While Darla tended to him, Mike said, "I shouldn't laugh." Then, his eyes growing stern, he continued. "Especially now."

I knew where he was going with that, and I knew it was inevitable we'd get there. Following him to the Walloon had ensured that. Not that I'd had any choice. Cutting and running hadn't been an option. Like I said, Mike was a good detective, and he knew there was something I wasn't telling about Jeffries' death. The fact that he didn't know what it was gave me a slight edge, but I had to give him something to keep him at bay. I just didn't know what it might be.

So, me being me, I decided to play dumb. "Yeah, I can't believe Nelson went after me again. Holding a grudge is one thing, but this is ridiculous."

Mike flicked his eyes at me, as if to say, "Nice try, asshole." He took a long sip of his drink, surprisingly his first, since it had been sitting there for all of three minutes. He closed his eyes, savored it, and sighed. "I wonder why Jeffries decided to go swimming," he mused.

I played along. "It is a little late in the season."

"Especially with all his clothes on." Mike's tone let me know he'd just tossed that one out there, sort of a reminder of how friends like the friends we used to be could sweep things under the carpet, look the other way. But not now. Those were the old days, back when we could trust each other. I wanted to ask him how it had come to this. What went wrong? Had he turned a corner, or had I just opened my eyes?

"So what did you have on Jeffries?" he asked.

Oh, I liked that. That was a good question. That was a question I could answer, honestly and fully. Well, almost fully. If at all possible I wanted to leave Karin's meeting him last night out of it. Hell, I wanted to leave her out altogether, but I wasn't sure that was going to work.

"Like I said, I never talked to him. He went walkabout about the time Jon took his stroll down memory lane, but what I heard, he was working with Jon to crack open the money behind the drug scene."

"Finding 'Mr. Big'?" Mike's sarcasm was palpable. "So how far'd he get?" Something just a little too offhand about that question, I thought.

"He got pretty close, he and Jon, at the end."

Mike swivelled on his stool. "Yeah, and how'd you find that out?"

I toyed with that one. The old me, everything would've been on the table. I would've been asking Mike for advice. We were beyond that now, and I had to figure out how to play this. Bottom line, I had to give him something, but if it came too freely, he'd be wondering what I was holding back.

"We're getting close to that whole client confidentiality thing," I offered.

"So you got all this from Deborah Wade?" He obviously wasn't buying that one. "Or the other one, what's her name? Your little nurse maid."

"She's got nothing to—"

"Or is it Williams?" he spat. He slapped the counter. Darla headed our way, thinking it was refill time, but she ran into the force field of our tension. "Jesus Christ, Jim, how many clients you got?" he snarled.

"Well, Deb's out," I said. "Karin was never in the picture—" What the hell, it was worth a shot. "And

Williams, he's the new kid on the block."

I checked my watch. 5:00. "Listen, I got time for one more, but that's it. I gotta meet Karin at six. She's going to help me buy a cell phone."

"Get out," Darla said, seizing on my lighter tone to jump back in. "You're going digital? You sure?"

I shrugged. "I don't know, maybe it is early, but I got some cash on me, I figure I'll take a chance for once."

She chuckled as she set down our glasses. "So you two kissed and made up?"

"Well," Mike drew it out. "I'm not sure we're ready to start dating again..."

"You never know," I put in. "I'll have to check with Karin."

"You guys really an item?" Mike asked, a crease of concern in his voice. "You sure that's a good idea?"

The reference was obvious. I didn't like it, but there wasn't a lot I could do about it. I'd spent the last five days asking myself the same question. "It'll be fine," I finally mustered.

"So, what? I'm back on the bench?"

"You had your chance, Darla. D'you ever think there's such a thing as playing too hard to get?"

That set her off again. While she was gasping Mike gave me a look and said, "You gotta give me something here, buddy."

I sighed. "Yeah, I know. Look, all I know is what I heard. They were getting close. Maybe they got all the way, I don't know. Maybe that's what got Jon killed."

"So you're down with that now?"

"It's gotta be." I shrugged. "There're too many corpses for it to be anything else. Doesn't Jeffries prove that?"

"But you don't know who it is." A statement, not a question, with the emphasis on "you." Which meant somebody did.

"Jon left a box with Karin." I gave him that one.

"That's where I found the notebooks, the one about me, and the one about Jessica." I'd leave the one about Justin out of it for now. A strategy was starting to open up for me.

Mike's interest was clearly piqued. "You think there might be something there? Something that'll give us a name?"

I shrugged again. "Who knows?"

"You didn't go through it?"

"I started to, but then you showed up." I took a long drink. "Hell, I should've just stayed there."

"Why didn't you?"

"I don't know. I guess I started feeling hinky about the whole Karin-Williams connection. Didn't know if I could trust her."

"Hold onto that thought," Mike advised.

"Why? You know something?"

"Naw," Darla butted in. "Mikey's just jealous."

"Williams doesn't trust her either," I noted.

"Williams doesn't trust anyone," Mike said. "It's in his job description."

I checked my watch. "Listen, Mike. I've got to get out of here."

"Well, take a look at that box. Let me know what you find."

I said I couldn't do that.

"What do you mean you can't?"

"It's not there anymore."

"Where is it?"

"Search me. Whoever tossed Karin's apartment took it. Ask me, I think that's why they tossed it.

"They took it?" I think that's the first honest reaction I'd gotten from Mike that afternoon. He thought he was playing me, that he held all the cards, but the look of astonishment on his face spoke volumes. If he didn't know it was missing, that meant he didn't know who had it. Interesting.

I told him I'd keep him posted, blew a kiss at Darla, and headed out to my car. The respite from the weather had ended while I was inside, and Detroit was shrouded in a crepuscular mist. I drove back downtown, back to my decrepit block, and the little haven of my flat. I had to get to the office to give Karin a call. Yeah, it was definitely time to get a cell phone. Okay, way past time.

She didn't pick up, so I left a voice mail saying I was home and waiting. Then I dug Jon's package out of the safe. Keeping it from Mike I counted as a major victory. As far as I was concerned, nobody was going to know about it. And that included Karin. Maybe that's not the best way to go into a relationship, but so be it. I thought I could trust her. Hell, I wanted to trust her, more than I could say, and maybe I would someday. But this was my hole card. This kept me one step ahead of everybody else, whoever everybody else was.

Not knowing who they were was galling. Or knowing too many of them, but not knowing for certain who was whom. Like I said before, I like my good guys wearing white hats, and my bad guys wearing black ones, or Balaclavas, or even berets, I suppose. Maybe Jon could help me out. But instead of opening the envelope, I just sat there. Maybe I didn't want to know. Maybe I was afraid Mike's fingerprints would be all over the case.

I had to believe Mike was dirty. There were his clothes, for one thing. And the big wad of hundreds. And, to be honest, I'd always known it. I'd known it for as long as we'd been drinking buddies. I shook my head. That meant even before Sara. I guess after Sara, and the hell that came with it, I got a little cynical, a little jaded. I guess I stopped believing.

I let things slide. Probably adopted some of that trial lawyer's philosophy. Which was basically screw the law, screw them all. There's no such thing as justice, which means there's no such thing as right or wrong. You just go where life leads you.

I did that with Mike. I just let it slide. He was a good drinking buddy, and that was all I needed. Speaking of which, I reached for the bottle of Jack I kept in my desk drawer. Grabbed it by the neck, and then I stopped. I'd had two already, maybe I should keep myself fresh for Karin.

So maybe being a good drinking buddy wasn't enough any more.

I always figured Mike was run-of-the-mill dirty, which is to say just crooked. Take a few bribes, look the other way now and then, and an envelope full of cash would magically appear. Now, I wasn't so sure. Now I was starting to think Mike might be a hell of a lot dirtier than that. Mike might be up-to-his-ears bent. It was starting to look like Mike was in the middle of everything.

The way he warned me off from the very beginning, cleverly laying it all on Deb. "What are you doing messing around with the Wades?" he said. Talk about misdirection. It was like he was worried about my feelings. Didn't want to see me get hurt again, and all the while he was trying to keep me from looking too closely into Jon's death. Which means he knew how Jon died. Maybe he even had something to do with it.

I sat up straight. One thought led to another. The way Mike waited for me to recognize Jeffries. How'd he recognize him? What'd that cop say? "No watch, no ring, no wallet."

I went back over it. At no time did Mike even hint at knowing him. First time I mentioned him, nothing. Even with the crack house it was "your buddy Bill Jeffries."

So if he knew it was Jeffries, he knew how he got in the drink. Which means the last thing he expected was for some codger to reel him in. No, Jeffries was supposed to stay missing for a long time. At least long enough for the fishes to nibble away at the evidence.

So Mike was out at the pier doing what? Damage control?

What was my role? Was I supposed to recognize

him? Then what? Did that make me a suspect? Was Officer Nelson supposed to get another shot at my nose?

I grinned. Going after him was turning out to be a brilliant move. Not that I'd planned it that way. No, I just wanted to jerk his chain, but in so doing, I put Mike off his game plan. But that's what instinct is all about. You don't know why you do it, you just do it, and it turns out to be the right move. That's the way it always worked for me, back when I was on top of the world. Back before Sara.

But enough of that. I'd been down that road too many times for way too long. Starting now, I was moving forward. Eyes fixed firmly on the future. Speaking of which, it was after six. Karin should have called by now.

I put in another call, and again it went straight to voice mail. I left another message, trying not to think too much about how much I was starting to sound like her the other night.

Which raised another question. Why'd Mike even pretend to come to my rescue? Granted, it was Carmine who'd sprung me, but why did Mike get involved? Maybe so I'd drop my guard, not suspect him? Then he'd have a better chance of finding out what I knew. On the other hand, he spent most of his time that night trying to talk me into cashing Deb's check and dropping the case. Well, I could square those two. Find out what I knew, and keep me from finding out anything more. Made sense. I didn't want to think about what he might have done if I actually had found something.

I opened the envelope, pulling the pages out face down, to spare me the sight of Sara's photo. I slipped it out from the bottom and stuck it in a desk drawer. I didn't want to look at it, but I didn't want to throw it away, either. Let it remain as a cautionary device. Keep me from getting too high, too cocky. "You're not infallible," it said.

I read the introductory letter again, pausing at Jon's reference to "people you think are allies but turn out to be playing you." Williams? It sure sounded like it. But if I was right about Mike, wouldn't that put Williams in the clear? It made sense that Mike wouldn't want me joining forces with the lawyer. If I were sufficiently suspicious of him, there was nothing Williams could say that would change my mind. Another conundrum. Maybe Jon had that answer, too.

I leafed through the sheets. There were bank statements, tax statements, real estate tax bills. What the hell? They were all Justin's. I looked a little more closely. They were probably photocopies of the statements in Jon's office. The same ones Williams had confiscated from Karin.

I checked my watch. It was after seven, and she still hadn't called.

Maybe she'd gotten the messages, but chose to ignore them. Maybe she was suffering from buyer's remorse. Maybe there was someone else she hadn't told me about. Maybe she was out with Mr. Wonderful right now, sharing a glass of wine, laughing at his wit, gazing into his blue eyes...

I had no right to be jealous. All I'd done was help her finish trashing her mattress. After the number the goons had done on it, it hadn't taken much effort to pound the stuffing out of it. And we had gone after it pretty hard. Thinking about it, I smiled, despite my growing concern.

I'd entertained hopes of enjoying round two, on my bed this time, on a mattress equal to the task, but if she had other plans, that was okay. Okay, not okay, but definitely better than some other options. I kept thinking about the violence displayed in her apartment. There was nothing professional about that job. That was personal. Especially after they found the box. That was just crazy. That was Justin Wade crazy. I spent some time sizing up Justin for the job. I'd seen him flip the switch from normal to balls outrage enough times in the past to believe he was capable of that kind of destruction. But in the end, I couldn't make it work.

Forget about means and opportunity, there was no motive. He had no reason to toss Karin's apartment. Like she said, they had never even met. I shrugged. There were plenty of other vindictive people in Greater Detroit. Howard, for example, though he had an alibi. He and Rafe had been busy securing the premises while Williams I had our little tete-a-tete.

I kept trying to make the case for Justin. A waste of time? Maybe. Let's just say I'm sentimental. On the other hand, it did spare me having to spend that ten minutes worrying about Karin. Too many fists, too many guns, too many bodies. I didn't like the way this case was going, this case I thought I'd gotten out from under. I liked it even less that I'd dragged her into it. Plus, I didn't like the way Jon was orchestrating things from beyond the grave.

 Add Jeffries to that equation, and her making love to Mr. Wonderful was starting to look like a best case scenario.

I tried her phone again. No go. Just her cool, professional voice telling me to leave a message. I didn't bother this time. If she was bouncing with Mr. Bountiful, it'd only make me look like a sap. If there was another reason her phone privileges had been cut off, leaving another message wouldn't make any difference.

Feeling the need to move, to do something, I got up and started pacing. Each time I passed the desk I gave the drawer a look. A longer look each time. The second one down, on the left side. The one where I kept the bottle. It was starting to look like old Jack was the only friend I had left.

But no. I had to keep my wits about me. I might need them tonight.

Back to the desk, back to the rest of Jon's "evidence." I put that in quotes because what I was seeing wasn't a road map to Mr. Big. What I was seeing was just another piece of Jon's vendetta against Big Brother. I flipped through the pages, giving each one a cursory glance, thinking I should have asked Williams for the originals last night, after he hired me. What could he do, turn me down? Not the most reassuring way to start a professional association.

After the financials came another shock. Jon had included a photocopy of the "Detroit News" article about Jessica's drowning.

"Jessie, Jessie, life's so messy," I thought ruefully. What did I have here? Some kind of sick joke? Or a puzzle?

It would be exactly like the Jon I used to know to leave this as a joke, except for one thing. He knew he was going to die when he put it in the mail. Not he thought he was going to die. He knew it, and even the old Jon wasn't that bizarre.

On the other hand, if it was a puzzle, it was too complicated for me to figure out. I'm a simple guy, and that's the way I like my clues. Straightforward. I don't want puzzles. I don't want flow charts and chains of evidence. "Olly Jensen is Mr. Big, and here's where he's hanging out these days." That's the kind of clue I like. Olly Jensen is Mr. Big. Or Kendall Williams. Or Mike Wallis, or, hell, even Justin Wade for that matter.

I sat back in my chair. Back to Justin Wade? That was empty speculation. No way it made sense. It was wrong on so many levels. But that's where Jon kept pointing. Obviously, I needed to spend a little more time with those statements. But first, the rest of the package. Maybe Jon had spelled it all out at the end.

I gave a quick once-over to Jessie's story. Someone, I had to assume it was Jon, had scribbled in the margin, "Where was Jonathan Wade? Where had he gone? What didn't the reporter tell you?"

Okay, good questions. The article said he'd run to get help. Not true? How could I find out, and was there really any reason to? It was a little late to assuage Jon's residual guilt.

I grabbed the phone before the first ring ended. "Karin?"

"Hardly." It was hard to mistake Kendall Williams' cool, almost patrician tone. "Have you misplaced Ms. Champagne? I should have thought you would have learned to be more careful with your clients by now."

Williams' formality was starting to get under my skin. Not to mention his constant mocking references to Sara. In fact, just about everything about the guy had started to get under my skin, from the moment I met him. Okay, not the exact moment. Not when he was the guy getting me unshackled from the hospital bed. Right then he was the exemplar of nobility, a regular Dudley Do-right. But shortly afterwards, and pretty much constantly since then. Still, as I like to say, a client is a client.

When I explained that I was expecting her to call, he said I sounded awfully frantic for a casual phone call.

"Well, she's supposed to help me buy a cell phone, and I'm afraid the stores will be closed."

Williams chuckled. "Well, well, a cell phone. Welcome to the 20th Century, Mr. Corcoran."

Yeah, I know it's the 21st Century. I think that was his point. "Thanks, Ken." He wanted to call me Mr. Corcoran, fine. But I was strictly a first-name-basis operator. Next time he called me Mr. Corcoran, maybe I'd say, "Welcome to the 19th Century, Mr. Williams."

"Since you're expecting a call, I'll get to the point."

"Which is?"

"Which is, what, if anything, have you managed to learn?"

"Well, I learned Bill Jeffries isn't going to do us much good."

"You mean, now that he's dead?"

"How'd you hear about that?"

"It's my job to hear about things," Williams replied pointedly. "And by the way, the reason I'm paying you is to find out things from you."

"Well, you already know the one thing I had to tell you." To be honest, I wasn't exactly thrilled with the petulance I heard in my voice. "As for anything else I might have learned, let's see. Jeffries was talking about skipping town. He was afraid of what might happen to him. Looks like he had good reason."

"You met with him?" he asked with some urgency.

"No, not me. I never laid eyes on him until it was too late."

"Then who?"

"Let's not go there."

Williams chuckled again. "I'm glad to see you've finally learned the value of protecting the interests of the client."

The bastard. The smarmy bastard. "She's not a client," I barked, then jutted the base of my palm against my forehead.

"She is no concern of mine," he said, with a harsh inflection on "she." "But what she knows may well be."

"I'm working on it. Maybe tonight, if she ever gets here." This seemed like as good a time as any, so I gave it a shot. "You know what could help? How 'bout you let me look at that material Karin got from Jon's apartment?"

Williams said no. "I examined the documents, and they are not germane to the matter at hand."

I pressed it, suggesting he might benefit from a second set of eyes. "After all," I added, "I am a professional investigator."

His laughter, I suppose, would have to suffice as his answer.

"Look, Ken, I really need to wrap this up. I should be able to do a full court press tomorrow. I had some other business I had to finish up today, then Mike Wallis dragged me down to Riverside Park to look at Jeffries' body."

"Wallis, eh?"

"He's a detective with DPD."

"I am well aware of who Detective Mike Wallis is. The question is, are you?"

"Let's just say I'm starting to figure that one out."

"So can I conclude you were interrogating him today?"

"Not interrogating him, no. More feeling him out, trying to get the lay of the land."

"All that booze, that was what, an attempt to loosen his tongue?"

"All what booze? What are you talking about?"

"Isn't that why people frequent the Walloon Saloon? I can't imagine they go there for the cuisine."

"You tailing me, Williams?"

"Yes, Corcoran, I am." He imbued "Corcoran" with such iciness that I grew nostalgic for the "Mr."

"Why the hell would you do that?"

"It is only prudent to protect my assets."

"Assets?" I snarled. "You mean investment."

"If you wish."

"You think you can buy me for a lousy five grand? Listen, I still got that check. How 'bout I send it back to you? Or better yet, I'll just tear it up." I was feeling pretty extravagant, considering I'd only been flush for a couple days.

"Cash the check, Mr. Corcoran," Williams said in his best world weary tone. "Just get me some results." And then he was gone with a resounding click.

What to do? Go back to Jon's saga. But first, another futile call to Karin. This time, though, it was busy. I hung up, grateful for that sign of life. Unless it was her assailant or assailants unknown, reporting in on an untapped phone. Nothing for it but to wait a couple minutes and try again.

Then my phone rang. "Jim, I was just trying to call you."

"You're all right?"

"Of course I'm all right. Why shouldn't I be?"

I said I was just worried, because I thought she'd be

done by six.

"My last session went long, and I always turn off my phone when I'm with a patient. It was a young woman, I'd been working with her and her fiancé. They both had substance abuse issues, but were making good progress. Then he went on a binge and ended up OD-ing. She's a wreck, and I just couldn't say, 'Well, time's up. See you next week.'"

"Did it remind you of Jon at all?"

"Oh, don't you know it." After a commemorative sigh she continued. "Anyway, I just listened to your messages. Is everything okay? You sounded worried."

She laughed when I reprised my line about the cell phone store closing. "I thought private detectives were better liars than that. Like Sam Spade or Philip Marlowe."

I insisted I could prevaricate with the best of them. "But I really, really want a cell phone. How soon can you get here?"

"I'm just leaving the clinic now—maybe twenty minutes?"

"Great, I'll be—" Then caution reared its ugly head. "Is there a security guard who can walk you to your car?"

"I imagine—might take awhile. Why?"

"Just do it, please. Humor me."

She laughed again. "Might take another twenty, but I'll get on it. Hope the cell phone store doesn't close!"

Twenty minutes minimum, forty at the outside, Probably not enough time to get all the way through the package, but I could at least make some progress. I found it at the bottom of the stack. Six pages in all. Single spaced, front and back. Typed. Interesting. Like he was afraid of leaving any evidence behind on a computer.

I was halfway through the sordid tale when the bell rang. I pressed the buzzer, then quickly scooped up the pages and stuffed them back in the safe. What I'd read was hard to fathom, but it made sense in a perverse sort of way. Just the same, I still didn't want Karin to know about

Jon's package. Not that I couldn't trust her. If Jon's letter had made one thing certain, it was that Karin was definitely in the clear. I could trust her with anything, even my life. It's just that, if she knew about it, she'd want to read it, and I didn't know if I could prevent it. Like Jon, I didn't want her to have to know this story.

I moved to the door, thinking she was taking her own sweet time getting up the stairs. I was eager to hold her in my arms again. So eager that suddenly I wondered what time cell phone stores did close, and did we have to head out right away? Maybe it could even wait another day. After all, I'd gotten this far without one.

He must have gone part way up the next flight, because as I started down the steps, I heard footsteps behind me. I whirled, or started to, and ran my face into some kind of heavy object. A baseball bat, or lead pipe, gun butt, or sap.

Next thing I heard, my phone was ringing, distantly, hollowly. Don't know how long I was out, at least long enough for whoever it was to trash my office. Must've been him who rang my bell. Fool not to check. Phone had long stopped ringing by the time I pulled myself back to the door. Careful, might still be here, but phone—Karin, had to be. I launched myself from the doorway, barely snagging the edge of the desk before I fell. Like I was drunk, reeling drunk. Spent a couple weeks like this after Sara.

Had to call her—Karin. Picked up the phone. Set it back down. What's her number? Last in, first out. How these things work. No redial. No Star 69 or whatever the hell it was. Sixty-nine, interesting choice. Never thought of that before. Must be key spots on phone pad. Yeah, that's the ticket. Right.

Then it rang. Pick up. "Jim? Jim? Are you there?"

Something s'posed to do. Oh, yeah. Talk. "Karn. S'you?"

"Jim what's going on? I've been waiting for half-an-

198

hour, and this is not the kind of neighborhood to loiter in."

"Loitring wuh intent," I managed. I thought it'd be funny.

"What?" Aghast, nice word. Not used much any more, but yeah, that captured it. Her tone.

"Out sigh? Side?"

"I'm driving around. I don't even feel safe sitting in my car."

"Come baa. Ring. Le you in."

"Oh my God, you sound awful." A catch in her voice. "Please tell me you've been drinking." Like alternative is worse.

Somehow I managed to stay conscious long enough for her to get back. Long enough to buzz her in—hope it's her this time. Long enough for the tears, the warm wash cloth, the incoherent attempt to explain, the call to 911. Then the glance around the office, her, "Oh no, they got you too?"

I held her hand, touched her face, her lips, the wetness around her eyes. "Thought we stay here tonight." Weak laugh. "No Star 69 tonight, best laid plans."

"What?" A little laugh, a little bewilderment, a tender touch, an "I'll stay all night with you—at the hospital."

A sudden jolt of lucidity. Whoever it was would come back, or was waiting to see who showed up. Cops or ambulance. Had already marked Karin. Cops come after ambulance. Mike would show, or was it him already? Don't know, but want the safe open. Gotta trust her. Gave combination. "Take envelope. Don't read. Go Book Cadillac Hotel. Go with ambulance. Don't let follow."

"I'm staying with you."

Could hear siren. "Get envelope. Go hotel. All answers. Don't read."

"Jim, you're not making any sense."

"Safe. Envelope. Open. Now. Close after."

She sighed, but went to the safe. I managed to get the numbers out again, then she had it.

"Stuff in skirt band, in back, jacket over." And I was out.

CHAPTER 14

This business of waking up in a hospital room, cop standing over there next to the window, you hurting like hell, and not knowing what day it is, let me tell you, it gets old after awhile. I lifted my arms. At least there were no shackles this time.

Karin was by my side in an instant, giving a sharp glance at the cop. Then Mike Wallis strolled in. "Jesus, Corcoran. Don't you ever get tired of this?"

Tired? Yeah, tired. That was a good description. Tired, beat down, worn out, washed up. How 'bout fucking miserable? I grabbed Karin's hand.

"They weren't going to let me in," she said.

"Yeah, but I greased that one. Some guys are just too diligent for their own good." He jutted his chin at the uniform. "Isn't that right, Henry?"

Henry? Not Henry Nelson. I groaned.

"Okay, you can go now, Henry," Mike said, adding over his protests, "No, no. I can handle him. Plus I've got this nice lady as back up."

Nelson scowled at us, and stalked out. As the door

hissed shut, Mike got down to business. "What happened, Jim?

"He got hit in the head, obviously," Karin said impatiently.

Mike got a kick out of that. "Bingo! Got it in one. Hell, buddy, she's a better detective than you are."

Karin tried to muster a little laugh, tried to pretend Mike meant it in jest, but her eyes remained somber, dead if you want to get technical. I stared at her, waiting. She had to look at me. Sooner or later, she had to. She shifted them, close, but then she cast them down. Demure. Most women can't do demure any more. No call for it, I guess. A dying art. But Karin, if demure made a comeback, she was way ahead of the game.

I didn't really need her eyes. I was pretty sure already. The somberness was a hell of a clue, but when I looked in her eyes I would get the confirmation. Which would mean I couldn't trust her. She did the one thing I told her not to do. Like Pandora, she had to open it, and now all the evils in the world had escaped. And the hell of it was, now as she finally gave me her eyes, eyes welling with tears and confession, the hell of it was, she had nothing left, not even hope.

Considering how many times he'd been married, Mike couldn't read a woman. Then again, considering how many times he'd been divorced, maybe that made sense.

"Oh, hey, Karin, don't worry," he said, not getting the tears at all. "Jim here, he's tough as nails. This is nothing. I've seen him lots worse."

Wasn't quite true, but I appreciated the gesture. Not for long. Not after he started questioning me, but right then? Yeah, it was a good turn.

I figured sooner or later I was going to have to face it. I was going to have to give it a shot. Open my mouth and see how badly scrambled my brain was. I had to see if any words came out. There were plenty of them running around inside my head. Gamboling. Yeah, that's the word. Gamboling like sheep in a sunlit pasture nestled up against the slopes of, what was it? Yeah, the Harz Mountains. Reminded me of a painting I saw once at the DIA. Doane, that trial lawyer, sometimes he'd use the Art Institute for the exchange. I'd meet him, usually in the American Landscape Gallery, hand off my report. Sometimes we'd exchange a few words about the case, but usually he'd just accept it, maybe say "Check's in the mail," often without even glancing my way, his eyes glued to some oversized Hudson River School painting.

Sometimes, if I didn't have anything else on my plate, which is to say, usually, I'd take a turn around the museum myself. That's when I saw the Harz Mountains. It was a 19th Century landscape. It was called "Harz Mountains," or "In the Harz Mountains." Something like that. Funny thing is, I don't recall there being any sheep.

Always liked art. Back in college, thought about majoring in Art History. Probably should have, even though it would have sidetracked my career. My career. What a joke.

Okay, enough of this. I was starting to feel like one of those plaster-cast victims in Pompei. Mike on one side, Karin on the other, both staring wordlessly at me, their respective faces bearing expressions of speculation and mounting concern. It was a real Dalton Trumbo moment, believe me.

Okay, here goes. Sheepdog comes bounding into the field, herding all those sheep together. Or would you say flocking them together? Flock of sheep, not herd. But then again, its shepherd, not shepflock. We'll go with herding them. The sheep dog. Herding the flock. Well, this is pretty damn ridiculous. Maybe I'll just go back to sleep.

Karin was still there when I woke up again. She was dozing in a chair off to my right. I glanced left. No Henry Nelson. No Mike Wallis. This time, no speculation, no fever rush jumble of thoughts and images. No hesitation.

"Hey babe, you all right?"

Her eyes popped open, wildly dagger-drawn to my face. "Did you—you spoke?"

"You okay?"

She burst into tears. Always liked that phrase. Burst into tears, like somebody just explodes into giant salty rain drops. No, enough of this!

She was on me, or close to me, touching my hands, tentatively my face. "Am I okay?" she cried. "Are you okay?"

Good question. Was I okay? With the love of a good woman, how could I not be okay? Of course, I couldn't be sure it actually was love, but the tears were promising. I reached for her and she came softly to me. Not the most comfortable setting for coupling, so we settled for a tender, gentle embrace. Eventually she got herself under control, and between sniffles, she repeated her inquiry.

I said I thought I might be okay, but only time would tell.

"That's what the doctor said—only time will tell. Oh, and I'm supposed to let them know when you wake up. They'll probably want to run some tests to check your cognitive and motor functions."

"Oh, my motor functions just fine, let me assure you."

She grinned and brushed my lips with a kiss. "I love you," she said, just as lightly and ephemerally as the kiss. "I'll just go tell—"

"Karin," I said, my voice almost as guttural as Darla's. "Wait a sec."

She hesitated at the door. "What is it?" she asked, without turning around.

"What's today?"

"Tomorrow," she answered lightly, then turned and came back to me.

"Tomorrow..."

"You haven't lost a day." She glanced at her watch.

"Only just though. It's almost eleven. You've been out for the most part of 27 hours."

"I was awake though, wasn't I? You and Mike were here."

Her face clouded. "Oh, it was horrible. Your eyes were almost rolling. It was like you were having a seizure, but you weren't moving. Your lips were, as if you were trying to speak but couldn't. I kept calling your name, saying 'What is it? What are you trying to say?'"

"You were talking? I don't remember that at all."

"I should get the doctor."

"No, wait. I need to ask you something."

Her eyes began to fill again. She knew what I wanted.

"You read it, didn't you." Not a question. A statement. She nodded. "The whole thing?" Another nod. "Then you know more than I do."

"What are we going to do?"

"Try to stay alive, for starters. Where's the envelope?"

She gestured at her bag. "Right here."

"I guess that's okay. As long as nobody knows we have it."

"Let me get the doctor," she repeated.

The intern wasn't up to speed on the fine points of neurological analysis, but she gave me a once-over and announced that I'd live. She smirked when I asked her If I could get that in writing. Then she told Karin she could stay the night if she wanted. It wasn't hospital policy, but they were short staffed and someone needed to wake me every hour or so.

"Just as a precaution," she added. "You woke up, so you're probably out of the danger zone."

After she left, Karin pulled the chair next to the bed. We held hands and talked about what she'd read. More lives would be destroyed when this came out. If it came out. How could I prove it? No doubt a forensic accountant could build a case out of the documents Jon had left, but I wasn't sure it would stand up in court. Without a smoking gun, all we had was a dead man's rant. How to prove that? Did I even want to?

"You read the whole thing?" I confirmed. She nodded, wearily. "Is there anything there? Anything I can take to Carmine?"

"Maybe—" Karin tried, and failed to stifle a yawn. "I'm so tired, Jim."

"But who's going to wake me up?"

"I'll just rest my eyes." They fluttered. "I won't really—" Then she rested her head on the mattress.

I chuckled, and lay there, my fingers brushing her hair, watching her sleep, and realizing I hadn't told her I loved her, too. Well, I had just suffered a serious head trauma, after all. That's what the intern called it. Serious head trauma. That was two concussions in a week, and I didn't even play hockey.

Karin was a beautiful sleeper. Not all women are. Some of them are actually quite repulsive. Now, I'm no expert, but I have watched a few. Karin was in a league of her own. Her features softened and a slight smile played on her lips. I fell asleep myself, lulled by the gentle whish-whish of her placid snores.

The headaches started the next morning after I woke up. Karin had left while I was sleeping, but had told the day nurse she would be back after a quick dash home for a shower and change of clothes. That wasn't such a good idea, but what could I do about it? Anyway, it was about that time someone put my head in a vise and started to squeeze.

I pressed the call button and kept the pressure on until the nurse returned. I begged her to give me something, but she said she couldn't. "Doctor says he needs your head clear."

I tried to laugh at the absurdity. My head might have been many things, a penny on a railroad track, an egg in a microwave, a ping pong ball in a Rottweiler's mouth, but one thing it most emphatically was not was clear.

"Doctor says headaches are normal in cases like yours," she said brightly. I don't know where they learn that particular form of bedside manner, that sunshine and lollipops sing song cheer. Maybe Sadism 101. All I knew was I wanted to strangle her. But that would require me to get up and wrap my hands around her neck, and that wasn't going to happen. Apparently movement is contraindicated for post-concussion syndrome.

The nurse did tell me it wouldn't last. According to "Doctor," the pain would be intermittent. She added that she was going to have a tray brought in, because I must be starving.

Yeah, sure. Those hunger pangs were murder. I was pretty damn lucky some bastard had just cranked that vise another half turn. Otherwise I'd be feeling hungry.

And what about that vise thing? Seems like every hack suspense writer has to convey the strength of either the hero or a villain by describing his vise-like grip, or his vise-like handshake. It's vise, you idiots!

Vice is what middle-aged, mid-level bank executives wander down seedy city alleys in search of. Just before they get rolled and their credit cards get maxed out.

You know why the hookers always leave them with one card and their driver's license? So they can get home. They're so damned ashamed, all they want to do is get home as soon as possible, call the banks, stop the cards, and swear, again, that's the last drink they'll ever drink. If they can't get home, they have to call the cops, and that brings the heat down on the hooker.

Hell, cops probably know who they are. They probably skim off a percentage of the take. As long as there's no police report, the system works just fine. That's vice, baby, and that's nothing like what happens when the vise starts tightening.

Then just as quickly as it came, the pain went away. Good concept, this intermittence, I thought. I wanted to sigh with relief, but I was afraid to do anything which might set it off again. So I just lay there, wondering what body parts the hand actually grasped in a vice-like handshake.

Karin got back about the same time the food arrived. Nurse was right, I was starving. I was so hungry, hospital food actually tasted good. You know, there's a reason hospitals call their food preparation staff nutritionists and not cooks.

Karin had packed an overnight bag, because "I don't know when I'm going to get back there."

"What about work?"

"I had some vacation time, so I took it." She ran the back of her hand across my cheek. "You know, we need to find some place safe to sleep, " she said.

I knew that. I just had other things on my mind lately, I told her.

That's when she brought up the cottage. The one where her parents had that fatal fight. It was still in the family. She went there now and then. Always, in the back of her mind, she thought she might run into her father. So far that hadn't happened. The old guy who took care of the place said he hadn't seen him in years.

She shrugged. It was one of those things you never really get over. "Kind of like Jon and Jessie," she said.

Interesting leap, I thought. But she had just read Jon's letter, and seen the documents, including the annotated article. Maybe, too, it was the reference to the cottage, which carried its own sense of loss.

She'd grown silent, and somber again after mentioning Jon, so I said, "You were saying something about a cottage?"

"What? Oh, yeah." She looked brightly into my eyes. "I thought maybe we could go there for a bit, while you recuperate."

It seemed as good an idea as any. Neither of us felt safe in our respective homes, and staying together in either wasn't an option since I wasn't in any kind of shape to protect her. It wasn't a long term solution, but until I got back on my feet? Why not? I said as much to her and she went outside to call the handyman.

While she was gone the neurologist finally arrived. He put me through the paces, then they wheeled me off for an MRI. Later, after my reunion with Karin, and a more successful stab at interrogation from Mike, the doctor returned to say I'd be okay. "Close call, though. I've seen permanent brain damage from lighter blows than the one you suffered. It's amazing he didn't fracture your skull."

"I've got a hard-headed man," Karin observed.

"Sounds like a blues song," I quipped.

The doctor laughed and said, "I see you still have your sense of humor."

"Actually, I never had one before. I was always dead serious."

He cheerfully ignored that, and told me, "You'll be fine. Just no heavy lifting or hard exercise for a few days." Then he wrote me a prescription for the headaches, and said I could get out of there as soon as they finished processing my release papers.

Karin surprised me by pulling a new shirt and some jeans out of her bag. "I stopped at The Gap while I was out," she explained. Then she reached into her purse and presented me with my very own cell phone. "It's just a basic flip phone," she said. "But I didn't know if you were ready for a real high tech one."

"I really wanted a boysenberry," I pouted.

"It's Blackberry."

"Whatever." I started tapping the screen with my fingertips. "Nothing's happening."

"It doesn't have a touch screen. You have to—" she stopped and looked at me. "Are you for real?"

"In the commercials people just—" I tried to keep it going, but couldn't do it. I started laughing, but quickly stopped when my head started pulsing again. I just lay there while Karin ran down to fill the prescription.

I lay still, breathing shallowly, trying to ignore the pressure and avoid going off on another rant. I thought back to Mike's questioning, about how he did the good buddy thing so convincingly, and the good cop thing with consummate skill.

He started with the basics. Did I see who did it? Did I have any idea who it might be?

I tossed out Howard's name, simply because he was big enough. "Hell, he didn't even need a weapon to put me in a coma." But that didn't make sense, I added. "Howard works for my client."

Mike scowled when I said that. "I told you to stay away from him."

"Well, you know how it goes. A client—"

"Is a client," he finished for me. "Yeah, yeah. If not Howard, who else?"

When I suggested maybe it was the guy who tried to kill me out at Ruggles Creek Park, Karin let out a gasp. Oh, right, she didn't know about that one. "It's okay, babe. I'll tell you about it later."

"Aw, what a sweet couple." Mike's sarcasm was tempered by what seemed to be genuine affection.

"It could've been AT&T," I said. "I've been behind, you know."

"Doesn't sound like the MO of a major corporation."

"Oh, really?"

Mike shook his head. "No, they'd of used a sniper."

We all got quiet on that one. Then Mike got back to work.

"Know what they were looking for?"

I shrugged.

"Something in your safe?"

"Safe still closed, then?"

"Was the last time I was there."

"And when was that?"

"Just before I came over here."

"What were you doing at my office?" I asked, struggling to sit up.

"My job."

"Your job? What are you doing handling a robbery? You're homicide."

"Like you said, you almost died. Plus, you're my friend. I didn't want it treated as just another Detroit B & E. Guys on robbery get a little jaded you know. They go over, dust for prints, do a quick survey for witnesses, then punt it to the back of the file cabinet." Mike raised his hands in a gesture of supplication. "I'm not actually working the case, just making sure it gets worked."

Okay, I'd give him that one, though it was equally plausible that he was over there to finish the job, to find whatever it was whoever it was who hit me was looking for. "Well, thanks, then," I said.

"So, the question remains. What was he looking for?"

I shrugged again. "Hell if I know. I figure it's got to do with the case. Can't imagine it was Herman Gallup."

"Herman Gallup?"

I said it was a divorce case I'd just worked. Then I was struck by the obvious. It was what Karin had said, "Oh no, they got you too."

"Must be the same ones that hit Karin's place."

"But I thought you said they already got the box."

Did I? I scrolled back through the past couple of days. I told Williams, that I remember. Or did I? Was it Mike I told? I was pretty sure I told somebody, but had no memory of who it was. Maybe it didn't matter. Maybe they were working together, or one was working for the other. Or Williams had a leak. Maybe it was Howard who hit me. That would explain Mike's involvement in the case. Not to protect my interests, but to make sure Howard's name stayed out of it. How many angles was Mike working?

"Jim? Jim, are you all right?" Karin's voice sounded distantly.

Then again, there were huge gaps in my memory. Maybe my telling Mike was one of the things that had fallen through.

"Jim?" Her voice was closer now, and sounding nervous.

"I'm right here, honey," I said, taking her hand. To Mike I added, "Where were we? The box? When did I tell you about the box?"

"At the Walloon. Just before sweetie pie here knocked you out."

"I did no such thing," Karin replied in high dudgeon. Oh, she was a keeper. She blushed. She did both aghast and demure, and now she aced high dudgeon. Mike howled, and I had to laugh, too.

Then Mike resumed his speculation. "Can't see it being the same perp, though. If they had the box, why come after you? Must've been somebody else."

"Unless what they wanted wasn't in the box."

"So that means you have it?" Mike jumped on that one, like a Congressman on a bribe. "Did they get it?"

"Mike, I swear I don't know what they're looking for, so even if I knew what they took, I wouldn't know what it was." Then a thought stumbled through the door. I asked Karin, "When you went back to your place, how'd it look?"

"Awful," she replied. "But no worse than before."

"You really ought to have an escort whenever you go back home," Mike said, reaching for his cell. "I'll call the Eastpointe Chief. He and I go back."

After he finished I asked, "What about me? I need to inventory my office once I get out of here. Can you lend me a uniform?"

"What about me?"

Yeah, what about him? Best way to find what's missing, be there when I figure it out. But, what the hell. "Why not?" I said.

It was after six when they finally wheeled me out of

there. I signed the papers which stated they could have my car, my cell phone, and my new Gap jeans if I couldn't scrape up the cash to cover whatever was left over after my scrawny insurance bit the dust. Then I called Mike and told him we were rolling.

He showed up and shadowed me around the office. I quickly sifted through the scattered papers. To tell the truth, there wasn't that much there. Not a lot to document the past ten years. I'd lived, and almost died, more in the last week than I had in the last decade.

"You figure out what's missing?"

"Yeah, a good part of my life."

Karin slipped her arm around my waist. "Don't try to do too much," she cautioned.

I said I wouldn't, just pick up a bit, then pack. She said she could do that for me, and passed through the door into my apartment.

Mike asked where we were going.

"Just away for a couple days, let me rest up. Maybe things will settle down while we're gone."

"Where?"

"Karin's got—" Was this such a good idea? "Karin's got a conference in Indianapolis. She thought I should come along, chill in the hotel." Not bad, I thought. Pretty quick on my feet for a guy with a concussion. The skepticism on Mike's face put paid to that burst of self-congratulation.

"Don't do this, Jim," he said softly enough that Karin couldn't hear.

"Don't do what?"

"Don't shut me out. I'm on your side. I'm your friend." His gesture took in the office, my apartment, hell, the entire city. "I may be the only one on your side."

"I'll just check out the safe," I said, not exactly in reply, but on one level, exactly in reply. Mike followed me over, and when I swung it open, said, "It's empty."

"Damn," I muttered.

"What'd they get?" He was locked onto it like a pit bull on a gas meter reader.

"Nothing. I was hoping maybe they'd put a little cash in there."

His lips curled up in a rueful grin. "You little shit."

It felt good, getting him back, suckering him in. For a second there, it felt like old times. I wanted to let him back in, but I told myself, no. That bond was broken. It couldn't, it wouldn't be repaired.

But I had to give him something. "They did come back, though. Must have brought a safe cracker this time."

"What'd they get?"

"All I had in here were some tax documents, and the file from Sara's case—" I glanced at him. "You don't think—"

Mike frowned. "What would Sara have to do with—"

"If the two cases are connected."

"You think Jon's death had something to do with Sara?" Mike's skepticism was eloquent.

"Not Sara," I corrected him. "With Olly Jensen." Now here I was straying perilously close to letting him know what I thought was going on.

Mike's laughter drew Karin from the bedroom. "You sound like a guy with brain damage." Another burst. "Oh, that's right, you are."

Naturally, Mike discounted my idea. "Olly's dropped off the face of the earth," he reminded me. "Whether he was who you said he was is immaterial. He's ancient history. Just let it go."

I almost blurted out Carmine's revelation that Olly was back in play, but remembered in time to keep my trap shut. As it was, mentioning him was a nice piece of misdirection. I'd leave it at that. "Maybe you're right, " I conceded. "This case has pulled me inside out."

Spotting the flashing light on my answering machine, and knowing I didn't want to listen to any messages in front of Mike, I suggested he escort Karin to her car. "I'll be right behind you."

The first two were a telemarketer and a collection agency. Maybe someday I'd get around to writing some checks. Prompted by that thought, I grabbed my checkbook and a stack of bills from the drawer. I had a nice little cubby hole in there for them, where they could languish, or breed, or whatever unpaid bills did, without spoiling my view of an otherwise spotless desk.

Next call was from Williams, which was the one I didn't want Mike to hear. As it turned out, it didn't matter. "Mr. Corcoran," he began, as courtly as ever. "I heard you had an unfortunate accident." Unfortunate. That's a nice turn of phrase. I wondered who he heard it from. Howard? Did he happen to check his knuckles?

Williams put on a show of being a good employer, solicitous of my well being, and urging me to give him a call when I was ready to get "back into the fray." Back into the fray. Don't you just love it? Then he added, "You might want to give me a call anyway. I've unearthed something which may be of interest."

Wondering what that might be, I absently punched the play button for the last message, and got punched back from an unexpected source. "Jim," she began, and after a long pause, concluded flatly, "It's Deb. Call me. We need to talk."

CHAPTER 15

It was after eight by the time we hit the Interstate, too late to go the distance. But we could at least get outside Metro Detroit, maybe find a motel near Lansing.

I suggested a Holiday Inn Express. "Who knows, maybe it'll make me smart enough to figure out this case."

She smiled, then accelerated around a slow-moving RV, a big one, the one like a bus, with a Jeep in tow. Did you ever notice, anytime you see one of those monstrosities, it's almost always towing a Jeep, either a Liberty or Wrangler?

"Pretty late in the season for one of those," I remarked. "Usually they're in deep hibernation by November."

"Going the wrong direction, too, " she mused.

I laughed. She was right. It should be heading south, to Florida or Arizona. "Contrarian retirees," I said. "A new breed."

Karin asked how I was feeling. "Okay. A little tired, and always afraid the headache will come back."

"It's been awhile, hasn't it."

A WHILE

"Not since the last one at the hospital."

"Why don't you try to sleep? I'll wake you when we get to the motel." She said the last bit with a healthy grin.

"You sure you don't want me to keep you company?"

She assured me that she was fine, but she'd wake me if she got drowsy.

I offered to go over the case with her, maybe talk about what she'd read. No, emphatically no, she didn't want to do that. Not while focusing on the road. She wanted to look in my eyes for that. She wanted me to hold her for that.

The miles drifted past, and I drifted away, and when she woke me up it was after ten. She'd already checked us in, and she helped me to the room, left me lying on the bed, and went back for our things.

Then it was morning and I was lying still dressed on the bed, with my arms around her. She woke slowly, dreamily, while I watched. Her eyelids fluttered on the edge of opening, as if reluctant to surrender slumber.

Then they popped open. And she laughed. When she'd returned back with the bags, I was completely out, she explained. " I just lay down for a moment. Guess I was more tired than I thought."

I said I was starving. She wasn't surprised. I'd only had one meal in the past, what, sixty hours?

"Yeah, I've probably lost ten pounds. Hey, maybe I can market this. Dr. Corcoran's Bat to the Head Diet."

"How about Dr. Corcoran's Concussion Diet?"

"Dr. Corcoran's Broken Head Diet?"

I won, or she got tired of the game. They'd taken all the old bandages off at the hospital, so I suggested a shower. When I pulled off my shirt I announced I was good as new.

"When was the last time you looked in a mirror?" she wondered.

"That bad?" She didn't say anything, so I checked for myself. Black eyes were back. Raccoon redux, and there was a massive, livid bruise on my forehead. All in all, not too bad. Another glance, and I realized if I hadn't heard the footstep, if I hadn't started to turn, that bat would have hit the side of my head, and I wouldn't be there looking at a battered man looking back at me, drunk on the wine of astonishment.

She slid in behind me, slipped her arms around my chest, and rested her head against my shoulder. "It was a close one, wasn't it," she murmured.

"Closest ever," I mustered.

She got the shower running while I finished undressing, then we stepped beneath the spray. We soaped each other, until I responded. Then I was sitting in the tub, holding my head in my hands. That was clinical proof. Arousal counts as exertion. Or heavy lifting, I suppose you could say.

Though the pain had chased all thoughts of food from my head, Karin insisted I eat. So I popped a couple pills, to keep the barbarians at bay. The motel's "free continental breakfast" offered the usual stale Danishes, liver-spotted bananas and dishwater coffee. Undeterred, I managed to wash a couple pastries down my gullet with the ersatz brew, scalding my tongue in the process.

With my headache in remission, and some food on my stomach, I discovered a resolve for something more substantial. Prospects were slim on the highway, which featured the usual fast food suspects loitering around every other Interstate exit. Fortunately, the desk clerk commuted each day from a hamlet called Pettigrew, just eight miles away, where, he said, the best breakfast in the world could be had at Karla's Kitchen.

Karla's Kitchen was everything the clerk had promised. The food was fresh, the portions ample, and between us, we consumed six eggs, four rashers of bacon, three orders of hash browns, a short stack of pancakes, and one biscuit with sausage gravy. Karin mentioned, in self defense, that she hadn't eaten much either the last couple of days.

The others customers ate as much as we did. They sported baseball caps emblazoned with the names of tractor or feed companies. They all joshed with the waitress and ribbed each other, while sprinkling their conversation with inside-baseball farming lingo. For just a little while, all was right with the world.

Then it was back to the road, with Karin behind the wheel and me playing the role of an eight-year-old. Alternately sleeping and whining, and asking how much longer we had to go, I was a miserable companion, but the headaches were becoming both more painful and more frequent.

Karin was worried, but I told her, between grimaces, that it must have to do with the motion of the car, or that biscuit and gravy had been a side too far.

We reached the cottage late that afternoon. Nestled at the base of a grass-shrouded dune, closeted by giant maples and pines, it gazed upon a small, placid lake. "Lake Michigan is just over the dunes," Karin told me. See p. 239 "But we can follow the lake shore south, where the dunes dip down. Sometimes there's a stream connecting the two lakes, other times it's walled off by sand."

It grew dark early, and was much colder than in Detroit. Before long the caretaker rolled up in his ancient, rusted Chevy pickup, and unloaded a stack of firewood. "Thought you might want this. S'posed to blow tonight."

"Blow?"

"A big storms's coming," Karin translated. "Early November's when the biggest gales hit the Great Lakes." She hugged herself, wrapped in snug denims and an oversized wool sweater. "I love it when there's big weather."

"You got a good place here," the old fellow allowed. "Good shelter," he added, nodding at the dune. "If it don't bury ya."

"Hasn't yet, Mr. Petersen," Karin chirped.

Then Petersen noticed me for the first time. "Ut happen to you?"

"Car accident," I replied. <u>What the hell</u>, if you can't lie to a stranger, what's the use of living?

Petersen was kind enough to lay and light a fire, "since your fella don't look so handy." What is it that makes people think it's perfectly okay to mock me from the moment they meet me? That's what I'd like to know.

After getting Karin's assurance that we were well-provisioned, the old caretaker took his leave.

"Your fella don't look so handy," I scoffed.

Karin replied that all I'd done so far is sleep and whine and complain and sleep some more. "Who had to do the grocery shopping? Me. Who's going to have to make us dinner? Me. Who'll probably have to carry you to bed?"

I looked around the sparsely furnished log cabin. "You?" I ventured.

She grinned and came into my arms. "I love you," she said, this time more forcefully.

"I love you, too." My voice was gruff, almost breaking as if I'd had to force the words out.

She frowned and eased away. "Don't say it if you don't mean it."

I swore I meant it. did. "It's just, it's been so long since I said it. So long since I thought I ever could again, or ever would. But Karin, believe me, I do. I love you."

Loved, she eased me into a chair, adding, archly I thought, perhaps even gratuitously, "Just call me if the fire needs tending." Then she laughed and danced out of the way as I tried to give her a swat. She disappeared into the kitchen, leaving me to look around the spacious room. It had a vaulted ceiling, with exposed rafters hewn from the same logs, by the looks of them, as those framing the walls. There were two bedrooms off the living room, and a loft reached by a ladder. It consisted of branches lashed together, and didn't look too sturdy. I hoped we were sleeping downstairs.

The wind picked up while I gazed at the fire. I could hear it howling over the crackling of the logs. Soon, rain began lashing the windows. If this is sheltered, I thought, I'd hate to be out in the open. I mentioned that to Karin when she called me to the table. It was simple, hearty fare, as befits a northwoods supper.

"It is terrifying," she agreed. "But awesome, too. To feel the power of the wind, and to see the huge waves crashing against the shore, there's nothing like it. I love it."

I wished I could go see it with her, but we agreed it was too risky, too soon. Though I was feeling better. I felt strong, well, stronger. Almost human. So much so that I helped Karin with the dishes.

Then we retreated to the sofa. We snuggled in front of the fire. In time, as the temperature outside continued to plummet, she hauled a big old comforter in from the bedroom. We snuggled beneath it, until it grew too warm. Shedding clothing, we soon were more than snuggling beneath that big old comforter. I was definitely feeling better, we discovered, as arousal no longer equated with exertion.

The comforter fell away, its task accomplished. I lay back and watched the firelight flickering on Karin's naked body. She did the bulk of the work, so it was only fair she derived the bulk of the pleasure. My excitement, my passion, my sheer joy at this union, was tempered by fear that my head would implode again. That distraction resulted in far greater endurance than I was accustomed to. For awhile I was starting to feel like a cautionary tale from a Cialis ad. Karin had no complaints as she rode me home, though I hoped she would remember that past performance is no guarantee of future results.

Eventually the sight and feel of her body, and the enveloping sensation of her pleasure propulsed me into a state of disregard. I plunged into a chasm of passion, free falling into the neverending depths of this woman. No fear of pain now, only a rising, roaring, raging desire to fulfill her unstinting demands.

I did, finally, and we collapsed together on the sofa. I reached down and drew the comforter back over ~~our bodies,~~ and we lay together, savoring the contact of our slickened bodies.

After a few minutes I put another log on the fire. The wind whistled and howled as it swept across the dunes and swirled through the branches of the trees. While heavy raindrops drummed on the roof overhead, and shattered against the window panes, Karin lulled me to sleep with bedtime stories about shipwrecks on the lake.

There was no sun when we awoke, and no lessening of the storm. There was a good reason they called them blows, I decided. Karin said sometimes the storms would last for several days. "It's because of the residual warmth in the lakes. When the winds shift out of the northeast, as they do this time of year, they pick up so much energy crossing the water that they just howl. Later in the season, when it gets even colder, the same principle produces heavy Lake Effect Snows along the shoreline."

She continued at some length, explaining how Buffalo, New York, at the eastern end of Lake Erie, often felt the most extreme impact of the Lake Effect. "It's not unusual for them to get five feet of snow in a single day."

"I never knew you were such a meteorologist."

She smirked. "Just call me your Weather Girl." She jumped up and started moving her hands around in front of an imaginary screen.

"Yeah, I can see you on The Weather Channel, saying, 'Richmond, Virginia, you've got upper air turbulence, which means severe thunderstorm warnings for the next three hours.'" I gave it a beat while giving her the eye. "Though maybe not in that outfit."

We hadn't quite managed to make the transition back to wearing clothes yet, and the way she reacted, I thought it might still be awhile before we did. She proceeded to create her own upper air turbulence, complicated by a warm front rising from the south, which produced a high pressure zone. Somewhere in China a butterfly flapped its wings, and the ensuing storm shredded the sheets.

But even the greatest chaos reaches an end. Showered, dressed and breakfasted, we finally settled down to the business of interpreting Jon's affidavit. That was the only way to describe it. Jon's letter was a sort of Forensic Accounting for Dummies. He told me what to look for on each document, which he'd labeled alpha-numerically. It was a complex system, with various letters denoting categories, and then each document numbered consecutively in its category.

Now, I know I'm not the brightest guy, probably in the same class as your average Congressman, without the deep-seated greed, that is. But I was having a little trouble following all the directions. Karin suggested we sort the documents by category, and put them in order, which took about an hour. After that, things went better. Still, it seemed like there were whole chunks of evidence missing. A strange omission considering his detailed annotations.

He drew a picture of cash flows in, and cash flows back out, and a whole slew of money-losing convenience stores and gas stations throughout Metropolitan Detroit. Justin must have had an army of accountants to keep it all straight.

Which gave me pause. How could Williams not know about this? When I broached the subject with Karin, she said, "Maybe he was feeding the information to Jon?"

"Maybe, but if he was on the inside, why did Jon need Jeffries? Why'd they have to go around hacking into data banks if Williams was giving them the goods?"

"What if he was just giving them hints, and making them figure it out on their own?"

"Why would he do that?" I wondered.

"To protect himself. What was that phrase he used?

Plausible deniability?" Gotta hand it to Karin. She was sharp. "Besides, isn't there something called attorney-client privilege?"

"That's true. And Williams has a good thing going with Fleigher, Kermit, and Schneid. If word got out that he violated confidentiality, not only would he lose his job, he'd get disbarred."

Karin looked at me. "Doesn't that seem wrong somehow? If by doing the right thing you somehow violate a code of ethics?" She pouted. Karin was a study in complexity. A strong woman, and smart, yet able to play the classic, perhaps sadly passe role of utter femininity. She would have been perfect as an on-screen foil for Humphrey Bogart. She was an enigma. She was fascinating. I looked forward to spending a long time unwrapping the layers which comprised her.

Jon said it all started with Butler Woods. Which means it all started with Olly Jensen. It gave new meaning to the "The Wall Street Journal" reference to offshore financing. Jon seemed to suggest that it had been Justin's first step on the wild side. But why? That was what continued to mystify me, the part that made me think Jon had made the whole thing up.

Justin was one of the leading men in town. He came from wealth, and he used his privileged perch as a springboard to create more wealth, both for himself, and for his clients at Wade Investments.

He had a glamorous wife, as I well knew, two photogenic children, and a future limited only by the scope of his ambitions. The papers, not just the local rag, but "The Detroit News" as well, published glowing accounts of his achievements, of sightings of him at local restaurants, at charitable benefits and at the ceremonies where he claimed yet another Man-of-the-Year Award.

The only person on earth who didn't love him was me. And I hated him. Okay, maybe Jon did too, but his vote didn't count any more. His citizenship had lapsed. Of course, if the rumors were true, it was possible Deb had decided to vote her late brother-in-law's proxy.

Still, the animosities of three little people didn't amount to a hill of beans compared to the problems I hoped to heap upon Justin Wade's head. But the heaping depended on the why, and that was the brick wall I kept butting my head against.

"I just don't get it," I complained. "I mean, he had everything. Why would he start laundering drug money?"

"Maybe he wanted more," Karin speculated. "It happens, you know. We even have a name for it, The Midas Syndrome."

"But that's the thing. He was getting more. Wade Investments was a gold mine. He had a name, connections, and a performance record that was off the charts." I thumbed through a stack of documents until I found the prospectus. "Look at these numbers. Nobody was getting returns like that, and he'd been doing it for years."

She shrugged. "I don't know, Jim. Yes, it's a mystery to me, too. Are you saying Jon made this up?"

I didn't want to give that question the time of day. My doubts were legitimate, but Karin was exhibiting signs of resistance. That whole don't speak ill of the dead thing is doubly significant when the recipient of the news had once spread her legs for the deceased. The significance ramps up exponentially when the speaker is entertaining thoughts of her spreading them for him again at bedtime, if not before.

"I wouldn't say I doubt him," I temporized. "But there's something missing. It's that old motive thing. Opportunity, means and motive. And in this case his means obviate his motive."

"Maybe his means weren't all they were supposed to be."

"What are you talking about?" I demanded. I don't know, maybe the frustration was getting the better of me. "I knew him, remember? I was part of that world. His means were exactly what they were."

"But you left a long time ago," she reminded me. "Things change in time."

Such wisdom. It took my breath away. I started pawing through the piles. "Maybe we've been going at this from the wrong direction. Instead of working backwards, maybe we should start at the beginning."

"Works for me," she said brightly. "What exactly are we looking for?"

"Jon said it started with Butler Woods, so let's find anything that relates to that."

Another hour of work, interspersed with lunch, and frequent rests for me as I discovered brain work was more fatiguing than physical labor. "Post-Concussion Syndrome," Karin reminded me when I went for a lie down. "But at least the headaches have stopped, haven't they?" She propped herself up on an elbow next to me, because of course it would be wrong to expect her to slog away on her own while I was shirking duty.

"No, the headaches are gone," I agreed. "Guess that means I'm cleared for heavy lifting."

"We'll see about that," she chuckled, and set about testing the theory. So, after another longish interlude, we returned to our task. The light was lowering, and the wind hadn't let up. Though the rain was intermittent, we hadn't seen a hint of sunlight all day.

In the end, all we had were the effects of Butler Woods. Tax statements, cash flows, sales documents, but nothing to do with the origin and funding of the project.

"Why wouldn't Jon have included that?" Karin complained. "It doesn't make sense. If we're right, that's the whole basis for his case."

'Unless he didn't have it any more," I said eagerly, insight suddenly dawning. I went back to his cover letter, and his reference to the box he'd left with her, that had additional documentation that I'd need. I told her about the notebook devoted to Butler Woods. "I didn't get all the way through it, but that could be the smoking gun."

"Then it's gone," she said. "That box was what they were looking for."

"Not necessarily," I countered. "I took that notebook, and a couple other ones, with me."

"You stole them?" she said, aghast. There it is again. Lovely word. "From me?"

"No, not from you," I explained patiently. "You'd given me the box to work through. I assumed I could take anything in there that pertained to the case."

"And you thought they did?"

"Not at the time. Or yes, but in a completely different direction."

She just stared at me.

"It was the reference to Olly being one of the backers."

"And you thought it might have something to do with Sara," she concluded. "It wasn't about the case at all, was it?"

I insisted it was.

"You wanted to wallow in self-pity again."

I couldn't blame her for being upset, though in all honesty I thought her tone left a lot to be desired. Still, it's got to be hard competing with another woman, especially if the other woman's dead. Two other women, I mused, thinking how I'd come to her through Deb, which made me the second man she'd had to share with her. Under the circumstances, bitterness was justified.

I told her she was right, in a way. "But I'm not the same man I was back then." I let out a laugh. "Hard to believe it's only a little more than a week. It seems a lifetime ago." I gave up. I waved the white flag. "Yeah, it was about Sara," I admitted. "I took the notebook because I thought maybe there were answers there. I guess I was lying to myself when I said she was ancient history. I guess she was more than just an unsolved mystery." I shrugged. "I honestly thought I'd moved on."

"But you hadn't, had you." Sometimes it's good when your lover is a shrink.

I shook my head. "I guess not. The thing is, though, I didn't dwell on her."

"By refusing to do your job?" Or maybe not so good.

"Oh, I did my job."

'But you weren't very good at it, were you."

Hard to argue with that one. "Yeah, okay. Maybe you're right."

She gave me one of those looks they probably offer entire courses on in the psych program.

"All right. You're definitely right." I surrendered with a grin. "But here's the thing. After years of consciously not thinking of Sara, of not dwelling on her, that notebook wasn't the first time the two cases started overlapping."

She just sat there waiting. Not for the first time I thought how much analysts and detectives have in common.

"It was the first time I met you."

"Met me?"

"Yeah. It was something about you, the way you just assumed you were in the case, driving me out to Jon's condo. No, even before. I wanted you from the very beginning, just like Sara. Not that I expected anything to happen with her, but that's how it played out. To be honest, I didn't exactly put up a fight. As soon as I figured out the feeling was mutual, I didn't waste a lot of time worrying about standards of conduct."

She scooted over next to me, and gently caressed my cheek. "You know, if a woman came to me about a relationship with a guy like you, I'd tell her to let it go. There's too much emotional baggage."

Fair enough. Don't know what I'd do in her shoes. Probably should've kept those thoughts to myself. I couldn't really blame her if this was the start of the long goodbye. It'd make for a couple more uncomfortable days in the cabin, or a long, miserable drive home through the deluge outside. But what the hell, at least I'd gotten laid, and it had been awhile. Still, I wasn't just going to roll over.

"So what do you say now? Now that it's you?"

She gave a lusty grin. "I want to get naked again."

She came into my arms, and nestled against me. We kissed, a long, turf-building kiss. "Getting naked is tempting," I said. "But we've got to work through this." I gestured at the stacks of documents. "Besides, I don't know that I'm fully recharged. I'm not seventeen any more."

"Well, okay. If that's the way you want to play it."

She laughed, and gave me a kiss. Then she got back down to business. "You said you took a couple other notebooks?"

I told her about the one Jon had kept on me, starting with Sara's death. "At the time it was just so bizarre, but now, I'm thinking it all ties in together."

Karin shifted to her knees. She took my hands in hers, and gazed deeply into my eyes. "Please tell me you're over her. Look into my eyes and tell me."

I could do that. It was easy. Karin had exorcized so many demons. Not just Sara, not just the last decade, but Deb, too. "I'd be lying if I said I don't want to find her killer. That's still unfinished business, and professional pride demands it. But I swear to you, other than that, I'm finished with her. I would have said the same thing a week ago, but I would have been lying." I gave her hand a squeeze. "Almost from the first this case started pointing at her. At first, I didn't want to follow, because, to be honest? I didn't trust my instincts. I accused myself of the very thing you want me to convince you isn't true. That I was fabricating the connections, that I was seeing lines between you and her because I wanted to. Mike's been doing it, too. Telling me I'm crazy, that A is A and B is B, that they're totally unrelated."

I sighed, then plunged on ahead. "Now, if I'm following Sara, it's not because I want to, it's because I have to. I mean, there has to be a reason, hasn't there, that Jon put her photo in the envelope? That it wasn't just, as he put it, to get my attention."

"What photo?"

"Oh, that's right. I took it out." I got up, relaid the fire, and lit it. One match. Take that, Mr. Petersen.

"It was the death scene photo. Don't know how Jon got a hold of it, but you didn't need to see that."

Karin nodded. "So where do we go from here?" she wondered.

"I guess when we get back, I'll work my way through those notebooks, see if we can make a case. Then I'll—" I was going to say I'd turn everything over to Williams, but I couldn't be sure. What if Mike was telling the truth? What if Williams was in the middle of this? "Maybe I'll turn it over to the DA, see if Carmine's serious this time. Or I could give it to Stewart Cooper, let him win another Pulitzer in The Detroit News."

"If there's anything there."

"Exactly. I mean, Jon kept the other notebooks from the age of five. I have no way of knowing if these are any different."

Karin wanted to know more about them, so I gave her a run down. "He even made one about Jessie's death."

She started. "What did it say?"

"I don't know, exactly. I didn't get all the way through it. The poem kind of threw me for a loop."

"What poem?"

As I recited a loose paraphrase, her face turned grim. "Was there a cassette tape in the notebook?"

"I don't think so. Like I said, I didn't go through the whole thing, but a tape's kind of hard to miss. Why?"

"Something Jon said in his note—" She got the look on my face. "Oh, you don't know."

"Know what?"

"There was another note, at the end. About Jessie."

I started to paw through all the documents. "Where is it? I don't remember seeing it."

"It's not here."

"Why not?"

"I—I took it out."

"Why would you do that?"

"I don't know. I was upset, I—"

"So where it is? Back at your apartment?"

She shook her head. "No. I put it in the mail. To Deborah Wade."

I sat back, stunned. "Why would you do that?" I repeated.

"I don't know. I was so angry. I just wanted her to know."

"You wanted her to know, but not me." I didn't really try to conceal the disgust in my voice. This was a massive act of betrayal. It was hard to fathom.

"I didn't know you didn't know," she protested. "I wasn't trying to conceal anything."

Well, she wouldn't know, would she. I told her to take the envelope, said it had all the answers. I didn't say I hadn't read it all the way through.

"So what did the letter say?"

She recited woodenly, whether because of the contents or from a belated recognition of her blunder, I couldn't say. "He wrote, 'Can you imagine what it's like to go through life with your sister's blood on your hands?'"

"So the rumors were true? Jon did kill her?"

"Let me finish," Karin snapped. "I don't remember it word for word, but I can give you the gist of it." She sighed deeply, as if preparing to perform some onerous task. "Imagine what it would be like to have a brother who never let you forget it. Imagine a lifetime of him threatening to tell. Now imagine a boy who has absolutely no memory of this ever happening, who has no memory of that day whatsoever.

"The only memory I ever had, for most of my life, was the one Justin put in my head. He told me I drowned her. He told me I got mad at her that day, and I pushed her off the diving raft, and I jumped in and held her down. Justin said he thought we were just playing at first, but by the time he realized what had happened, it was too late. She was gone. He said I swam to shore, went into the woods, and just curled up in a ball. He made up the story of me going for help to cover for me. And he's been doing it ever since. That's what he always told me."

I grabbed the *Detroit News* article. "That's what all these notes mean, then."

"Hold on, it gets better. Jon said he always felt, deep inside, that the story wasn't true. He couldn't imagine wanting to ever hurt Jessie. They'd always been so close. It was always Jon protecting Jessie. Justin was a bully, a real tyrant. He was terrifying, but their parents always took his side. In their eyes he could do no wrong."

She stared soberly into my eyes. "That 'Big Hurt' as you called it? I had it pegged. Jon wrote that after he started seeing me, he really started trying to focus. He focused on what felt wrong about that day, or Justin's version of it. He said it was hard, at first, to see clearly through the haze of drugs and alcohol that shrouded the best part of three decades, but after he got clean, after he detoxed, he started making out images. And they weren't the ones Justin had always painted."

Karin wore the saddest expression.

"You thinking about him?"

She nodded, eyes brimming. "It's just so sad to think about the burden he carried for all those years. Justin really was a monster."

"You mean it was Justin?"

"That's what Jon wrote. He said one day it came to him like a vision, how he came upon Jessie down by the lake. She was crying. At first she wouldn't talk about it, but he insisted. At last she relented. She said Justin was doing things to her. 'Down there,' she said."

"Some sick loving," I said softly. From Jon's poem.

"They were both too young to really understand," Karin continued. "But they knew instinctively it was wrong. Jon said they had to tell Mommy and Daddy. She was reluctant at first, saying they wouldn't believe them, as usual, but Jon finally got her to agree. That night, as soon as they returned.

"Then Justin popped out of the woods. The hearty, fun-loving Justin, who challenged them to a race to the raft. Justin must have been listening. He must have figured his parents wouldn't be able to ignore that accusation. So he decided he had to act.

"Even though Jessie was the youngest, she was the best swimmer. Only this time, every time she got an advantage, Justin would grab her ankle and dunk her. When Jon tried to stop him, he got a dunking of his own. Justin was laughing the whole time, as if they were all having the time of their lives. Jessie took advantage of the boys' struggles to put some distance between them, but he caught up as she was climbing the ladder."

Karin stopped to dab at her eyes. I offered my arms, but she shook her head. I got it. She had to do this one on her own. This was her doing penance for professional failure. Yeah, like she said, she'd pegged it. But she couldn't finish the job. She couldn't draw it out of him. Jon had to do that on his own. No doubt she figured Jon had died because she didn't do her job. And she might have been right.

"So what happened?" I prompted. "At the ladder."

She smiled. A sad one. One consumed with regret. Well, I knew a little bit about that kind of smile myself. Then she sucked it up, and went on. Because that's what you do, you go right on to the end.

"Justin pulled her off the ladder. She screamed just before he pushed her under. And, Jon wrote, that's where things got hazy again. He thought he had a memory of swimming away, back to shore. He didn't like that thought, because it was so wrong. It's probably true, though, otherwise Jessie would still be alive, or he would be dead, too."

She broke off with a choking sob. "Which he is," she squeaked.

"And he carried that memory with him for the rest of his life."

She shook her head furiously, and fought through the flood of emotion. "No. This is where it gets interesting. He said it was actually worse once he realized what had happened. It's one thing to go through life thinking you murdered your sister. It's even worse to go through life knowing your sister died because you are a coward."

"When he had worked out that Justin was laundering drug money, he arranged to confront him at Williams' house."

"Oh, very interesting. So that proves Williams was working with Jon."

"We don't know that."

"But if he set up the meeting?"

"Jon told Williams he was leaving town. He was heading up to Alaska, had lined up a job working on a fishing boat. Why would he make up a story if he and Williams were on the same side?"

I had to give her that one. Which was a pity. It would be nice if the good guys still wore white hats.

"He told Williams he wanted to ask Justin to bail him out one last time. Give him enough money, and he'd clear out. Justin would never hear from him again."

"And Justin bought that?"

"Williams did, at least. Jon told him to get Justin there, he'd do the rest. So Justin shows up, Williams heads out, and they get started. Jon wrote that he intended to confront his brother with what he'd uncovered, that he was going to tape the conversation. The only problem was, when he saw Justin with that smug look on his face, he just lost it. He threw out his script and called Justin a murderer. He just blurted out his recovered memory."

"And?"

"Justin, as cold as ice, said, 'So you finally figured it out.'"

"He admitted it?"

"More than admit it. He bragged about it. He was proud he'd gotten away with it, prouder still that he'd convinced Jon that he'd done it. He said the only truth in the story had been finding Jon curled up in the woods. 'You were always so weak,' he sneered. 'It was the perfect murder.'"

"If Jon believed he'd killed her, Justin owned him. If he confessed, case closed."

"And if he accused Justin, who'd believe him? He really is a monster."

"And you sent all that to Deb?"

She nodded. "I really regret it now. It was such a stupid, childish thing to do." This time she accepted my arms, and let me hold her awhile.

"You know, she called me," I said once she regained her composure. "Said we needed to talk."

"When was this?"

"Must've been while I was in the hospital. It was the last message on my machine."

"Are you going to?"

I nodded. "I was going to give her a call, but now I think it should be face to face."

"What if she asks you for the tape?"

"We don't know where the tape is."

"The letter said he'd put it somewhere safe. He said it was his get out of jail free card. As long as it was out there, Justin couldn't touch him."

"But Justin would have to know about the tape," I pointed out.

"Well, obviously, he did."

"Then it didn't work, did it?"

That one stumped us for awhile. Karin went and rummaged up some cheese and crackers, and a nice Chateau Fontaine Pinot Blanc. We ate them on the couch while the fire crackled and the storm continued to rage. It was an idyllic setting, an almost perfect moment. Except for the mess of revelations, the as yet unproved conjectures, and the question of how to proceed.

"So first Justin killed his sister, then three decades later, he kills his brother." Karin said this flatly, finding it hard to reconcile his iconic public image with fratricide.

"He might not have done it," I theorized.

"Who else could it be?"

"It'd be interesting to see if there've been any Olly Jensen sightings recently."

"You can't let it go, can you?"

"It could be Howard, I suppose, doing Williams' bidding. Or even Mike for that matter."

Karin pointed out that all three of our suspects were men of power, influence and prestige.

"All I know is the hits just keep on coming."

Karin's expression froze. "They're not going to stop, are they."

I shook my head. "Probably not. Not until they get what they want. I mean, think about it. First Jon's condo, then your apartment, then my office."

"Don't forget about Jeffries," she murmured.

"No, can't forget about him, and you can be sure he didn't tell them what they wanted, or they wouldn't have come after me."

"Unless he knew about the envelope."

"Let's assume he didn't. Jon was playing things pretty close to the vest." I sat there, idly brushing my fingers through Karin's hair. "What I'd like to know is, did Jon confront Justin again, or did someone else decide to get proactive?"

"If they went after Jon first, he might not have had a

chance to tell Justin about the tape."

"He would have given it up," I insisted. "If nothing else, as a bargaining chip, to stay alive."

"But if it wasn't Justin, if it were Williams or Jensen, would they care?"

I thought that one over. "It wouldn't be enough to keep Jon alive, but they would definitely care. Williams especially. He's the architect of Justin's political career. Imagine if he had something like that on Justin. He'd own him."

"That's a scary thought."

"Jensen, too. If he's involved, he'd be happy to own Justin, too."

"What are we going to do?" asked Karin.

I suggested maybe we could change our names and just stay where we were. "You could hang out a shingle. There's got to be some towns somewhere on the coast."

She rested against my chest, snuggling up to my proposal, and sighing contentedly. "There's towns all along the coast," she said. "And I'm sure people have problems, even here in paradise. But what about you?"

"I could be a part time detective, help kids find lost beach balls and stuff. Maybe get a job in a T-shirt shop to supplement my income."

"What would you do in the winter?"

"Try to stay warm."

"How?" she asked, though I suspect she knew the answer. I demonstrated a couple approaches I might try. She suggested certain refinements. Then she jumped up and began clearing away the detritus of dinner while I banked the embers. Then we headed to the bedroom to work on technique.

Later, her head resting on my chest, I nuzzled her hair and talked about the future. "We have to go back to Detroit so I can get those notebooks out of the safe deposit box. I'm thinking we should stay at the Hyatt, out at the airport, and just lay low until we know what we have. The

237

tricky part will be meeting with Deb."

In the best case scenario, we'd have a strong enough case to take to the DA. I was pretty sure Carmine would listen to me this time. If there was something there, it would come out in his investigation, and it would finally get that monkey off my back. Even though I'd been cleared, there were still a lot of people who figured I had to be involved in Sara's murder. They had no proof, but they just knew it. To be honest, if I were in their shoes, I'd feel the same way. An Occam's Razor kind of thing. She was killed with my gun, she died in my arms, ipso facto, I killed her.

Karin said she couldn't just lay low. "If I'm back in Detroit I'll have to go to the clinic. I owe it to my patients."

"Yeah, and I have to go see Deb," I agreed. "So we can't be incognito. What we need to do, then, is be as public as possible."

By that I meant we had to be out in the open, where they'd be less likely to hit us. "I mean there's still a risk. If they want to take us out, they will. Yours wouldn't be the first clinic to get shot up by some wacko."

"You paint such pretty pictures," she murmured drowsily. I was happy to let her drift. Out here, snuggled up against the dunes, we were safe. Tonight, we were safe. We might as well enjoy it.

CHAPTER 16

Next morning when we awoke, I feigned panic, because that's the kind of person I am. "It's sunlight, silly," she laughed. She padded into the bathroom while I put some coffee on and fried a couple of eggs. The wind was still blowing, even if the sky was blue, so Karin suggested we head over to the lakeshore, "If you feel up to it."

I told her I felt fine. "I feel like I'm 100% for the first time in a long time."

"Well, you hold onto that thought," she replied. "Just don't look in the mirror," she added with a laugh.

Of course I couldn't resist, though what I found wasn't as bad as she'd led me to believe. The black eyes had faded to a pair of livid yellow haloes. I could live with that. The swelling was way down, and the bruise on my forehead had shrunk to a manageable, Gorbachev-sized blemish. I wasn't ready to compete for The Bachelorette's hand, but I was presentable enough for my line of work. That's the good thing about scars, they prove you're no stranger to the battlefield.

The hike took about an hour, including fifteen

minutes of exhilaration while getting buffeted by the wind. The waves curled, spume streaming off their crests, before hurling themselves at the shore. Between the crashing surf and the howling winds, it was deafening.

Back at the cottage, we packed up, loaded up, and headed out, stopping by Petersen's trailer so Karin could let him know she was through for the season. We made our way slowly southward, delayed repeatedly by road crews clearing uprooted trees and fallen branches from the highway. By the time we reached the eastbound Interstate, it was obvious we wouldn't reach Detroit before the banks closed, so Karin suggested we stop near Lansing again. "I want you to be at your best tomorrow," she explained with a grin.

She allowed that maybe she was just trying to postpone our return. "It's such a depressing thing we—you—no, we have to do."

Next morning, after a detour to Pettigrew, and a smaller, though no less fulfilling visit to Karla's Kitchen, we headed home. Home had never sounded less inviting, but there we were. After a quick visit to the bank, we ran by Karin's apartment so she could grab some of her professional garb. Then she dropped me at my car, and I followed her out to the Hyatt.

That was one of the things we agreed on. We wouldn't be alone. Sure, she'd be on her own at the clinic, but she'd be with people. That was the key. I'd pick her up when the day was done, and we'd go back to the hotel together. I honestly believed we were safe in the daylight, and as long as no one knew where we spent our nights, we should be okay.

At least, Karin would be safe. As for me, who could tell? I would be going into tight quarters with dangerous people. Maybe I'd come out, maybe I wouldn't. Of course, it's always more challenging going into tight quarters when you don't know who your friends are. It's tough having someone watch your back when you don't know if he's going to stick a knife in it. But the most important thing was keeping Karin out of the picture. We had our own tight quarters, and there were no knives or guns involved, just swords and sheaths and frantic, gasping cries of "I love you."

I dropped Karin at the clinic, and headed for the Art Institute, figuring no one would think to look for me there. I went to the café, ordered a sandwich and coffee, and got down to work. I owed Williams a call, but I couldn't figure out what I could or should report, so I called Deb instead. I apologized for not getting back to her sooner, fobbing my sloth off on being concussed. She didn't seem impressed until I mentioned that I'd nearly died. That melted some of the ice.

"So, what do you want?" I figured ignorance, and a gruff version of it, was the best approach.

"We need to talk."

"Yeah, I figured that much. Where and when?"

"I don't blame you for being upset."

"I'm not upset," I growled. "I'm a professional doing his job."

There was silence on the other end. I figured she was trying to decide whether to insist that I was in fact upset, to snort derisively at my assertion of professionalism, or maybe, to apologize for treating me so contemptuously. The silence went on for so long I started to wonder if this was a dropped call. If it were, it would be my first. Maybe I should celebrate. I could get another cup of coffee, and some of those pastries in the café looked tempting. Come to think of it, they even had splits of champagne. That might be a more appropriate way to commemorate my first dropped call.

Then she had to spoil it all by saying something stupid like "I'm sorry."

"For the check?" I offered, resigned to waiting for some other crucial moment to be interrupted by the inevitable dropped call. "Don't worry about it. I thought of tearing it up, but that would have meant acknowledging the insult. So I cashed it to spare your feelings. " Sounded good, I thought. "Besides—"

"You needed the money."

I laughed. "Yep."

"You sound different," she observed in a surprisingly normal voice. I mean the kind of voice she used to use, back when we were us. Not a voice dripping with contempt, or freighted with grief, or awkwardness at what we had been and become.

"I guess you could say I've turned a corner. A lot of ghosts have been exorcized. Starting with Sara and running all the way through you." I gave it a beat to see if she wanted to respond. I got nothing, so I added, "I guess we can add Jon to that list."

"Jon."

"Yeah, just a shame he had to become a corpse before his ghost got retired."

"It's not really about Jon that I—"

"Of course it is. At least it starts with Jon. Where it ends is up to you."

"That's why we have to talk."

"Like I said, where and when."

"Today, as soon as possible."

"That's the second part. You want to do The Grill again, I'm game. Anywhere's fine, as long as it's in public. Someplace where there's no chance of an ambush, and preferably no cornfields."

"You wouldn't consider coming here?"

"Uh, no. Seems to me that exactly doesn't fit the bill. No cornfields though, I'll grant you that."

"Okay," she decided, her tone having lost that familiar and long too unheard playfulness. "The Country Club, then. One o'clock."

"You got it." Then, as an after thought, "Will Howard be joining us?"

Her disdain was palpable. "You want him to?"

"Not at all. I could happily go the rest of my life without seeing him again."

"From what I understand, the feeling is mutual."

"Oh, now I'm hurt."

She laughed. It remained a special piece of music. "He'll be around, I'm sure of it," she added more somberly.

"As long as he's not at the table."

Our date set, I gave Karin a call and filled her in on my social calendar. She didn't sound too thrilled to learn we'd be together.

"Has to be done," I assured her. "How's your day going?"

She said it was hectic, lots of sessions. "I'll be busy right up until six."

"I'll be there. Let me know if there's any changes."

She said her next client had just arrived. "Be careful, Jim. I love you."

I gave that one back to her, and spent the next hour working through the notebooks. It was frustrating because everything was there, yet nothing was. With Jon's road map it was easy to put things together on the Butler Woods thing, and while it all made sense, there was nothing pointing to the why of the matter. Without the why, everything else was useless. No way Carmine would investigate Butler Woods solely based on my say so.

"So you think Justin Wade is laundering drug money?" he'd scoff. "Based on what?"

"His brother told me in a letter."

"Which brother is this? The one who got shot to death outside a drug house?"

The only thing that would keep me getting laughed out of his office was if I told him over the phone. Then he'd just hang up and that would be that.

Speaking of phones, maybe it was time to give Williams a call. Maybe it was time to give the branches a shake, see which side he fell down on: mine, which is to say Jon's, or Justin's. Come to think of it, maybe I'd better cash his check first. I was pretty sure he hadn't hired me to dig up dirt on his most important client.

I finally called him on the way out to Grosse Pointe. It took some doing to reach him. I had to fight through a firewall of receptionists, assistants and secretaries, utilizing the old "He won't be happy if you don't put me through" line, then following up with the equally effective "Why don't you just ask him if he'll take my call?"

"Mr. Williams is in a meeting and can't be disturbed."

"Yeah, right. A minute ago you said he was out of the office."

"He is, or was. He just got back, and there was a very important client waiting for him."

"Was it Justin Wade?"

"I can't give you that information," she responded with the same sort of indignation as if I'd just asked if Williams was still sleeping with preteen boys.

"Because from what I hear, Justin Wade is the most important client your boss has, and Justin Wade is what I need to talk to him about. So unless you want your next job to be call screener for some all night talk radio show, I suggest you tell your boss I'm on the line."

It didn't take long, only about two stanzas of a particularly saccharine Celine Dion number, for Williams to pick up. "What's this about Justin Wade?"

I told him I was recovering nicely. No permanent damage from the concussion. I was pretty much firing on all cylinders.

My little reminder got him back to his accustomed courtly manner. He expressed his great satisfaction at my recovery, even tossed in another "Mr. Corcoran." Then he repeated the question.

"Your buddy left me a package that points a giant red finger at Justin Wade."

"What on earth are you talking about?" Williams

spluttered. I counted myself fortunate. It's not too many private eyes, or anyone else for that matter, who have had the privilege of hearing Kendall Williams lose his composure.

"According to Jon, his brother has been laundering drug money for unknown individuals and has been ever since Butler Woods. Given its onset, I believe that puts Olly Jensen back in play."

Williams was gobsmacked. "I don't believe it. It's—it's impossible," he blustered. Then, his tone suddenly harsh, he demanded, "Where's your evidence?"

"Well, that's the thing," I replied. "Jon laid the whole thing out, but I'm missing the smoking gun. I don't have definitive proof."

"That's because it doesn't exist. All you've got are idle conjectures and irresponsible allegations."

"That's why I'm talking to you, to see if you can corroborate any of this."

Williams said even if he could, which, he stressed, he couldn't, he couldn't communicate it to me.

"Yeah, that's what Karin said."

"Karin? The girl?"

"Yeah, 'the girl.' She thought maybe you were feeding Jon clues, leaving it up to him to make the connections without violating attorney-client privilege."

Williams assured me there was no truth to Wade's involvement. "Just leave that one alone. It's a dead end."

"I thought you hired me to follow the money," I protested.

"I hired you to find out what the girl knows," he said bluntly.

"What about Olly Jensen? You dangled him in front of me."

"Fine, track him down, then we'll talk." Williams hung up. It wasn't a dropped call, but it had the same sort of abruptness.

I turned onto Moross Road and made my way

through the leafy contours of Grosse Pointe. Lawn crews were working the mansions, blowing up huge piles of leaves onto outspread tarps, the first of three weekly cleanups, before the trees were bare, the part-time yard boys were let go, and the crew chiefs attached plows to their pickups in anticipation of winter.

So I'd put Williams in motion. This was the end game. I had to get everyone talking to find out who was with me and who was against me. This is where it would get interesting. This is where it could get dangerous. My only regret, stop me if you've heard this one before, is that I'd gotten Karin mixed up in it. You could argue that she'd gotten herself mixed up, and maybe there'd be some truth to that. But I'd let her do it. I'd let her get involved. I could have, should have, kept her at arms length. Why didn't I stop her? Because I was a fool. A fool, and a stupid horny bastard.

Mike was the next variable, and only time would tell. If I didn't hear from him in the next twenty-four hours, then I would have to rethink things. Mike might prove to be an ally after all. If he was mixed up with Williams, he would get in touch with me right away. That would likely mean he was in it up to his eyebrows.

I remembered enough about the Country Club to know if I pulled up anywhere close to the front the valet parkers would be on me like Senators on a lobbyist. Even though my checking account was back in five figure territory, I figured I was alienating well-heeled clients at a steady enough clip that I'd be better off saving the obligatory $10 tip.

I swung off to the right, to the parking lot for golfers and other cheapskates. I had plenty of company. Grosse Pointe was filled with people who, though capable of pressing Benjamins instead of Hamiltons into grateful valets' hands, would spend up to twenty minutes searching for an after hours parking meter in order to save the cost of a parking garage.

I strolled up to the graceful, Tudor building, glad Karin had thought to pack a sports coat back at my flat. It wouldn't do to meet Deb wearing blue jeans and a flannel shirt. Not that I was worried about blowback from a fashion faux pas. They simply wouldn't have let me in.

I was five minutes early, which meant I had at least twenty minutes to wait. Grosse Pointers are incapable of showing up on time. It's a key tenet in their social Bible, which over the generations has gone from being indoctrinated from birth to being imprinted on their DNA.

The bar was different than I remembered. It was in a different room, for one thing. It had been moved across the broad, flagstone hall, and now occupied what had once been The Mixed Grill. It looked nice, comfy, very clubby with dark wood and a horseshoe bar with two flat screens dedicated to the Golf Channel. The only thing it had in common with the old bar was that it was completely deserted.

Deserted, but well-staffed. The bartender was on me before I'd pulled out the stool. She carefully wiped down the spotless counter and dutifully concealed her excitement at actually having company during the lunch shift.

"Ut can I getcha?" she asked. She was cute, young, with short blonde hair and a thin, perfectly proportioned face.

"Maybe some wine."

"Red? White? House?"

"D'you have a good Merlot?"

She gave me some options. I opted for the Newton, and was pleased to see her open a new bottle. When a place that does no business offers three Merlots by the glass, there's a good chance that any open bottles have been sitting there for a week or more.

I told her I didn't have a member number, that I was meeting Deborah Wade for lunch.

"Yeah, I didn't think I seen ya here before."

"Do you ever see anybody here?"

She laughed her appreciation, a healthy belt of a laugh that preempted any thoughts I might have entertained about us having a lasting relationship. In fact, given my gift for witticisms, and the utter lack of others to compete for her company, I was pretty sure that sound would grow old long before Deb made her appearance.

Good call on my part. Masochist that I am, I spent my time asking about members I recalled, and giving her my thumbnail sketches. She chimed in on cue with her bleats, and with some fleshing out of my assessments. She obviously wasn't Country Club staff material, lacking the discretion and instinctive loyalty that old school institutions demand.

She said she was studying to be a beautician, and had taken this job because "some guy I met in a bar" turned out to be the Club President. He had told the manager to take care of her, because she needed a job, and he was grateful. I wasn't surprised to learn it was Chip Mettler. It takes a certain kind of chutzpah to put your mistress behind the bar at the same place where your wife and kiddies might pop in for lunch. But that was Chip.

Chip had been part of our circle back in high school. Even then he had rough edges which he refused to get smoothed. His skin was thicker than the frames of his glasses. He flat out didn't care what you thought. His dad was the largest shareholder in National Bank of Detroit, his mother was a Proctor, as in Proctor and Gamble, and he was destined to make it any way he chose. He chose to make it by setting up a venture capital fund which invested in start ups far, far away from Detroit.

Before I even had the chance to learn if the barmaid was still seeing Chip, Deb made her appearance. She gave me a half-smile while signing my chit, and led us into the dining room.

Her clothing gave more than a passing nod to fashion, unlike her attire at The Grill, though it still wasn't anywhere close to cutting edge. That was in keeping with the Country Club ethos.

There were two basic rules regarding fashion in Grosse Pointe: First, it had to be expensive (though always on sale. In fact, the ideal scenario involved buying expensive clothes on sale in New York or London, during expeditions mounted solely to acquire expensive clothing on sale). The second rule was it could never be the latest thing. Not that Deb was wearing last year's fashion. She wore brown slacks, a cream-colored blouse and a muted orange jacket. Call it burnt sienna if you like. It was the obscurity of the shade that made it so expensive, and legitimated it as a standard part of the Grosse Pointe wardrobe.

She remarked that I looked no worse than the last time she saw me.

"Only it's a new set of contusions."

"I'm sorry I got you into this," she said in a tone that made me want to believe her.

We avoided pursuing that topic, or the one which had brought us together again, during the ordering, waiting, receiving and consuming portion of the afternoon. Then she asked if I wanted to walk.

I agreed, even with the risk of ambush. The golf course was closed for the season, but it remained a lovely setting. Wide, still-green fairways lined by stately oaks, elms and maples, it was more like parkland than a place devoted to something as mundane as golf. Whenever I saw the course, back in the days when I was no stranger to the Country Club, I always wished I played the game. Not enough to buy clubs, take lessons, and practice, practice, practice, but purely from an esthetic impulse.

As we headed down the first fairway, before drifting off to the left, through a stand of trees, Deb told me again how much she regretted getting me involved.

"Don't worry," I assured her. "Getting beaten up is part of the job."

249

"I wasn't talking about you," she corrected me. "I was talking about me."

I asked her what she meant, reminding myself that her disregard for me couldn't hurt because I was so well, truly, and irrevocably over her.

"My life has been utter hell," she replied, her eyes brimming. "I just wish I'd let it—let him—go."

"I'm not following you."

"I wasn't completely honest with you at The Grill."

"Well, that goes with the territory. Nobody tells you everything in this business."

It's boilerplate language, part of how the game is played. The client, or ex-client in this case, confesses to concealment. I absolve her, then she comes clean. Only Deb wasn't playing according to the rules. She simply continued to walk. We were getting deeper into the woods now. I'd forgotten how extensive they were, a copse, around which the course revolved. I started to get my back up, wondering if it actually was possible to get set up out here.

"So what didn't you tell me?" I gave in, broke script, but figured if it's the end, I at least wanted to get some answers.

"I knew exactly what Jon was up to, he and Bill." She hugged herself as she walked, veering to the right, much to my relief. Her route was taking us back toward another fairway. "I tried to talk him out of it." She stopped, turned to me. Her arms were pointing down, her palms open and facing me. She was totally open, entirely vulnerable. "I was worried about myself, not him. I never thought he'd get killed."

Then she was in my arms, the trees absorbing the sound of her sobbing. I let it flow. It's a good technique. If there are enough tears, some of the truth will wash out in the flood. I was also mildly amused at the irony of finally getting her back in my arms. I was aware of her body pressed against mine, my right hand resting on the small of her back. It had been so many years, yet my body remembered those contours.

Yet, it wasn't the same thing at all. Deb was, to my gratified amazement, truly in the past. She'd lost her power over me. Whether she realized it or not was immaterial. What I held in my arms wasn't just a former lover, but something even more desirable. She just might be the break I'd been looking for.

"What exactly was Jon up to?" I asked after a suitable delay.

She broke away from me. "He was going to destroy Justin."

"And by extension, you."

She nodded. "It was my life. He—was my life. Oh, not that he defined me, but his status, our status, our—I don't know. Our life was what it was. It was the life I was meant to live."

"The life I couldn't give you," I murmured.

"Or wouldn't," she countered bitterly.

"We all do what we must," I deflected her recrimination. "So which of Justin's sins was Jon trying to reveal?"

She started. "What do you mean?"

"You brought it up. Whatever it was Jon wouldn't leave alone."

"Oh, that." She looked relieved. You don't know it, I thought. But I know, and it will come out before I'm through with you.

"So what was it?" I repeated, starting us walking again. Moving deeper into the woods, thinking if I'm leading we can't be heading into an ambush.

"Justin isn't what he appears to be," she said, finally. "He plays this role of being a pillar of the community, but we're basically living hand to mouth."

I laughed out loud. "Come on. I've seen his bank statements. If you're living hand to mouth it's with hands and mouths most of the world would kill to have just once."

"It's all a lie," she blurted. "And it has been for the last ten years."

Ten years? That was the Butler Woods time frame. And Olly Jensen. And Sara.

"What happened ten years ago?"

At first she wasn't answering the question, but talking around it. Eventually, though, she talked around it in smaller and smaller circles until she found herself in the middle of the answer. It was the answer I needed to hear, but that doesn't mean I was happy to hear it.

She talked about what Jon had been, "when we were all a thing," what he'd become, and then what he finally became. How at first she was with him every step of the way. "It made perfect sense, in a holistic kind of way, for him to follow the money. If he could find the answers, to locate 'Mr. Big,' as he always—"

"Mr. Big," I said. The air got suddenly closer. I found it hard to breathe. The case was cycles within cycles and I found myself in a cyclone of memories and despair.

"Are you okay?" There was genuine concern in her eyes. I told myself it was fear of inconvenience if I were to keel over. The hassle of slogging back out, calling 911, leading them back here. The scandal of her being out in the woods with me. The questions from the cops, the leering insinuations from Andy Parsons–hey, that bastard still had my gun. Had to get it back from him.

She repeated her question, this time a tinge of panic leaking in.

I nodded. "Just an after effect from the concussion." I cleared leaf fall from a nearby stump and suggested we sit awhile. Then I asked her to continue.

"Are you sure? We could do this another—"

I shook my head, slowly. I thought I knew what had caused my stupor, but I wanted to be sure it actually wasn't my post-concussion brain acting up again. "Tell me about Mr. Big."

"He was the money behind Detroit's drug trade. Jon said he needed to track him down. 'These things don't just happen,' he said. 'If I can finger him, maybe it will stop.' Oh, he knew it wouldn't stop," she amended, with a shake of her head. "But he always said, 'If we can slow it down, and even more important, make those bastards pay, then maybe I can make good on a debt.'"

"He was talking about all the people he took down with him?"

She nodded. "Especially the ones who didn't make it back."

"So how much did he—"

"At first, he told me everything. I even helped, giving him advice, listening to his speculations, and suggesting directions he should pursue." She ran her finger along a crack in the stump. "I had no idea where it was leading."

"To Justin."

She looked up, astonished. "You knew?"

"I'm figuring it out."

"Then you can see why I—"

I shook my head. "It's too big. It's too dangerous."

"Justin wouldn't—he couldn't—"

"Deb." It was a chastisement, and with that one word she knew. She started to cry again, and I held her again, and this time my heart went out to her, and I loved her again. But this time like a brother. I held her, and stroked her head, and kissed her forehead. I shed tears of my own. And then I said, "Tell me about it."

"After a few months Justin's name kept coming up more and more. Naturally I didn't want to believe it. I kept demanding proof, and he kept bringing it. But it was all so nebulous, so much based on speculation. I told him, 'This isn't proof. This isn't real.' He said, 'You think I'm making it up?' I told him no, but I thought he was letting his resentment for Justin cloud his judgement. He just flew into a rage, and said he had damn good reasons for resenting him, and if I wanted to defend that sick fuck, I could just go to hell with him. And then he stormed out."

"That was it?"

She shook her head. "I didn't hear from him for a couple months. He'd taken up with Karin by then, and I guess she was playing my role—without all the baggage."

I said, "Yeah, that's what I got from her."

"Then, it was a week before he died, he called me, said he wanted to make amends. We met on his boat. He apologized for what he said the last time. 'I didn't want it to turn out like this,' he said, and then he laid it out to me. Everything he had. It looked awful, it really did. You can't imagine what it's like, hearing that your husband, the father of your children, the man who shares your bed each night, is responsible for tens of thousands of young lives being thrown away on drugs."

I offered my arms again. She took them. No tears this time. The time for tears had passed.

"What did you do?"

"What could I do? I listened to his story. It was convincing. In a way, I knew it was true. But in another, I didn't. 'But why, Jon? ' I asked. 'Why would he do that?' And Jon said he didn't know. Everything was pointing at Justin, but he couldn't figure out why."

"Damn. Jon built the perfect case, but he didn't finish the job. We've got nothing."

Deb was very solemn when she spoke. "After I had lunch with you, after I hired you, Justin and I went up to New York for a couple of days. We were going to take in a play, have a couple nice dinners, do some shopping. It was just the two of us. Sort of a second honeymoon, an attempt to salvage our marriage. To be honest, it was starting to run off the rails."

When I said I'd heard rumors to that effect, she was dismayed. That meant it was out there. That meant it was all over town, and that wasn't good news for a Grosse Pointe fixture to hear.

Then she shrugged. "Well, I guess it doesn't matter

anymore." Then she told me how in New York, Justin was so kind, understanding, and dammit, fun. "It was like he used to be. Everywhere we went we left a trail of laughter. I couldn't help it, I started to fall in love with him all over again. I started to believe things could go back to how they were."

But always at her back she heard Jon's accusations, and she knew before the weekend was done she'd confront him.

"When I did, I expected him to deny it. I expected him to get upset, to curse his dead brother's name. I didn't know how I'd react, but that's what I expected from him."

"But he didn't?" You didn't have to be a good detective to make that leap. It was what we in the trade like to call a no-brainer.) SEE P. 135

She shook her head. "He broke down. He started to cry and he told me he couldn't keep it inside any longer. It had been ten years of hell and he hated that he couldn't tell me."

"Tell you what?"

Tell her about Wade Investments. As it turned out, Karin had been right. Justin's means weren't all they'd been made out to be. At first, the company was a gold mine. He could do no wrong. He made some brilliant calls. Sure, he did the research, but at the end of the day, when it was time to pull the trigger, he always aimed at the right target.

He was adding staff, expanding the office, bulking up on analysts. Clients were flocking to his door. Why not? Wade Investments was outperforming the benchmarks by ten percent or more, based entirely on Justin's calls.

"It got so he believed he was infallible. He had an unerring instinct. He could do no wrong. He told me he started overruling the analysts. They'd say he was making a mistake, and if they didn't let up, they were out the door."

"Sounds like hubris to me."

"True, but it was also the middle of the dotcom bubble. There was plenty of hubris to go around."

I conceded the point, adding, "So what went wrong?"

Suddenly Justin started making mistakes. In the middle of the biggest bull market in history, he couldn't pick a single winner. "In 1996 his funds lost ten percent while his investors were expecting at least a 25% return. He said if it weren't for the fact that everybody else was getting rich, he would have just bitten the bullet. But it was just so embarrassing. And that's what made him lie. It wasn't the risk of losing some clients, it was the shame of being a loser."

"It wasn't like he was going to go broke, " I noted.

She looked at me with a dazed expression. "No, that's exactly what it was like."

"How can that be? He was worth, what, fifty, a hundred million?"

She shook her head. "He should have been, but he rolled the whole thing into Wade Investments."

When I said that wasn't very smart, she snorted. "You got that right. In fact, that night in New York, I basically told him that." She shrugged ruefully. "Oh, maybe I threw in a few adjectives."

I chuckled lightly in reply to her sheepish smile. Then I asked what happened.

"He still had plenty of new money flooding in, so he added that to the returns and claimed a 28% gain for the year. It was just an accounting trick, he insisted. He'd make it up the following year when he got back on track. The new money gave him cash flow for the distributions. It wasn't like anybody was pulling out of the funds."

"But the next year was more of the same?"

She said it was worse. He doubled down on a handful of sure things, which turned out not to be, and his funds lost 15% in 1997. "He claimed a 30% return."

"And made up the difference with new money," I concluded. "Your husband was running a Ponzi Scheme."

"It didn't start out that way. He wasn't trying to rip anybody off. He was just trying to save face."

I wondered why nobody caught on to it.

"I did, too. He said when he first started the company he was the only one who ran off the statements. You remember how he was always fascinated by numbers?"

"Sure."

"Since he had the structure already in place, it was easy to keep it going. And in those days, before Enron blew up, accounting firms would just basically sign off on whatever the client gave them. He even cited it as a strength in his prospectuses. Because everything flowed through him it reduced the risk of rogue traders, the kind of thing that brought down other funds."

"So how'd it fall apart?"

"The following year one of his biggest clients wanted to pull out half his holdings."

"Olly Jensen," I surmised.

She nodded, and scowled. "Justin said he never knew if Olly actually intended to do it, or if he just figured out what was happening and was playing him."

"Either way, Justin was trapped."

"Once word got out, even if he was just diversifying his holdings, as he claimed he was—"

"Which actually would have made sense," I noted.

"But he was already diversified. You ought to know that."

Oh, I knew that all right. Ten years ago I'd been so busy digging into Olly's assets, I still couldn't see a dollar sign without shivering. "Everybody knew that," I chimed in. "So the question would have been, 'Why's Jensen pulling out?'"

"And maybe I should, too."

"Which is when the shit would hit the fan," I agreed. "Why didn't it?"

"At first Justin tried to talk him out of it. When that didn't work he asked for thirty days, explaining that everything was so structured, every penny doing the work of five, that that was how sophisticated financing worked."

"Bet Olly liked that."

"He had a huge ego and he didn't appreciate being talked down to. He told Justin he wanted his money first thing the following Monday, or he'd be hearing from his attorneys."

"Which would have started a run on his bank."

"So Justin caved. He explained what had happened, how it had happened, and how he was going to make it better. But he needed more time."

"Did he realize how dangerous Olly was?"

"Did any of us?" she replied.

That earned a pause to contemplate the consequences of Olly's power and his rage. "Sara did," I muttered. "I thought I did, but I was wrong."

Deb placed a hand on my arm. "I am so sorry. It there had been anything I could have—"

"There wasn't," I assured her. There was, of course, but it really didn't matter. "It's all history now," I said. "But Justin was lucky he didn't become history right then."

"Oh, he knew it. He said he knew he was putting his life on the line, but there was no other way out. Either way, his life was over." She stood up. "Can we walk? It's getting late."

I checked my watch. It was. It was after three. Still plenty of time to wrap this up and get to the clinic by six, though.

Deb returned to her story, saying how surprised and relieved Justin was when Olly didn't go ballistic. "'He was so understanding,' he said, just before he started to cry again."

Olly said it could happen to anybody. He knew he should be angry that Justin had pissed away his money, but what the hell, he'd always considered him a friend. His solution was simple. He had a large chunk of cash which he was willing to move into Wade Investments.

"He was going to invest more money with the guy who'd just lost him I don't know how many millions?"

"No, not invest, just move it in. He said it would be an off book transaction, and Justin was going to have to figure out a way to clean it up. And then he was going to need Justin to front him on other investments from time to time."

"Like Butler Woods."

"That started the following month."

"And all the other real estate, the liquor stores, the gas stations?"

"He just signs his name whenever and wherever Olly tells him to."

"Tell me, did Justin know he was laundering drug money?"

"How could he not have known?" Her exasperation was manifest.

"That's not what I asked."

"Not at first. Obviously he knew it wasn't good. But, you know what he told me? He thought maybe it was guns."

"Olly an international gun runner? Makes sense."

"When we came back, that's when I called you. I wanted to call you off. I knew if I gave you a big enough check you'd go away." She gave me a wry smile. "I guess I was wrong. At that time, all I wanted to do was make it disappear. I wanted to protect Justin."

"And yourself," I noted.

She nodded ruefully. "But when the shooting started, I knew that it would never end. I knew Ken Williams had set that up, which meant Justin's finger prints were all over it." She shivered. "I honestly don't know if he was going after you, or me."

"Or both of us."

"Or both of us," she agreed. "My first thought was he regretted breaking down to me, and he wanted to limit the damage."

"But you don't know that," I insisted. "If it was him, it's more likely he was after me. Otherwise it doesn't make sense."

"It doesn't have to make sense," she countered.

I said I wasn't following her.

"Justin hasn't made sense for years," she said. "And lately, it's gotten worse."

"What do you mean?"

She shivered in reply. "You know how Justin always had this manic quality?" I nodded. "It was part of what made him so dynamic. I know it was what attracted me to him." She gave a rueful smile. " From the time I was born, I was so locked into the Grosse Pointe social straightjacket. You know, how to act, dress, talk."

"Sure, I was part of that."

"But you escaped," she countered.

"Escaped or was expelled," I replied with a shrug. "Maybe it's the same thing."

She smiled sadly. "I wish I'd gone with you."

I laughed. "But you were one of the reasons I had to leave."

She acknowledged that truth, and then she said, "I was more of a rebel than you knew. I just didn't know how to express it."

"So how does this relate to manic Justin?" I wondered.

"Well, that's just it," she said impatiently. "Justin was so—I don't know—out there? He was all over the map, and yet, he played the Grosse Pointe game so perfectly. You wouldn't know it, unless you really knew him, the way I got to know him, but his grasp on, I don't know, reality? It was so tenuous. I loved it at first. It made me feel so alive. But lately?" She hugged herself. "Lately, and especially since New York, well, it's kind of frightening."

"Whoa, come on, Deb. You can't be serious." I don't know why I was so determined to defend him. Maybe it was residual affection for Deb, but I just couldn't go down that road. Not right then.

I touched her on the arm. "Hold on a sec." We were approaching the edge of the woods, nearing the eighteenth fairway which would take us back to the main building and end our conversation. I didn't expect us to ever have another one.

"Maybe Williams set it up on his own," I offered. "After all, we don't know how much he knows about this."

"Maybe you should ask him," she said sharply.

"Maybe I have."

"Well, it's nothing to do with me. We don't exchange small talk, let alone secrets."

That was a bit a of a shock. "But you're neighbors. And what about Howard?"

"What about Howard?" she threw back at me.

"Howard works for Williams. Since he's moonlighting as your bodyguard, I figured you and Williams must be—"

"Howard is not my bodyguard." She enunciated every word. "Howard is my minder. Howard's job is not to keep me out of trouble. Howard's job is to keep me from causing trouble."

"I wonder why he let you come out here with me, then."

"Maybe Ken wants to know how much I know, and expects to find that out from you."

I supposed she was right. "After all, it's what he's paying me to do." I assured her that I wasn't about to start singing. "Still, I need to know whose side he's on."

"Ken is on his own side," she replied dismissively. "And right now his side is interested in keeping Justin's nose clean."

"Keep his political career on course."

"Can you imagine just how excited I am at the prospect of being a Senator's wife?" she asked, her voice dripping with doleful sarcasm.

"Not part of the game plan?

"Especially not now. Can you think of a scenario in which this doesn't come out? It will be humiliating. Not just for me, but for the children. Him, I don't care about," she added bitterly. "But it's just insane. That's why I think Ken must not be aware of it. He's too smart for that. I mean, Justin's life will be under a microscope. People are going to find out, and you can't keep buying them off, scaring them off—"

"Killing them off," I added softly.

"What do you mean by that?" she challenged.

It was time. It was getting late and I still had miles to go. Not to mention promises. "Tell me, Deb. Where was Justin the night Jon died?" My perverse bout of loyalty was over, and now I was back on Justin's tail.

She whirled to face me. "You can't be serious. You think Justin had something to do with his own brother's death?"

When I suggested it wouldn't be falling too far from the family tree, her face fell. It simply caved in. Her skin shrank, her cheekbones stood out. She looked haggard, like a heroin addict, or a teenaged supermodel.

"You know about that?" she murmured.

"It was in the package Jon sent me." I told her I'd never actually seen that letter, explained why, and apologized for Karin sending it to her.

"No," she said defiantly. "I'm glad she did." She'd had no idea where it had come from, though. "I never considered her."

"What are you going to do?" she wondered.

"What are you?"

"I'm leaving him. Ruggles Creek decided it," she announced. Then she laughed. "I should have done it a long time ago. You know, not all abuse is physical. I've never been happy, but I've been trying to hold things together. It was my life, you know."

I said I was sorry.

"Maybe if I had left him, everything might have turned out different."

I said things usually turn out the way they're meant to do. "But what will you do?"

She shrugged, and we finally emerged from the trees. "I'll be okay. It's not like I don't have any money of my own." She barked a laugh. "You know, that bastard tried to get me to invest in Wade, to turn my trust over to him." She hugged herself again and kept walking, striding really, up the fairway. "Things will be different. We might have to leave Grosse Pointe. Probably should."

When we reached the giant sand traps guarding the green, she turned to me, with the brick and half-timbered facade of the Clubhouse looming behind her.

"I obviously don't care what you do about the money, but can I ask you one favor?"

"Depends on what it is."

"Can you just ignore the stuff about Jessie? Especially if he's going down for money laundering, can you just leave the other thing alone? It won't change anything. Me, I don't care, but the children? It'll be bad enough for them knowing their father's a crook. But a murderer? Of his own sister? I just want, if it's at all possible, to spare them that." the

I shrugged. "I can't promise you anything. If the DA opens an investigation, it's anybody's guess where it'll end up. The FBI will get involved, the DEA. It'll be a feeding frenzy." I took her hands in mine. "But I can promise this. They won't hear anything from me."

She thanked me. She hugged me. She kissed me on the lips, and it wasn't a social kiss either. Not that she slipped me the tongue or anything. Not on the eighteenth green she wouldn't. Even if her carefully constructed life was about to implode, she wouldn't go that far. Not on the eighteenth green.

The kiss fell somewhere between chaste and intimate,

close enough to the latter that it spurred memories and put paid again to my valiant oaths concerning sleeping dogs. I did resist the urge to reflect on old times, old feelings, old habits. I just let it go. Maybe she read my mind, or maybe she realized where we were standing, but she broke away, and stood away, and babbled something about being so, so grateful.

Me, I babbled in turn, ignoring the kiss and reiterating my vow of silence. "If I had the tape that'd be a different matter, but without it all we have is Jon's word. Not only is it hearsay, but given Jon's history and the way he died, it would be dismissed as nothing more than the drug-induced rantings of an unstable—"

I stopped. She'd gone pale. "What is it?"

"You mentioned a tape?"

"Yeah, the tape he made of Justin's confession."

"I never thought—I never put it together. I never, I didn't."

The hell with the gossips. I wrapped my arms around her. I tried to slow her down, and eventually did. Then I asked for an explanation.

"The last time I saw Jon, when he told me what he thought Justin was doing, he gave me some things. Like he knew. There was a little cassette tape. He told me not to listen to it, that it had nothing to do with me, but it might save his life."

"You never listened to it?"

She shrugged, and said listlessly. "He said it didn't concern me."

"But—"

"He said it would save his life," she continued in that same lifeless tone. "He was wrong."

"But when he mentioned it in the letter, didn't you—"

"Oh, the letter!" She flounced away from me. For a minute I thought she was just going to march away, out of my life one final time without even saying goodbye. She stopped after a few strides, though, and turned. "I was so upset by the end of the letter," she recited. "I was crying, and I really wasn't paying any attention. I never put the two together. I wanted to believe Jon was lying, or imagining things. If anything, it more likely meant he had killed her."

"That's what I thought, too," I lied. Then, almost as an after thought, "What did you do with the letter?"

"I burned it."

"Do yourself a favor, Deb. Burn the tape, too."

She nodded, gave a tearful wave, and walked stiffly away. She was gone. Gone out of my life forever, again. I knew this time she was gone for good. I felt sorry for her. I felt bad. But I felt good, too, as if somehow this ending made more sense. Really, if you looked at it, in many ways this ending was the same as the first.

After an intense connection, Jon and Justin Wade came between us. They made it impossible for us to be together. We said good-bye. She disappeared into the Country Club, and I left town for the last time, forever.

At least, that's the story I told myself. That was the happy—okay, not happy—how about conclusive? Would you settle for that? It was a conclusive ending, as endings should be, but happy, too, because I was on my way to pick up Karin, the woman I loved. And she loved me, and by God, we were going to make ourselves a happy ending. If things went right, it was going to last a long, long time. Sort of like the ending of the third "Lord of the Rings" flick, though a lot less painful to sit through.

I'd pick her up, we'd go back to our hideout, order from the room service menu, then after dinner, lay out our own erotic buffet and pick and choose those items we wanted to sample. Tomorrow after I dropped her at her office, I would put everything I had together. I'd draw a road map for Carmine. It would be out of my hands then, and everybody would know it. Williams would find out first, because, like he said, it's his job to find things out.

Everybody would be too busy covering their own

asses, or skipping town, to worry about something as inconsequential as revenge. No, they'd leave us alone. Everything they'd thrown at us had been about stopping it. Well, it couldn't be stopped once Carmine got involved. That meant we were out of the picture.

I truly believed that. We were home free. Karin and I were about to begin a beautiful life together.

Ain't happy endings grand?

CHAPTER 17

After I left the Country Club, I figured I had just enough time to pick up a few things at my office before meeting Karin at the clinic. Traffic was, as Detroit traffic is, not a problem.

The office was in the same state I'd left it the other day. A jumble of file folders and their far flung contents covered the floor. Dictionaries, reference manuals and the stack of great books I'd worked through over the course of a decade while pretending to do my job, were scattered around. Some of their spines were broken from the impact with the walls or floor. Others looked like they had been slit with a razor. The search had been thorough, and as was the case with Karin's apartment, gratuitously destructive.

My computer was toast. Like Jon's, it looked like it had been attacked with a sledgehammer. Which meant they weren't looking for files or documents. Unless, of course, it was Jon's envelope. Maybe he'd admitted mailing it before he died. I suppose facing the business end of a shotgun makes you rethink the value of certain commitments. Like making sure you could nail your brother's ass from beyond the grave.

It was then I started getting nervous. We weren't out of the woods yet, Karin and I. That envelope, and Jon's notebooks, were crucial to my case. Right now they were sitting in the trunk of my car, which wasn't parked in its usual secure parking lot, but a couple blocks away. My thinking had been that anyone who knew where I lived probably knew where I parked. Rather than stake out my building, it would be more efficient for Williams, or Mike, or hell, even Justin Wade, to have someone sweep the lot periodically.

Suddenly all I could think of was the life expectancy of a car, even a ratty old one like mine, parked at the curb in on a Detroit city street. I could see my well-constructed end game foiled not by one of my adversaries, but by some opportunistic Detroit thug.

I tore out of the building and returned as quickly as I could to my car. I tried sprinting at first, but the effort revived the headaches. As it was, I was winded when I reached the car, and relieved to see it intact. Just to reassure myself, I popped the trunk, retrieved the crucial documents and slid them under the driver's seat. Then I made my way to Karin's office, where I killed time reliving Olly Jensen's Cheshire mourning and the horror of Sara's death.

Then I came out of it. 6:15. I glanced up, half expecting to see Karin standing outside the car, staring in horror at the specter which must have been my face. But no, she wasn't there.

I figured her last session must be running late, like the last time. I figured I might as well go in, make my presence known, help the latest serial addict achieve her latest life-altering breakthrough.

The building was a hexagon, with the lobby in the center, accessed by a wide hallway lined with posters depicting cool mountain peaks and placid lakes. Yeah, yeah, I get it. Actually, the hallway would have been bright, only half the lights had been shut off.

Same with the lobby, a two story atrium affair with a band of rectangular windows lining the cupola. Clusters of offices radiated from the center. It was straightforward, efficient. I wondered if anyone who worked there realized the layout mimicked the latest in prison architecture. I'd have to ask Karin, once I tracked her down.

I finally located the directory, and the map which gave meaning to offices labeled A3, D6, or C4. Karin's was C4, which meant I wanted the 3rd corridor to the left. I was headed that way when I heard the distinctive key, flashlight and hand cuff jingle of a rent-a-cop double-timing it behind me.

"Place is closed," he panted, as I stopped and turned to spare him further exertion.

"I'm looking for Karin Champagne, Mr. Fortune," I said, peering at his name tag. "S'posed to pick her up."

"She ain't here."

"What do you mean she isn't here?" I demanded, before racing down the hall. I figured security wouldn't chase me. More likely he'd be on the phone to the cops. Karin's office was third on the right. It was locked and the lights were off. Fighting panic, I returned to the lobby.

Sure enough, lard-ass had the phone to his ear, the other hand gripping his flashlight like a club. I wanted to go up and take it away from him, on general principle. But he was saying, "No, he's back. Doesn't look dangerous, but hang on." My first instinct was he was bluffing, though he didn't look smart enough to mount a bluff.

I wasn't that worried about the cops, but I decided I should make nice. After all, he was as close as I had to a connection to Karin.

"Do you know when she left?"

"Yeah, about two hours ago."

"Two hours? Where'd she go?"

He scanned the register. "Doc's are s'posed to log out during office hours, and give their destinations.

Sometimes they do, sometimes they don't. Alls I can do is ask. Can't make 'em." He ran his finger down the page. "Your lady, she's pretty good about it." Maybe I had this guy pegged wrong. I was glad I hadn't taken away his flashlight, which I noticed, he'd casually slipped back into his belt. The phone, too. He'd hung up without saying good-bye.

"Went to the Medical Center. Says here, emergency. You wanna call?" he offered, gesturing at the phone.

"Thanks," I said. "I'll use my cell. Sorry to come off like a hard ass," I offered as I turned to go.

"Yeah, me too," he answered, leaving me to wonder if he meant he was sorry I came off like a hard ass, or that he had. I glanced back. He unleashed a belly laugh. I gave a grin and a wave, and headed out. Officer Fortune was all right.

IS A RENT-A-COP AN ?

I hadn't thought to turn my cell back on when I left the Country Club. The rule against cell phone use at the Grosse Pointe Country Club was similar to those regarding doing business on the golf course or not sleeping with another member's wife unless your handicap was lower than his. The only difference was, the cell phone rule was rigidly enforced.

It was back up and running, all the bars in place, and the standard issue photo on the little screen. I'd have to figure out how to put a personalized photo in there. That cool mountain peak—the same one as on one of those posters inside, come to think of it—must be the same sort of thing as the snapshot of Jacqueline Bisset which used to come with new wallets, to show what those glassine slips were for. It had been so long since I'd bought a new wallet, I wondered whose pictures they used now, or if they even did that any more.

A voice mail waiting message popped up before I could retrieve her number, which I thought was encouraging. It was Karin telling me she had to go to the Medical Center. "One of my patients, she needs me." She sounded upset, but that made sense. Hectic day, having to rescramble her already scrambled schedule. Plus having a client OD, or whatever it was, must feel a lot like a private dick having his client get shot.

No, mustn't go there. For a second I thought about just burning the damn notebook, but no, I knew I'd have to go through the whole thing, preferably with Karin sitting beside me, holding my hand. She said she wasn't sure when she'd get out of there, but she'd just take a cab back to the Hyatt. "Call me when you get this. I love you."

Okay, it was fine. I could relax. I'd just head to the hotel and wait. My serenity had a hiccup when her phone went straight to voice mail, but I remembered how she said she never had it on when she was in session. I suppose being in session in the ER made it doubly important.

My complacency took a few hits over the next two hours during which Karin didn't call and didn't answer. It finally went down for the count after I called the hospital. It took some doing to reach a real, live person, and quite a bit more to reach one who actually cared, but that's okay. It's one of the things I do. Keep pressing buttons, redialing, and pressing more buttons until I get the answers I need.

In this case, I got an answer, just not the one I wanted. Because Karin worked at the Detroit Psych Clinic two days a week, she wasn't an unknown quantity there, so when I learned she hadn't checked in with anyone, anywhere, at the hospital, I realized something was terribly wrong.

As soon as I suggested that being as big and busy as the Medical Center was, maybe she'd slipped through the cracks, I knew how wrong I was. Sure, someone who wanted to could slip in and out without leaving any evidence of her visit. But that was the exact opposite approach she would have taken. The one thing we had agreed to do was to make sure people knew where we were. Plus, I was informed, it would be impossible to visit a patient without checking in.

The hospital played host to so many shootings and stabbings that its own Emergency Room had an Emergency Room. Its level of security was on a par with that of a prison.

So where did that leave me? Helpless, verging on despair, reduced to repeatedly punching buttons on my stupid phone, only to learn that Karin Champagne wasn't available. I didn't know what to do, who to call. I raged at myself, "You're the goddamn detective, start detecting."

I called Williams, caught him at the airport, where he was about to board a flight. Seems he had to fly to London on some important, last-minute business. He seemed amused to learn why I'd called. "Why, Mr. Corcoran, the way you keep misplacing, or shall I say mislaying women, strikes me as rather careless."

That shot should have been beneath a man of his sophistication. I didn't need to hear it, especially now, having just been so brutally immersed in Sara's murder. Even his going out of the country on business was eerily reminiscent of Olly's alibi.

"If you know anything, Ken, I'm begging you."

"Why would I know anything?" he asked blithely.

"It's your job to know things. Isn't that what you told me?"

"If it's my job, then why am I paying you? Good bye, Mr. Corcoran."

I was left staring at the phone nestling in the palm of my hand. I wanted to hurl it across the room. I wanted to–

It rang. "Karin!" I cried.

"Not lately," Mike said.

Mike Wallis. Right on schedule. Doing Williams' dirty work while he skipped town. Pity that. No, beyond pity. Mike could have been a friend. He maybe could have helped me find Karin. I headed for the door.

"What do you want?" I asked, then, struck by an even

more important question, asked it. "How'd you get this number? It's a new phone."

He laughed easily. "God, your ignorance knows no bounds. I need to know, I know. It's that simple."

The elevator doors opened. "What do you want?" I repeated.

He slipped into his business voice, his cop voice. "There's someone you need to see."

"Now's not a good time," I said, passing into the lobby and veering to the right. "Got an old buddy waiting for me in the bar."

"I'll pick you up," he said. It wasn't an offer, it was a fact.

"Hell, you don't even know where I am."

"Right. The Hyatt's about half-an-hour away. I'll meet you in the bar."

"How the hell?"

He should have laughed. The words he used should have come wrapped in laughter. I could hear it, and the tone in which he said things like that. But there was no laugh, just "God, Corcoran, hard to believe you've stayed alive this long."

I told him I wouldn't be there.

"I think you will," he said. "You don't want to make the same mistake twice."

"Wait. Is this about Karin?"

"See you in a few."

I did it. Told myself I wouldn't. Told myself I shouldn't. Told myself I needed my wits about me, but what I kept seeing was Karin's starring role in the blockbuster hit, "Sara Redux." She didn't look any better than Sara did with half her face missing. I guess it's just not a good look. Maybe that's why it hasn't caught on.

I did it. I ordered the drink. Got reacquainted with my old friend Jack. What a pal. No recriminations, no "Where ya been? I missed you." Nope, he just grinned and invited me in for a swim.

Just one, I told myself, as I ordered another one. I'd leave that sitting on the bar for Mike. I checked my watch. 9:50. Pretty late to go visiting. I wracked my brain trying to figure out somebody else who might want to see me this time of night. But Karin was missing. She was incommunicado, and Mike was all business.

Who had her? Not Williams, he was on a jet. Or not. He said he was flying out, but I had no way of knowing if it was true. I suppose Mike could have snatched her, hidden her away somewhere no one could find her. Or he could have snuffed her already. Or maybe Olly really was back.

I took another sip and waited for Mike. Another sip, and I watched the condensation beading on his glass. Maybe I'd finish this one, down his and make him buy his own.

Don't know how that one would have played out because Mike grabbed it before I could make up my mind.

He drained half of it one go, set it down with finality and said, "You always were a good drinking buddy, I'll grant you that."

Then he said, "You set here?" I nodded.

He flared out his jacket, giving me a glimpse of his holster. "Then let's go."

"Like that is it?"

His face was set. "Yeah, buddy. Like that."

I shrugged. Whatever it was was what it was, and I wouldn't know how to play it until I knew what it was.

He was parked right outside. Amazing what a DPD shield on the dashboard will do for you. Mike opened the door for me, which I thought was a nice touch.

"Sure you don't want me in back?"

"Just get in."

Mike headed east on the Interstate, through downtown Detroit. "Where we going?"

"You'll see."

So he was giving me the silent treatment? My

carefully constructed happy ending of just a few hours ago was shattering before my eyes, and he was going to play the stoic? Not if I had anything to say about it.

"I never figured you for a dirty cop."

"You should have," he replied. "If you were any kind of detective, you would have."

"Well, it didn't take a detective to know you were a crooked cop. Even Darla figured that one out."

"Crooked, dirty, what's the difference?"

"You know the difference as well as I do, Mike. Hell, better than I do."

He said, "Humor me."

"A crooked cop maybe looks the other way now and then, pockets a little cash to pay for his suits and alimony, but he does his job, which is to uphold the law. A dirty cop breaks it. A dirty cop is a bigger scumbag than the criminals he's supposed to be putting away." Mike kept quiet, kept his eyes on the road. But he was working his jaw muscles. So I went for it. "A dirty cop doesn't just break the law, he invalidates it."

He shot me a glance, and muttered, "You have no idea."

"So tell me. It'll help pass the time."

"I told you to leave the case alone. I practically begged you."

I said maybe I should have listened. Maybe then I'd still have a good drinking buddy. "But I wouldn't have Karin. That's not a trade off I'm willing to make."

"I wouldn't be so sure about that."

"Where is she? What have you done with her?"

"What have I done with her? Corcoran, you ought to hear yourself whine."

I said that didn't answer my question.

"In due time. In due time."

"What about now? Now's a good time."

Mike put on his blinker and slid over to the right, to take the Moross exit.

"Tell me we're not going back to Grosse Pointe."

"No can do, buddy."

Seems no matter how long you stay away, that town has a way of sucking you back in. "Can you swing by the police station? Maybe Andy Parsons will let me have my gun back."

Mike thought that was pretty damn funny. He laughed so hard I was afraid he'd run off the road. "You have no idea," he repeated.

I asked him why. He said it was a long story. "I honestly did want to keep you out of it."

"How'd you get in it?"

"It was Williams who did it. He set up a sting. Yeah, I was on the take, no better than some, no worse than most. Like you said, I was crooked. Then one night I'm on a stakeout, supposed to be some deal going down."

"Why you? You're homicide."

"This was the Wrecking Crew. Rivera, guy who took over for Kong? I wanted him bad. Half-dozen murders at least."

"I heard he did Kong."

"Yeah, well, I wouldn't have charged him for that one. Hell, I would've given him a medal." He broke off to swing around a slow-moving, diesel-belching double-bottom gravel truck. "But it was Narcotics' bust. I was just baggage. I was just there to cuff Rivera. But funny thing happened. Just before the deal goes down, the Narcs start bleeding away. When it does go down, I'm out there on an island. There's one of me, twelve of them, and any one of them has more firepower than I do. So I hunker down, hoping I don't catch a stray through the door, and that nobody makes my car."

"This is back when you were just crooked?"

"Yeah, just a lousy crooked cop," he spat. "Nice suit, unmarked car. Bunch of uniforms at my beck and call." He kept on Moross, crossed Mack Ave. We were getting close now, and Mike was talking too much for this to end well for me, or Karin.

I begged him to let her go.

"Not my call, pal."

I begged him. I don't know, maybe I shed a tear or two. He glanced over at me. "If I could, I would. I don't want you going off to hell with another Sara on your hands."

Mike was moving slowly now, just creeping along in the right lane at about twenty. Just half the speed limit. Cars raced up behind us, swerved into the other lane and passed us with blaring horns. I guess he wanted to finish the story.

So I let him. "What happened that night?"

"The way Williams set it up, the buyers were supposed to ambush them. They were supposed to leave the money behind, and when I picked it up, Williams would own me," he said, almost relieved to finally tell it. "Problem was, the Wrecking Crew'd decided these guys were getting too big."

"So the set up was a set up?"

"Yeah." Mike cackled, kind of a life's so fucked up you gotta laugh to keep from blowing your brains out kind of laugh. "Yeah, the set up was a set up. Then I had to pull Williams' bacon from the fire."

"How so?"

"When the shooting finally stopped, thing like that, it's kind of like popcorn. Lots of popping going off. Then fewer, then just one at a time. Then it's done and you get to eat."

"Get to eat."

"Yeah, get this," he said, pulling into a parking lot behind the Methodist Church. I looked around, thinking a church was a strange place to end it. But he made no move to get out. Guess he just wanted to finish the story.

"When I got out of my car," he said, hands at ten and two, eyes staring straight ahead at the soaring edifice in front of him. "Everybody's dead 'cept one guy. He's got the money and he's trying to crawl away. So I take out my throw down, cap him, wipe it off, grab the case and run. Couple days later Williams wants to see me. We set up a meet. He shows me the photos his guy took, and introduces me to my new best friend."

"Olly Jensen," I said.

"Justin Wade." He ignored my protests. "Olly doesn't do hiring and firing. He has his minions handle that shit."

Justin Wade as a minion? That was going to take some getting used to. Though based on what Deb had told me, it made sense.

"Did you kill Jon?" I asked.

Mike laughed, bitterly. "Not my job description. I'm an implementer."

"An implementer."

"Yeah, I set things in motion. There's other guys who pull the trigger."

"So you just pick guys up, and deliver them to the place where they get shot."

He turned to me. "Yeah, that's it. And sometimes I babysit broken-down detectives, make sure they stop looking under rocks." He rested his hand on my shoulder. "I tried like hell to get you to stay away."

I had more questions, and it felt like he wanted to answer them, but, no, it was time. Can't keep the boss waiting. We pulled back out on the road, heading back to Provencal.

I can't say I was surprised when we turned in Williams' driveway. Whoever set this one up had a sick sense of humor.

"I thought Williams was out of the country?"

Mike nodded. "Guess the heat is on."

"What's that supposed to mean?"

"Your old buddy, Carmine? He's closing in." We stopped. A jolt of hope.

"You mean—"

Mike pulled his gun. "Don't be a hero, Corcoran," he

warned.

"Not my style," I said.

A quick quiver of a grin. "Gonna miss you, bud."

Then we were out of the car, through the door, down the hall and to the left. Back in the dark, refined living room. Karin was sitting in one of the armchairs in front of the roaring fire. Justin sat in the one facing her. It was quite the intimate scene. There was even a snifter sitting on the table next to him. I noticed Karen didn't have one. Possibly because it's hard to pick up a glass when your legs and arms are duct taped to your chair.

"I'm sorry, Jim," she said plaintively.

Justin crossed the distance between them and backhanded her across the face. Before I could make a move Mike's gun was buried in my ribs. "Don't be a hero," he repeated.

"What did I just finish telling you?" Justin demanded.

"Not a word," she said through gritted teeth.

"Good girl." He caressed her cheek with the barrel of his pistol.

"I brought the goods," Mike said, unable to conceal his contempt, for himself, for Justin, for the whole scene? I couldn't say. "Are we finished?"

"Almost," Justin replied pleasantly. "Make our guest comfortable." He gestured at the armchair. "Over there, next to the girlfriend."

Mike gave my arms a couple quick wraps with the tape. It wasn't enough to hold me for long, but based on how diligently he avoided my eyes, I figured that wouldn't be necessary.

He stood back up. "Now?"

"Go, go," Justin said absently, waving his gun idly toward the hall.

Mike walked away without giving us another glance, but before he reached the doorway, Justin said, "Oh, there's one more thing, Wallis."

Mike turned back, his irritation evident. "Wha—"

The bullet caught him just below his right eye. Mike dropped and was still.

"I'd never shoot a man in the back," Justin observed. "That would be wrong." Then he returned to his chair, set the gun on the table, and picked up the snifter. He inhaled it deeply, sighed, and took a small sip. Another sigh, "Armagnac, '67—same age as me."

I just stared at him. I heard Deb's words again, and this time I didn't doubt them. Maybe carrying the guilt of raping and murdering your little sister takes its toll. Or maybe he'd been mad even way back then. Made me wonder how much Mummy and Daddy Wade had known, and when they had known it. Made me think some one should look into the circumstances of their deaths. I snorted. Yeah, brilliant, start making plans for the future.

"You laughing, Corcoran?" he said. "Aren't you taking that whole hard-boiled thing a bit far?"

I said I wasn't laughing. More like choking. "Hell, you just murdered Mike."

"No I didn't."

"What do you mean you didn't? I just watched you."

"No, you killed him." He showed me the gun. "Look familiar? I borrowed it from Andy Parsons."

"You bastard."

"Next, you're going to give me what I need, or you're going to kill your little girlfriend."

Karin. Karin killed with my own gun. This wasn't happening. "You can't do this," I pleaded.

"Again."

"You can't do this."

"No, you're supposed to say, 'You can't do this again.'"

"You?"

He grinned. "Bet you never saw that coming."

"You'll never get away with it."

"Oh, I think I will. I think I was out for a stroll, heard gunshots. Now, I know Williams is away, so I call the police. Parsons is here like a shot—" He chuckled. "Like a shot, I like that. So apparently what happened is you brought your little fluff up here because you're, I don't know, a sentimental sack of shit." He got up and began strolling around the room, casually waving his gun as he spoke. "But let's not go down that road just yet. There's still a way out for you."

He was lying. I knew that. After what I'd just witnessed, there was no way he'd let us go. But what the hell, I was ready to hear the pitch. "What's the deal?"

"You get me what I need, I'll let Little Miss Muffet here go."

Karin started to speak. I like to think she was going to say something like, "No way, I'm not leaving without the man I love," but before she could get the words out, Justin turned, brandished the gun and said, "Tut, tut."

I started talking fast, before he could pistol whip her. "Yeah, sure, Justin. I've got everything you need. The files, the dossier, the statements, the case I've compiled. But I don't have it with me. It's back at the hotel."

"Fuck the money!" he cried, swinging around on me, the pistol pointing at my head. "I don't want that. I want the tape!"

"I don't have the tape!"

He sprang at Karin, stepped behind her, wrapped his left arm around her throat and jammed the gun against her right cheekbone. "Wrong answer, Corky. I get the tape, or the girl dies."

I told him there was no tape. There never was. Jon was lying about it. "He sent me a letter, said he just told you there was a tape so you wouldn't kill him. I swear to you, Justin. You've got to believe me."

He stared at me for a minute, trying to decide. Karin was struggling beneath his hold, writhing around, trying to breathe. Then he laughed. "You almost got me, Corky." He relaxed his grip on Karin's neck, and she shrank, gasping, back in the chair. "I mean, it does sound like Jon.

That lying little weasel. I can hear him whining now, 'I got you on tape. You killed Jessie. You kill me, everybody will know.' I had to put up with that shit my whole life from him." He shrugged. "So I blew it. I should have found out where it was, but instead, I got pissed off and pulled the trigger."

"You're insane."

He shrugged again. "Sometimes you wear so many hats, you forget which one is real." Then he wrenched Karin's head up by her hair, and smashed the gun into her cheekbone again. "I'm sick to death of being lied to!" he roared. "Where's that fucking tape?"

"There is no tape!" I cried. I thought about giving up Deb, but what good would that do? She'd already destroyed it.

"Then say good by to Miss Deja Vu," he shouted. His finger was tightening on the trigger when Deb said, "I have the tape."

She must have come in through the service entrance from the kitchen. She was holding a pistol and aiming it at her husband. There were tears on her face, and a quiver in her voice. "I listened to it," she spat as Justin whirled around to face her. "And then I followed you here."

He held the gun ambivalently, not really pointing it at anything. His hand shook slightly. It wavered. I knew he was going to lift and fire.

"Don't do it, Justin," I cried.

He glanced over his shoulder, then turned and pointed it at me. "See you in hell, old pal."

His gun went off when the bullet hit him, but the shot went wild. The second bullet hit him in the back of his head. His finger spasmed as he went down, and I took a round in the shoulder. Another shot from Deb as she approached. Then she stood over him and fired again.

The echoes of the shots faded away, leaving only silence. Deb stood still, staring blankly at Justin's body. The gun wavered in her hand. I said, "Deb."

She glanced up slowly, with vacant eyes, and absently pointed the gun at me. Even as I prepared to die, I couldn't help but appreciate the irony. Then Karin cried out, and Deb seemed to come out of her trance. She looked about wildly, her eyes finally coming to rest on Justin again. Then she raised the revolver until the barrel pointed underneath her chin. Her eyes went blank again, and her tears flowed.

Karin and I both shouted, "Deb, no!"

"Think of your children," Karin said.

That brought her partway back. She dropped the gun, then sat on the floor beside her husband. I tried to figure out how to play this. Ordinarily I would have gotten out of the chair. Mike had done a cursory job of securing me, but with my right arm useless, I couldn't do it myself. Then I thought maybe I should just stay there until the police arrived. It might lend some credence to my protestations of innocence. Especially handy if Andy Parsons took the call. But I had to get somebody to make the call. It didn't look like Deb would be doing us much good for awhile.

More than the cops, I was starting to realize, I was going to need an ambulance, and soon. I was bleeding way too heavily for a flesh wound. Justin's bullet must have found an artery. Whatever happened was going to have to happen quickly, I realized, or there might be a third corpse in the room.

If Parsons did get here first, I knew who'd end up being the perp. Me, the dead guy. And with me out of the way, maybe Williams could come home again.

Then I realized Karin was calling my name. Must be awkward, I thought, tied to a chair in a room with two dead people and two zombies. Plus the fire needed tending.

I rallied, briefly. I told her I was in trouble. She said she could see that. A little impatiently, I thought. After all, it wasn't like I wanted to bleed to death.

"Can you get free?"

She was struggling, but not making much headway. I tried calling Deb's name again, to bring her around, but it didn't have any effect. Karin started shouting at her, shrieking, really. She glanced wildly back and forth between Deb and me, her eyes wide with growing horror.

I told her that I loved her, that I always would, but that I was cold, and tired, and then someone kicked the door in.

CHAPTER 18

The truck was rolling up the lane as I finished caulking the last gap in the logs. I climbed down the ladder. It was a hot day in June, and I was sweating, exhausted, and pretty damn proud.

It hadn't been easy, especially the last bit around the loft. I had to go precariously high on the ladder because I couldn't raise my right arm above my shoulder. Even at shoulder height, I couldn't exert much pressure, which meant I had to do most of the top four feet left handed. It was work. But it felt good.

They told me at the hospital that even with physical therapy I probably wouldn't regain full use of the arm, which meant my beach volleyball career was over. Lucky for me, I'd never played beach volleyball. Plus the Speedo, not a good look for me. So I figured I could live with the arm. What I really found irksome was the infection that kept me in the hospital for ten days.

By the time the ambulance arrived I'd lost so much blood they started a transfusion on the way to the hospital. The doctor told me, after I came out of the coma, that if the EMT's hadn't done that, I might have died. As it was, I almost died anyway.

He said they still weren't sure exactly what had happened, but somehow the blood was tainted. I snorted. How appropriate, I thought. Bad blood. That's what this whole case had been about. Bad blood. That was just six months ago, but it felt like a lifetime.

I walked around the front of the cabin and gave a wave to Dave Jenkins as he climbed out of his pickup. Dave owned the Ace Hardware in Grand Haven, and I'd gotten to know him over my two-month-long winterization project.

"Comin' along," he observed after we shook hands.

"Got the caulking done," I announced. "Now I just gotta put on a coat of varnish, and it'll be good as new."

"Yeah, she's solid," he agreed laconically. I wasn't sure I'd ever master the art of assigning the right gender to inanimate objects, which might prove the biggest obstacle to my ever achieving true backwoodsman status.

"Better get her done before fruit fly season," Dave added.

"Fruit fly season?"

"Little buggers love paint fumes, varnish, a good whiskey. They'll swarm the place. You'll be picking them outta your teeth for a month."

This constituted the longest speech I'd ever heard from him. Hell, it might be longer than the rest of his utterances combined. I wondered what he wanted.

"You got 'til August, though," he continued. "The rate you've been going, shouldn't be a problem."

I thanked him for all his advice. "Couldn't have done it without you."

He acknowledged that with a nod, then just stood there, gazing at the cabin. I stood there next to him, glad to have an audience for my achievement.

"Yep," he said at length, scuffing some of the dirt around one of the bluestone stepping stones I laid last month. Karin wanted to fill them in with moss, which meant my self-education was going to move toward horticulture before summer was out. Must be nice, having a live-in handyman, I thought, unable to resist a grin at the thought.

Dave grinned back, without showing any interest in being let in on the joke. He just scuffed the ground again, and continued gazing at the cabin.

"So, do you take this much interest in all your customers' DIY projects?"

"What? Uh, no," he began, then lapsed back into silent contemplation. I let the silence flow. Old habits die hard.

Then he began falteringly, "I got a, well, I got a problem." You could tell it took some effort to get that much out. I was beginning to understand that folks in Western Michigan were a self-reliant lot. They didn't go running for help every time they broke a nail.

Karin was discovering that this quality was what business consultants called a barrier to market entry. She had opened a practice in Grand Haven, and took a part-time position in the Psych Clinic at Forest View Hospital in Grand Rapids. That required a thirty mile commute, but at least being a city, even a mid-sized city, meant there were messed-up people who weren't too proud to admit it.

Unlike Dave Jenkins, who seemed to think his confession was enough for one day. Or maybe a year.

What sort of problem?" I asked, trying to speed things up. Of course, this time-awareness was another thing a backwoodsman had to give up.

"It's my boy," he said.

"Your boy—"

A lazy shrug. "Not a boy, I guess. Not now." A lengthy pause. "He's a Marine."

"You should be proud of him."

He glanced up sharply. "Of course I am. Third generation. Damn proud."

"So, what's the problem?" I asked brusquely. I figured if he was a Marine, he could deal. I had a pretty good idea where this was heading, though I couldn't say I was looking forward to being right.

"Just finished his third tour in Afghanistan. Had some leave, called to say he was headin' up here. Had something he needed to talk about."

"Any idea what it might be?"

"Figure he's thinking about leaving the Corps. Figured either he wanted my blessings, or for me to talk him out of it."

I asked him what he wanted to do.

"Depends on what he wants." Dave looked me straight in the eyes. "I'd be real proud to have him come work for me."

I nodded. "So, what's the problem?"

"That was four days ago. Said he was coming up. Since then, nothing. Cell phone goes straight to voice mail. Won't answer his emails. Contacted his CO. He hasn't heard nothing either."

This was, back when I was in the business, what was known as a slippery slope. Or the thin end of a wedge. "What makes you think I can help?"

"You're a detective, aintcha?"

When I asked him where he got that idea, he scowled, though his eyes remained friendly enough. "You don't come into a little town like Grand Haven, 'specially at the end of March, without folks noticing."

So much for dropping off the face of the planet, I thought.

"Plus, we do get newspapers," he added, with a nod that made it sound more like, "Yeah, we know how to read them, too."

I shrugged. "So you know who I am."

"Me, I don't care. Guys at the diner, everybody wants to know the whole story, but I tell 'em, 'If he don't want to talk, leave him alone.'"

I thanked him for that.

"But now it's different. I need help, and you're the only one who can give it to me."

I held his eyes, and nodded, letting him know I knew how hard that had been for him. I told him I'd retired. "That last case wiped me out." He just nodded, and kept staring. Finally I told him I'd try to find out something. "Give me a couple of days, and let me know if he shows up."

After he left, I finished cleaning up, and called Karin. I offered to drive into Grand Rapids. We could go to that Tapas restaurant she'd been wanting to try.

Then I sat there trying to figure out whether to tell her I was back in business. Which meant I had to decide if I was.

To tell the truth, I did miss it, from time to time, between chores. We'd talked about it, from the time we hatched this plan, when I was still in the hospital. If we lived simply, and kept our expenses down, she could probably make enough to keep us both fed and clothed. I didn't care much for that idea. Not that I had any qualms about being a kept man, just that I knew there wouldn't be enough to keep me occupied. I'd just come off a decade of doing nothing, and that had almost killed me.

Then again, Justin Wade had almost killed me.

Put that on the other side of the ledger. But up here, along this beautiful shore line? Help the odd resident find his wayward son? Maybe it wouldn't be too bad. Could involve some traveling. Might have to run over to Detroit every once in a while. It was surprising how much I missed the place. Especially since Karin and I had decided to move mainly to get away from it.

The city seemed to be going down for the count. Even with Carmine's investigation expanding almost by the day, its tentacles reaching deep into the police departments of the city and a half-dozen suburbs, sometimes it seemed like corruption was too entrenched to be rooted out. Even by someone as diligent as Carmine.

I shrugged. Carmine kept me appraised of new leads. Half the time he begged me to come back. He'd take me on as a special investigator. Even get me medical benefits. I had to consider that one. I owed him that much. Hell, I owed him my life. It was Carmine's men who knocked down the door that night. They'd shown up with an arrest warrant for Williams.

"That was your doing," Carmine told me. "I went back over everything you gave me on Olly Jensen, way back when. It didn't hold water then, and it still didn't when I reviewed it, until I thought maybe I was looking at it from the wrong end. So I gave Williams a closer look, and things started falling into place."

Williams had gotten sloppy. "I guess he figured with half the police in his pocket—and some of the people in my department as well—there was no need to hide his footsteps." So he had Williams for money laundering, conspiracy, accessory to at least three murders. He had everything but Williams himself.

"But we'll get him," he assured me. "Him, and Jensen as well."

When I told him I wanted to be there for that, he reiterated his offer. Finally, I had to tell him no. It was tempting, but I was too much in love with this land, and too much in love with Karin to consider leaving her for any length of time.

I would have to go back and testify of course, when the cases came to trial. What surprised me was how much I looked forward to it. Not just to showing up on the side of justice, but just seeing the city again. Ridiculous, I know, but dammit, I still had roots there. Maybe Mike was gone, but Darla was still there. Little pockets of life clinging to the edge of the cliff. Maybe the city did have a future. Maybe Carmine could make a difference. Maybe the citizens would get wise and vote Mayor Brown out of office.

What really gave me hope was when Carmine mentioned there were signs pointing at the Mayor's office. Made sense when you thought about it. Helped explain why he didn't seem too bothered about the state of the city. Maybe if he got sent away the people would wake up, and the city could begin the long march back to normalcy. Sometimes I thought I wanted to be there to help point the way.

Then I looked out at the special green light which comes from sunlight shining through the new leaves on the beech trees, and thought, "No. I'm here now."

I'm here, and Karin's here, and I've got to figure out how to make moss grow around the stepping stones, and maybe help Dave Jenkins locate his son. I'd been down for too long to look back. When Deb had called, she offered me more than she knew, and more than I knew. She offered me a lifeline. I took it, and caught Karin on the rebound, now nothing could force me to go back.

It was over. Deb was finally history. Sara had finally been laid to rest. My life, my future was here.

CPSIA information can be obtained
at www.ICGtesting.com
Printed in the USA
FFOW04n1814191213